Mar sighs and opens their eyes—then bites back a shriek. They stumble two steps back, away from a man who's silently joined them against the railing.

No, not a man. The edges of his black tailcoat shed wisps of smoke, and his heavy boots thud against the deck as he turns to Mar and smiles with eyes like coal.

"Ay, perdón," el Diablo says. "Did I startle you?"

SWASHBUCKLING ROMANCE
FROM GABE COLE NOVOA

The Wicked Bargain

The Diablo's Curse

THE
WICKED
BARGAIN

Gabe Cole Novoa

EMBER

Text copyright © 2023 by Gabe Cole Novoa
Cover art copyright © 2023 by Mia Araujo
Interior art used under license from Shutterstock.com

All rights reserved. Published in the United States by Ember, an imprint of Random House Children's Books, a division of Penguin Random House LLC, New York. Originally published in hardcover in the United States by Random House Children's Books, a division of Penguin Random House LLC, New York, in 2023.

Ember and the E colophon are registered trademarks of Penguin Random House LLC.

Visit us on the Web! GetUnderlined.com

Educators and librarians, for a variety of teaching tools, visit us at RHTeachersLibrarians.com

The Library of Congress has cataloged the hardcover edition of this work as follows:
Names: Novoa, Gabe Cole, author.
Title: The Wicked Bargain / Gabe Cole Novoa.
Description: First edition. | New York: Random House Children's Books, [2023] | Summary: Sixteen-year-old Mar, a transmasculine Latinx pirate hiding magical abilities, must learn to use their magia to save their papá and newfound pirate familia from losing their souls to el Diablo.
Identifiers: LCCN 2021043158 (print) | LCCN 2021043159 (ebook) | ISBN 978-0-593-37801-4 (hc) | ISBN 978-0-593-37803-8 (ebook)
Subjects: CYAC: Pirates—Fiction. | Magic—Fiction. | Gender identity—Fiction. | Fantasy.
Classification: LCC PZ7.1.N687 Wi 2023 (print) | LCC PZ7.1.N687 (ebook) | DDC [Fic]—dc23

ISBN 978-0-593-37804-5 (pbk.)

Printed in the United States of America
1st Printing
First Ember Edition 2024

Para Aya,

por ser la primera que me enseñó lo que

significa ser un luchador.

Te quiero muchísimo.

CHAPTER 1

August 3, 1820

Papá says water speaks to those willing to listen.

On the night Mar arrived silently in the world, the ocean danced and clapped in time with the roaring thunder and unrelenting rain. Mar's parents named them after the sea because the water had celebrated so fiercely, it nearly sank *La Catalina* when Mar took their first breath.

Of course, Mar has no memory of their birth, but they imagine it was probably a night like tonight: dark as ink and so wet that they can barely keep their eyes open against the downpour. Fitting, as today's their sixteenth birthday.

Mar leans against the rail of the crow's nest, squinting into the storm. The warm rain pelts their face and paints their lips, seeping into their mouth and soaking their clothes until their black linen shirt clings to their brown skin. Thunder like an army running through the tempest rolls through them. The rain is heavy and feels like drumming on their skin; though it's hard to separate the rain's embrace from the uneasy magia humming in their bones.

Mar presses their hands down their rain-slick arms, trying to ignore the fact that the edges of their black markings are glowing orange. The "birthmark" weaves over their arms and chest and down their legs like thick, black mazes. At least now Mar is old enough to pretend their markings are tattoos.

Mar shakes their head and takes a deep breath. They can argue with their magia later. Leo, the quartermaster, sent them up here to peer through the blurry, endless sheet of rain to the raging waters. *La Catalina* is supposed to be nearing Isla Mujeres, off the coast of la península de Yucatán. It's where Mar grew up, and Papá's crew frequently returns to deliver most of the treasures and resources they've taken from the Spaniards. It isn't really stealing—more like *returning*, since the Spaniards stole it from those living around the Caribbean Sea in the first place. Out of the Spaniards' hands and back to the people.

After five successful raids, the crew's haul is one of their biggest yet, but this storm is throwing them off course. If Mar's magia were *useful*, it might point them in the right direction, like a compass. But no, all Mar's magia ever does is cause them grief. It's a lesson they've had to learn the hard way, and one they don't intend to forget.

Mar swiftly climbs down the rigging, gripping the rope with their toes, careful not to slip on the water-slick holdings. They've climbed up to and down from the crow's nest on *La Catalina* so often, they could do it in their sleep. And a good thing, too, because it's dark tonight, Mar might as well be blindfolded.

Their bare feet have scarcely touched the soaked wooden slats of the deck when a crack of lightning slices through the night, followed by a rumble Mar can feel in their chest. Papá isn't navigating—not that Mar is surprised; navigating through a storm like this is like looking for fresh water in the ocean. Still, if anyone can navigate out of this storm, it's Papá. But as Mar squints through the storm, Papá doesn't seem to be on deck with most of the crew. So, then. He's inside.

Coño, you'd better not be doing what I think you're doing. Mar marches up the steps to the quarterdeck, bracing themself against the railing as a wall of wind slams into them. Mar leans into the wind, cursing under their breath as they grip the rail so tightly their fingers hurt. Still, they slip back inches at a time over the slick steps anyway. Flames burst from their fingertips and Mar yelps, clamping down on their magia abruptly, pain lancing through their chest. Their shaking arms burn with effort; it's all they can do to hang on without letting their magia slip again and incinerate the rail.

Mar glares at their orange markings. It's always the fire ready to explode out of them the moment their guard slips. Where fire always demands space and attention, their ice magia is quieter, steadier.

"¿Por qué no puedes comportarte como el hielo?" Mar grits out. Ice magia never causes problems, but the fire is wild, demanding. Deadly.

A wave of heat washes over them in protest, so hot Mar

sweats in the rain. But then the wind lets up just long enough for Mar to rush up the remaining stairs, to the back of the quarterdeck, and through the gilded double doors into el Capitán's quarters, slamming the doors behind them before the wind can catch them.

It takes all of a second for Mar to adjust to the dim golden candlelight of the cabin and register the thick smell of rum in the air. Two empty bottles lie on their sides on the floor beside the table strewn with maps, illustrations, and trinkets scavenged from various raids. Papá's favorite gun—which once belonged to the cabrón Manuel Ramón García López, the Spanish capitán who has made it his mission to hunt down the last of the Caribbean's pirates—teeters at the edge of the table.

Mar touches their own holstered flintlock pistol tucked under their soaked shirt at the small of their back. They run their thumb over the slick wax waterproof coating and onto their rope belt as they peer into the dim cabin. Not because it's likely anyone dangerous is here, but with the endless humming in their bones, the reminder that the pistol is still there is . . . reassuring.

"Mar!" The call comes from the far end of the room, doused in shadow, where Papá's bed is. Papá stumbles out of the darkness, his rail-thin frame leaning on Leo's large torso. Papá grins widely as he waves around a third bottle of rum, this one half-empty. Some of the amber liquid sloshes out of the thin bottle neck onto his stained white shirt, slapping the deck like the rain outside. Papá must be really drunk. He'd never let even a drop of precious rum go to waste unless he was neck-deep in, well, *three* bottles.

La Catalina's quartermaster grimaces as he gently helps Papá to the table, looking at Mar with something like disappointment. "¿Viste algo?" he asks softly. Leo sounds utterly exhausted, and it takes Mar half a second to recognize he's talking to them.

"Oh." Mar rips their gaze away from their completely drunk Papá. "No, it's impossible to see anything through this storm," they answer in Spanish.

Leo steadies Papá and releases him, watching as Papá balances on his own. Satisfied he won't fall over, Leo sighs deeply, gently cups Papá's cheek for a moment, then bites his lip and walks over to Mar. He rests his hand on Mar's shoulder and squeezes lightly. "I need to get back out there with the crew. Can you . . . ?"

"I can handle him," Mar says. "Let me know if you need help out there."

Leo nods. "Still the long night."

They meet his steady gaze. "Still the long night."

Leo takes two quick strides to the hatch, then hesitates, his hand on the door. He looks back to Papá. The pain in his face is raw—it hits Mar in the chest. "Te amo, Juan."

The smile that warms Papá's face makes him look ten years younger. "Y yo también te amo, mi corazón."

Leo smiles softly, then steps out into the roaring storm.

Mar sighs and turns back to Papá, not sure where to begin.

"¿Qué tal, mi tesoro?" Papá slams the bottle on the table

so hard, it's a miracle it doesn't crack. He stumbles forward, and his rings scratch the table as his hand trails on it for balance.

Mar isn't feeling especially treasured.

"I don't think I've ever seen a storm this bad—at least not while sailing," Mar says.

Papá gets close enough for the mixed stink of alcohol and sweat to flood Mar's nose, but they resist the urge to step back. The man may smell, but he's still Mar's papá. Besides, it isn't the first time they've found him borracho like this in his quarters. Still, when Papá clasps Mar's face in his hands, the reek is so strong, Mar tries not to breathe. They focus instead on Papá's rough hands on their cheeks. On the raised line around Papá's thumb where García López tried—and almost succeeded in—cutting off his finger. On the crinkles around Papá's smiling eyes in his brown skin; on the gray hair just barely speckling his mustache, even though Papá is still too young for gray.

"Just look at you," Papá whispers. He takes Mar's hands and runs his fingers over their still-glowing markings. "Incredible." Papá's gaze unfocuses, and a small smile carves his lips while he traces the lines on Mar's shoulder. Like he's looking at some paradise far away. *Magia.*

Easy to worship magia if you're not forced to hide it all the time, Mar thinks. They glance at their arms and groan aloud; their dark sleeves are rolled up, and their markings are glowing fully bright orange, which seems unfair because they haven't even used magia.

"¡Basta!" Mar hisses, shaking their arm as though they were trying to put out a match. It doesn't do a thing, of course; Mar's magia has been stubborn all day, bursting from them unprompted in sparks, demanding attention. Before it started raining they even accidentally set a rope on fire, a slipup they haven't made in months. All night their magic has buzzed uneasily under their skin, a never-ending hum, their bones vibrating like tuning forks. It swirls around Mar's stomach and collects—hot—around their heart. A warning, whispering—something. Refusing to be ignored.

Mostly it just makes Mar nervous. And a little angry. Life would be so much easier if they could just pretend their magia didn't exist.

Mar scowls and rubs their still-glowing arms, trying not to think about how they must look like some kind of demonio, glowing from collarbones to wrists to toes. At least on *La Catalina* they don't have to hide until their magia calms down. The schooner isn't just their home; it's their haven. The only place they don't have to worry about being executed for brujería.

They stuff their hands into their soaked trouser pockets. "Magia only brings trouble and death," they mutter.

But Papá shakes his head and takes Mar's face in his rough hands. "Your magia is a gift, tesoro. You need to stop fighting it and accept it—it's a part of you. A beautiful part of—"

"The storm is getting bad, Papá." Mar swallows their frustration and gently covers Papá's hands with their own. He always gets like this when he's drunk—sentimental and far too easily distracted. But the crew needs him to focus. Mar needs him to focus. Better: They need him sober. "The crew could have used your guidance out there. This was not the time."

Papá lowers his hands and sighs. "Sixteen already. Where have the years gone?"

Mar smiles weakly and lifts a shoulder.

"Here." Papá snatches the half-empty rum bottle off the table and presses it roughly into Mar's chest. "You should drink. It's your cumpleaños, after all, and you're a—" The sentence catches in Papá's mouth as his gaze darts over Mar.

Mar forces a thin smile. When Papá is sober, he doesn't have a problem referring to Mar neutrally like the rest of the crew does, calling them hije and niñe, fluidly making substitutions where o/a endings denote gender. After all, it's not like Mar is the first of their kind; before the Spaniards came along, many Mexican communities, including Mar's ancestors, recognized there were more options than just *boy* and *girl*. When Papá's drunk, though . . .

Well. Mar pretends Papá was about to say *man*, because that'd be much more bearable than the other possibility. *Man* may not be quite right, but it's not entirely wrong, and certainly nowhere near as wrong as *woman. Boy* feels better—good, even—though it's not completely right, either.

"Adult," Mar finishes for him. "Though I'm not sure I agree with you."

Papá laughs and brings the lip of the bottle to Mar's

mouth. Mar takes a burning gulp, partially to appease him and partially because with a storm like tonight . . . well, at least the alcohol will smother their nerves some and make the endless buzzing of troubled magia easier to ignore.

But the buzzing under their skin is a warning of impending danger. Sometimes Mar wishes they could turn the warning off, like when they're in the middle of a violent storm and the danger is obvious. But most of the time the warning prickle is not to be ignored; admittedly, it's saved Mar from walking into dangerous situations unawares more than a handful of times.

Mar sighs as the warmth of the rum mixes with the tingle of their magia's warning. Yes, this storm is unusually intense, but they don't need their magia to know that. Coño, Mar takes a second gulp just because.

"That's it." Papá proudly pats Mar's shoulder. Then: "This storm will kill us, you know."

Mar nearly chokes on the last of the rum trickling down their throat. "What?"

Papá nods somberly and puts the bottle back on the table—lightly, this time.

"Why would you say that?" Mar's face goes hot. It's one thing to utter a curse like that on one's enemies—but on their own crew? In the middle of a dangerous storm, no less? Does he *want* to die? "Take it back."

"I can't take back the truth." Papá pulls a chair away from the table and sinks into it, deflating like the life is leaking out of him. "I've known this storm would come for sixteen years. But now the time is here and—" His voice cracks and Mar's heart punches their chest. Is Papá *crying*?

Mar's magia hums intensely, gathering in their muscles and hissing lightning into their ears. The magical warning has only worsened since the storm started, and Papá's breakdown certainly isn't helping.

Mar shakes out their prickling hands and pulls a nearby chair over. They sit across from Papá, knees to knees, as Mar reaches over and pulls Papá's warm hands into theirs. "Talk to me. Why are you so worried? This storm is bad, but I don't— It's not the first storm we've weathered."

"My blood screams tonight," Papá whispers, so softly that Mar almost doesn't hear him above the roar of wind and rain. Mar shivers. Papá doesn't have magic to warn him about danger, not like Mar, but he *is* intuitive. Still, they won't tell Papá their blood has been screaming too. "This night fills me with fear, but not for myself. I've known my time was ending."

His time *ending*? Mar scowls. Sure, pirates often don't have the longest lives, but this storm is hardly the most dangerous threat they've faced. It's not like they're fighting the entire Spanish Armada at once out there.

This overblown lamenting isn't like him at all, not even when he's drunk. And honestly, Mar's quickly tiring of it. If the crew heard him talking like this, they'd be furious.

"You should be spared." Papá nods, and even though he's looking at nothing over Mar's shoulder, they get the sense he's seeing something else, *someone* else. "He saved you—that was the deal. You should be all right. I have to believe you'll be all right."

"Who are you talking about?" Mar asks. "You're not making any sense. Maybe you should get some—"

"El Diablo." Now Papá looks right at them.

"El Diablo," Mar says flatly. "Claro. Bueno, pues, Papá, te quiero, but you need some rest. You've had too much to drink."

Mar starts to stand, but Papá grabs their wrist too tightly. Mar hisses and sits back down. "That *hurts.*"

But Papá doesn't ease his grip. He leans forward, so close his nose nearly touches Mar's. "You have to listen to me," he whispers into the darkness. "I made a deal sixteen years ago. I was young and foolish and desperate. Your mamá—"

"That's enough." Mar has heard this fantastical tale just about every time Papá gets drunk. The night of Mar's birth, young Juan Luis León Rojas supposedly made a deal with the devil and asked for two things: fifty years of prosperity and to save his legacy—Mar, who was born not breathing. El Diablo offered him Mar and sixteen prosperous years that would make him legendary. With infant Mar turning blue in Papá's arms, he was too desperate to barter for more. Or to ask what would happen when the sixteen years was up. It's the perfect story to tell over rum and cards on dark nights when the wind sings canciones, but tonight Mar doesn't have the patience for it.

They yank their arm out of Papá's burning grip. "You need to sleep it off. Leo can handle the storm tonight, and I'll help, but you need to be ready to go in the morning, all right? I'll tell everyone you're not well."

"I tried," Papá says. "I tried to get us to Isla Mujeres before tonight, but the winds were against us." He presses his palms to his face. "So much gold, sugar, and weapons at the bottom of the ocean . . ."

"Will you stop that?" Mar snaps. "Keep cursing us and it'll actually happen."

"That haul is for the people—"

"And we'll get it to them—"

"I won't let el Diablo take you. I won't. I won't. You're my child, mi tesoro. He can't go back on a deal—that's the rule. I saved you then; I'll—"

"Papá," Mar pleads. "Basta, por favor. Everything will be fine. You're just drunk. You drank too much, understand? Everything will look better in the morning, I promise." But even as Mar says it, the words feel strangely hollow.

Maybe it's the bite of static in the air. Or the smell of rain and salt water thick enough to drown in. Maybe it's the warning edge of Mar's magia, or the terrible echo of Papá's words, but tonight . . . everything feels wrong.

"Just promise me you'll survive." Papá grips Mar's hand with both of his. "That's all I want. I don't care about the gold or the ship—just promise me you'll make it. Please, Mar, my death will be meaningless if you die too."

Mar is breaths away from being sick. How can Papá talk

about his own death like that—so certainly? How can he doom the ship, speaking of *La Catalina* like she's already at the bottom of the ocean? It isn't just bad luck—he's practically *asking* for the ship to sink.

But maybe if Mar agrees, Papá will relax. Maybe he'll finally go to bed, and Mar can forget this awful conversation ever happened.

"Fine," Mar says. "I'll survive. Now will you please get some rest? For me?"

Papá opens his mouth and a lightning strike splits the air—so close, the crash sends Mar's heart racing and they taste the burned night. Acrid and bitter, like biting into packed gunpowder. Mar takes a slow breath to try to still their panicked heart. Their magia prickles hotly down the back of their neck and washes over their back. Mar freezes. Their magia only ever reacts like that when . . .

Mar spins around, pistol out and pointed at—

A man. Gleaming, too-new polished boots; dark, unstained trousers; a fine, deep green ruffled silk shirt beneath a fitted black tailcoat with gold buttons. His trim black beard is the kind of perfect that takes meticulous hours to shape, and his dark hair curls around his pitch-black eyes like thorns. If a king were a pirate, this is what he would look like.

But it isn't his lavish style that makes the hair on the back of Mar's neck stand on end. It's something much stranger.

He isn't wet.

CHAPTER 2

"How precious." The man smirks at Mar. "The baby, all grown up."

"Who are you?" Mar demands, keeping the pistol steady despite the magic *vibrating* in their blood. They'd be impressed with themself if they weren't utterly terrified.

Papá stands and touches Mar's shoulder, pulling them back one step, two, as Papá shifts in front of them. "Let me handle this," he says calmly. "If he kills you, he can claim your soul."

Mar's mouth nearly drops open; after Papá's earlier hysterics, he's calm *now*. Like this stranger's inexplicable arrival is fine. Like greeting an old friend. And what's this about souls?

"It's good to see you, Juan," the man says. "I'd say your child looks like you, but Mar clearly takes after their mother."

Mar's eyes narrow. Most people who don't know Mar assume they're Juan's son, because girls don't dress the way Mar does or wear their hair like Mar does. Many still believe that nonsense about women being bad luck on a ship. So how does this stranger know Mar's name and to refer to them neutrally?

Papá lets his hands fall to his sides. No weapon. It doesn't make sense. Strangers are *always* greeted with weapons, especially strangers who appear on *La Catalina* without invitation. Juan always wears three guns—one on each hip and one at his back—in addition to the knives strapped to both thighs and ankles, tucked into his boots. But he doesn't move for any of them.

So be it. At least Mar has the intruder in their sights.

"Mar, put the gun down," Papá says, and Mar nearly screams in frustration.

"You can't be serious."

"I am, as always, entirely serious." Papá glances back at Mar. "Don't make me repeat myself."

Mar bites their lip so hard, it's nothing short of a miracle they don't taste blood. They let their weapon fall to their side. But Mar doesn't put the gun away. Papá may seem suddenly sober, but that doesn't mean he's making the right decisions.

"It's sweet how protective they are." The man smiles like a curved knife. "Foolish, but sweet."

Mar frowns.

Papá nods. "I don't believe you came here to discuss my child."

"Ah. Right to business, then? As you wish." The stranger steps forward, jingling with every smooth stride. He seems like he'd be heavy, weighed down with whatever is rattling in his pockets—it sounds like gold coins—but when he moves, it's as if his polished, engraved boots don't touch the ground. Now that the man is closer, Mar notes another curious feature: The edges of the man's black coat trail lightly with smoke, as if it were recently on fire. But what really strikes Mar are the stranger's eyes: They previously thought them blacker than night, and they are, but as the man nears, they reflect a faint red glow, like cooling coals.

The hum of magia in Mar's veins becomes an outright hurricane as the stranger idly walks closer, trailing his hand along the wall like Mar used to as a child. But there's nothing childlike in the gesture from him; he holds himself as if he's claiming *La Catalina* just by dragging his fingers along the wood.

Something feral and hot curls inside Mar. They don't care if this stranger and Papá have been friends longer than Mar has been alive; the broiling magia in their veins is all the warning they need not to trust this stranger with burning-coal eyes and a slicing smile.

"You know why I'm here, Juan." He comes to a stop just feet from where Mar and Papá stand.

"I do," Papá says.

"We made a bargain."

Papá nods. "We did."

Wait. *Wait.* A bargain? He can't mean—

"You've had a great sixteen years, made quite a name for yourself—I don't believe there's a sailor alive who doesn't fear the infamous Embrujado. And your child, though ill-mannered, appears to be in perfect health."

Mar scowls. They'll show him *ill-mannered*.

"You kept your end of the deal." Papá nods again. "I have no complaints. I understand it's time for me to pay my due." He turns to Mar and smiles, but the wild spark in his eyes makes Mar's stomach twist in nauseating waves. He's trying not to show it, but Mar knows every one of Papá's faces better than they know their own—and this one, a shade too pale in the wavering light, wide-eyed and sweaty—is undeniably fear.

But Papá doesn't tell Mar to run, or fight, or shout for the others. Instead, he says, "*La Catalina* is yours."

Mar stares. "What?"

"I want you to have her. She was always yours." Papá touches Mar's shoulder and smiles even as his eyes shine with unshed tears. Mar's stomach sinks; they can't remember the last time before tonight they saw Papá cry. They're not entirely sure they ever have before. And now he's giving Mar *La Catalina,* which he would only do if—

Clarity cuts through Mar like a frozen sword. "No," they say firmly, turning the heat of their glare on the stranger. Magia rushes from Mar's chest, down their arms, into their fists, buzzing like millions of red-hot insects under their skin. "You can't have him."

But the stranger only smirks again. "Touching."

Papá grabs Mar's fists before they can raise them, looking imploringly into their eyes. "Por favor," he whispers. "My time is over. I want this."

"¡Mentiroso!" Mar hisses, yanking their fists away. "Don't lie to me. You don't want to die."

"No, no, I don't." This time Papá takes Mar's face in his hands again, softly running his callused thumbs back and forth over Mar's smooth cheeks. The gesture aches bone-deep, and heat rushes to Mar's eyes, momentarily blurring the cabin before they can force back the tears. "But more than anything, I want you to survive. Take back what those cabrones have stolen from us. Fight for our people. I know you'll make me proud."

Mar's voice cracks. "Papá . . ."

The stranger laughs. Both Mar and Papá look at him, Mar with a scowl that would make most shiver and Papá with an arched eyebrow. "Amused?" Papá asks, with a tone that is anything but.

"Perdóname, perdóname." The stranger wipes his eyes as he chokes down a snicker. The bastard. Mar isn't about to forgive him for a damn thing. They could broil him alive with a thought, or freeze him solid, then shatter him with a mallet. But a warning look from Papá keeps them quiet, still, and fuming.

"It's just—" The stranger continues through his laugh. "It's so adorable how you actually think anyone on this ship will live to see morning."

A beat.

A slap of sheeting rain hissing against the walls like a steaming pan.

A flash of lightning and the deep-throated rumble of thunder like a giant pounding the ocean.

"Your bargain was with me," Papá says uncertainly. "The crew don't have to die. I'll come willingly—there's no need for anyone else to get hurt."

"That's true." The stranger smiles. "There's no need, but I never did agree to keep anyone alive once our deal was over."

Papá pales. "But—our bargain."

The man snorts. "What, did you expect me to be *merciful* at the end?"

Papá stares at him in horrified silence.

"Sixteen years of prosperity and the continuation of my legacy—my child's life," the man quotes. "I've done everything I promised: El Embrujado is infamous, your little crew's been unusually successful, and your child survived their tumultuous birth."

So Mar's panicked half guess from earlier was right. Sixteen years of prosperity and Papá's legacy, Mar's life: That was the deal Papá said he'd made with . . . with el Diablo.

"So you'd break that deal?" Papá's face flushes red, and the vein above his right eyebrow bulges. "If you kill everyone including Mar—"

"This is the devil you made a deal with." The words are

out of Mar's mouth before they can stop them. "It wasn't just a story. You were telling the truth."

"Surprise." The stranger says smugly. "And it seems no one told your papá you have to be *very* careful with your choice of words when you make deals with diablos. Deals can't be broken, but we pay close attention to *exactly* what was said—and what *wasn't* said." He chuckles. "Oh well, lesson learned, so on and so forth. Now, if you're done being uselessly sentimental—"

The gunshot rips through the air, so loud and close that Mar thinks they've been shot—but the pain in their chest is just their panicked heart punching them from the inside. Papá drew his gun so quickly, Mar didn't even see him, but the smoking barrel and their ringing ears say all they need to know.

That is, until the stranger laughs again, filling the room with a resonance like his laughter is amplified and coming at them from all sides. Like the cabin is full of the dead all laughing together, their voices echoing upon echoes until the terrifying chorus all but smothers them. The sound churns Mar's stomach and chills their buzzing blood to ice. Papá lowers the gun. He's as pale as Mar has ever seen him. Visibly shivering.

The candlelight casts deep, cutting shadows on the stranger's face as he takes one, two steps closer, smiling all the while. He brings his hand to his mouth, spits out a bullet, and puts it in Mar's shirt pocket. Then the demon pats it twice for good measure.

"It's good to know you, Juan," el Diablo says. "You're always so . . . entertaining."

Lightning crashes—too close—painting the cabin with blinding light and deafening Mar with the thunderclap. Just like that the devil is gone.

And so is Papá.

CHAPTER 3

The air is thick with burning wood.

When Mar stumbles out onto the deck blinded by unshed tears, not even the soaking rain can make them feel entirely awake. The night is superheated, burnished in orange and red, crackling and popping in Mar's ears. They must be trapped in a nightmare. This can't be real, because Papá can't be gone. He can't have just disappeared right before Mar's eyes.

And yet he has. There is no explanation at all except to believe the impossible: El Diablo has taken their papá.

"Mar!" Leo rushes up to them, brushing his dark, rain-slicked hair out of his wild eyes. "Where is el Capitán? *¡La Catalina* se va a hundir!"

It takes far too long for Mar to process what Leo is saying. What he's asking. El Capitán. Papá. *La Catalina* is going to sink— Wait. Sink?

And all at once it makes sense. The thick heat lapping closer by the moment, the plumes of stinging gray clouds wafting through sheets of endless rain, the threatening orange light behind Leo, growing brighter by the moment.

The flames dancing along the bow and climbing up the rigging.

The men desperately throwing buckets of seawater onto the fire, screaming at each other as it edges ever closer. The crew can't do anything to slow the advancement of the inferno.

But Mar—Mar can.

"He's gone, isn't he?" Leo's voice breaks, and so does something in Mar. Leo loved Papá; the whole crew did, but Leo is like Mar's second dad. The strong and steady one, even when Mar felt like their world was falling apart. But now, here, the pain in Leo's face bites deep.

"I—I don't understand," Mar says, their voice trembling.

"Juan knew what that deal meant for him." Leo's eyes shine as he looks at the chaos raging ahead of them. "I don't think any of us realized what it meant for the rest of the crew."

Mar shakes their head and wipes their eyes with the back of their hand. "I have to fix this."

Leo wraps his thick arms around Mar and squeezes tight. Mar presses their face against his soaked, smoky shirt, wishing the world would pause for just a minute, just so they could stay here longer, safe in Leo's arms. Then he holds Mar at arm's length by the shoulders. "You can do this, hije," he says gently. Then Leo releases them and throws his arm out toward the flames. "¡Vaya!"

And then Mar is running. Toward the heat, through

lungfuls of ember-hot smoke, weaving between panicked shouts and staggering men. A roar like the earth splitting open mutes the chaotic song for just a breath before a wave crashes into *La Catalina* so hard, the schooner dips sharply starboard, throwing Mar against a man and his bucket. The two of them hit the edge of the deck with an impact that steals the air from Mar's lungs. They cling to the railing, spitting seawater, blinking furiously through the rain as *La Catalina* rights again.

And still the fire rages.

Mar pushes off the railing, their entire right side throbbing. Two, three, four steps and the flames are upon them. There's no time to think. No time for Mar to prepare the magia inside them, like they've done before to create flames in their palm, to steal the light from a candle, to swallow fire and breathe it out again for a crowd, or a cute boy.

Now there's only time to take a breath, expand their aching chest, and step into a heat so fierce, the air ripples with it. Magia thrums in Mar's bones, always begging to be used. Roaring to the surface at a moment's notice.

Mar extends their arms, and flames leap onto them. They breathe the heat in and breathe it out. The flames race over their skin, but fire has always been a friend to Mar. They hum with the life of it until their blood sings. Until their markings glow as if the fire sits under their skin and not just on top of it. Until every inch of flame is within Mar's grasp. Until Mar is the fire consuming the crow's nest, looking over a raging ocean; until Mar is hungrily leaping toward the crew members, barely flinching back at the bursts of water; until Mar is clambering over the side of the ship, eating through wood like water through sugar.

Mar doesn't stop until every inch of flame is singing in their bones. They extend their reach until they're vibrating with energy, with smoke on their tongue and heat in their soul. It's only then, with the ship-eating fire firmly in their grasp, that Mar takes a breath like the final gasp before a plunge, drawing the flames to them.

Más. They clamp their mouth shut, holding in flame and breath, and inhale smoky air until their lungs feel ready to burst. Mar turns to the ocean clapping at their destruction, and with a bone-deep scream exhales flame, and fury, and agony into the sky. Away from *La Catalina,* and the crew, and everything and everyone they've ever known and loved. The heat pours and pours out of them, battling furious rain-heavy clouds and lighting up the night until it feels, impossibly, like a hazy day. Until the fire, and heat, and light are gone. Until their markings grow dim, then black. Until Mar is empty.

They sit on their knees on the blackened deck, sweat- and rain-drenched, the tang of magia thick on their tongue. As the endless rain batters the smoke rising from the sizzling sea, Mar stands on shaking legs, squinting through the darkness of the storm now that the light of the blaze is out.

How many survived? And how much of the schooner? If *La Catalina* holds, they can weather this storm. Mar doesn't know where it will put them, but that's a problem for the morning. Tonight, all Mar needs is for *La Catalina* to stay afloat. They can do the rest. Papá taught them how to make it through ship-eating storms as long as she fights along with them.

"You did it." Leo rests his hand on Mar's shoulder and squeezes lightly, his gap-toothed smile pained but genuine. "You saved us."

And then Mar is in the center of a mess of people laughing and crying and clapping them on the back. Even in their relieved huddle, Mar counts too few among the remaining crew, but they still have a crew, and they still have *La Catalina,* and the flames are gone and they're alive.

"Storm's not over yet," Mar says.

Leo nods. "Still the long night."

"Still the long night," Mar murmurs in return as Leo turns to everyone and barks out orders. As the crew moves away from Mar, a thrill of something sharp and tight—like the twang of an untuned guitarra string—strikes deep in Mar's chest. *It's just—it's so adorable how you actually think anyone on this ship will live to see morning.*

But they've survived el Diablo's fire. El Diablo has underestimated Mar.

A crack like a strike of lightning jolts Mar to the present. But the sky doesn't light up—the ship does, fresh flames licking at the wood once more. No rumble of thunder follows; just a low, creaky groan, like a giant stepping on an enormous old floorboard. Then screams and a tree-tall shadow plunging toward Mar—the crow's nest.

Leo slams into Mar's side and they hit the deck hard,

shoulder throbbing as they roll again and again, the world spinning dizzyingly as a deafening crash washes out even the unrelenting roar of the storm. *La Catalina* pitches sharply—Mar's back rams into the railing as the ship reaches for the sky.

No, not the whole ship. Blackened, jagged edges like burned teeth where the middle of the schooner once was, opening up a gaping maw of a fiery mouth in *La Catalina*'s center. A crack of lightning paints the halved ship in white, then—

Water. Salty ocean fills Mar's mouth and nose and eyes as they frantically swim for the surface, but the blackness is everywhere and the hold of the sea tugs them lower. Deeper. Into colder water as stars spot Mar's vision, as *La Catalina* sinks into the ocean's abyss and Mar with her.

There are many things Mar can do with their magic, but they never learned to breathe water.

As the darkness takes them and the sea swallows them whole, Mar can only think el Diablo was right. Morning will never come. Not for Mar.

Not for any of them.

CHAPTER 4

Mar doubles over, gagging on fire.

Not fire. Salt. It's salt water, pouring out of them as they heave, then gasp desperately for air. They are lying on slats of wood. A deck. A ship?

"Told you he wasn't done for."

He. Mar could cry with relief; the flattening cloth wrapped tightly around their chest must have held together.

They blink blearily into too-bright light gleaming through the darkness. A boy is standing over them, holding a lantern. A tall boy, with brown skin a little lighter than Mar's, a scar on the right side of his pink top lip, and deep brown hair the same tint as *La Catalina*'s wood. He wears a white linen shirt and brown trousers, like most nonnavy sailors do. Like most of *La Catalina*'s crew does.

La Catalina—oh, Dios. It all crashes back into them: el Diablo, Papá, the fire and the ship and the crew. All now at the bottom of the ocean somewhere.

Mar's stomach churns and eyes sting as they wipe their

mouth with the back of their hand. Just about everything from the waist up hurts, inside and out. They suppose getting thrown around a ship before drowning would do that to someone. Mostly they're just glad their chest still looks flat; they can't imagine a fate any worse than waking on a ship full of men who mistake them for a girl.

Being seen as a boy, conversely, feels like the ocean breeze filling Mar's lungs, even if it doesn't always fit perfectly. But that's all right. Mostly right feels good too.

The boy with the scar turns to his peers; Mar quickly counts twelve who've circled around them, in addition to the boy and the majority of the crew still continuing their work on the ship. Something about the bustle of a full ship, so familiar that part of them wants to believe they never left *La Catalina,* hurts worse than throwing up ocean water did.

The boy grins far too brightly at a man with curly black hair and a mustache, who is absolutely drenched. So drenched, the black tattoos on his golden-brown skin are clearly visible beneath his soaked linen shirt. "Certainly worth the quick dip in the ocean, wouldn't you say, Tito?"

The man, who Mar supposes is Tito, spits on the deck.

"Perfecto. I knew you'd see things my way." The boy flings his arm over Tito's shoulder and beams. "You listened to me, and I saved his life! And you got to be a part of it! How exciting, how very exciting. I knew today was going to be a good day, didn't I? I said so this morning, and you all ignored me!"

"That storm nearly sank us," a man with long dreadlocks, rich umber skin, and shoulders wide as a doorframe answers with a bored expression, cleaning his nails with a knife. "And you almost fell overboard."

The boy tsk-tsks. "Yes, well, it *didn't* sink us and I *didn't* fall overboard, now did I?"

"And what's this about *you* saving him?" Tito asks. "*I'm* the one who jumped in to fish him out."

The boy sighs heavily. "After *I* spotted him. You wouldn't have jumped in if I hadn't pointed him out to you."

"I wouldn't have jumped in if you'd gone and actually saved him yourself," Tito answers stiffly.

"Ah, but why would I do that when you are clearly the superior swimmer? I was just looking out for his best interests."

Mar stares at the two, hardly believing they're bickering like children about who saved them when Mar is just . . . there. Back from near death (did they actually die?). Sailing away from the ruins of *La Catalina*, from Mar's home, and familia and—

Mar closes their eyes and inhales deeply through their nose, resisting the urge to cough anew. It hurts too much to think about earlier, and they can't break apart in front of these men. Mar doesn't even know what the crew will do to them now that they have, evidently, survived what was supposed to be unsurvivable.

"Did—" Mar chokes on their own croaky voice, coughing after all.

"Oh!" The boy laughs. "Where are our manners? We forgot all about our guest." He grabs Mar's hand and yanks them up—only Mar's coughs conceal their yelp as pain streaks up their arm and down their side. The boy then slaps Mar's back firmly, which, oddly enough, actually shocks them out of their coughing fit.

Mar glances at the strange boy warily and rubs their shoulder.

"My name's Sebastián, but call me Bas." The boy—rather inexplicably—winks at Mar. "This is Tito and Joaquín, our quartermaster and boatswain."

"Um. Thanks." Mar's voice appears to have recovered somewhat, so they clear their throat and try again. "Did you pull anyone else from the ocean?"

"Hmm, afraid not," Bas says. "What was left of the ship was still burning when we arrived, but it seems you're the only surviving member of your crew. Lo siento."

Mar swallows hard, fighting the pain creeping up their throat. They don't trust their voice not to betray the storm brewing inside them, so they focus on even breaths instead.

Bas tilts his head to the side as he gives Mar an appraising look. "What's your name, my sad new friend?"

Sad new friend. Bas speaks to them so simply, breezing right past the death and destruction they've just endured. Not that Mar really expects compassion from a stranger, but his ease is just so . . . cold. "I'm Mar."

Bas's entire face blooms into a full-bodied grin, which feels somewhat inappropriate, given the circumstances. "What a perfect name for a pirate! Did you choose it yourself?"

Mar just shakes their head.

"Well, your parents have excellent taste, though I imagine

it's probably for the best if we don't speak of them at the moment, ¿verdad?" Bas doesn't give Mar a chance to answer before plowing forward, which is probably also for the best, because Mar has nothing kind to say to a boy who speaks so lightly of their parents' deaths. "Not a problem. I imagine el Capitán will want to meet you in any case. No sense in wasting time becoming friends before I know whether or not we'll be throwing you back into the ocean." Bas pats Mar on the back and laughs, like the thought of throwing Mar overboard after saving them from drowning is genuinely funny.

No, they have nothing kind to say to him at all.

Mar's distaste is irrelevant, because at the first pressure of Bas's hand on their back, Mar is moving forward with the crowd of a dozen other men, which seems like a bit of overkill in terms of a protective entourage. It's not like they know Mar's magia could send this ship to the bottom of the ocean as fast as *La Catalina*.

Though, truth be told, Mar isn't sure how much magia they have left to spend.

El Capitán leans casually against the wheel of the ship. The ruffled collar of his white linen shirt moves gently in the sea breeze, and unlike many of the barefoot men, he wears black boots over his matching trousers. With his thick black beard, long dark hair, and scarred bronzed skin, he doesn't look much like Mar's papá, but the air of confident authority certainly reminds Mar of the way Papá carried himself. When he wasn't drunk, that is.

Their eyes sting and Mar squeezes their hands into fists, digging their nails into their palms. They can't think about Papá right now. They won't break in front of a group of strange men about to decide their fate.

"¿Quién coño es este?" The man looks at Mar like one might at a spoiled fish.

"His name is Mar," Bas says. "I spotted him floating in the wreckage and convinced Tito to fish him out." Bas looks rather pleased with himself at that, which seems odd given he just said he isn't sure whether they'll be letting Mar stay on board. Besides, Mar can't imagine there'd be much reward for bringing another mouth to feed, particularly one who isn't worth anything.

Not like Mar knows anyone who would pay for their return.

Not like Mar knows anyone who would give a shit at all. They're all—

"I can speak for myself," Mar says, forcing their thoughts to stall.

El Capitán smirks and crosses his arms over his chest. They're large arms. Like cannons. The kind of arms that could easily break their thin neck. "Then speak for yourself," he says. "Who are you, and why shouldn't I shoot you where you stand?"

"It'd be a shame to stain the wood," Mar answers.

Someone snickers behind Mar—they suspect it's probably

Bas—and el Capitán's eyes widen, just slightly, just for a moment. Then he barks out one quick, short laugh. "Do you really think your blood would be the first to paint this ship?"

Mar lifts a shoulder. "You've no cause to want me dead."

"You're trespassing on my ship. I have every cause in the world."

"I didn't come on board your ship of my own free will. I wasn't even conscious when your men brought me aboard."

"All the more reason you should be on your knees, thanking me for my mercy and begging for your life."

Mar pulls their shoulders back and looks el Capitán dead in the eye. "A pirate doesn't grovel."

"Is that what you are? A pirate?" The lantern light casts deep shadows on el Capitán's face. He tilts his head and looks Mar over carefully. "How old are you?"

"Fifteen," they lie, shaving a year off their age as they always do when someone asks. Mar can pass as a boy—prefers to pass as a boy—but only a young one. At sixteen most boys are more angled, even starting to get scruffy, and Mar . . . Well, Mar is Mar.

"Hmm." El Capitán pushes off against the wheel and stands at his full height, towering over Mar's small stature. "And from what ship's wreckage did my son save you?"

Son? Mar resists the urge to glance back at Bas, who's undoubtedly looking as full of himself as ever. It makes sense, though. It's easy to get a big head when you're the captain's child. Mar would know.

But here—here is the topic Mar has been strictly trying

not to think about. The reality that, once broken open, might break Mar in return. It's all Mar can do to take a shaky breath and prepare for the pain of speaking the words into being.

Of admitting their papá—and everyone they love—is dead.

"*La Catalina*," Mar says, willing their voice not to give out before the words touch their tongue. "Me llamo Mar León de la Rosa. I'm el Embrujado's child and . . . and only surviving family or crew."

Whether by coincidence or Mar's imagination, the ship goes quiet for several moments while el Capitán's face settles into a deepening frown. Mar thought it ironic that it was Papá who picked up the name Embrujado when it was his child who had magia, but until tonight *La Catalina*'s crew hadn't lost a member, or had an injury, since Mar's birth. It didn't take long for rumors to spread claiming some sort of magical reason—some even saying the whole crew was immortal—but Mar brushed it off as a combination of skill and luck. Now they can only assume it was part of the diablo deal; having an unbeatable crew was certainly one way to guarantee success as a pirate.

El Capitán shakes his head. "No. ¿El Embrujado? Taken down by a storm? No puede ser."

A storm and el Diablo himself, Mar thinks. But they know all too well that's a level of honesty that would be met with skepticism. Papá may have frequently told the story of el Diablo, but it was thought to be just that: a story. And anyway, even if they *were* believed, Mar isn't willing to take the chance that this new crew might opt to throw Mar off the ship out of sheer superstition.

El Capitán turns and runs his hand through his long hair. "If el Embrujado is dead as you say . . ."

"He's gone," Mar answers, and this time they can't keep the shard of pain from their voice. But it's at that tight strain of Mar's words that el Capitán turns back, and Mar sees it on his face. He believes them.

"If you're truly el Embrujado's son," el Capitán says, "then I've heard stories about you."

Mar tenses. La Catalina's crew has always done their best to keep Mar's magia secret, but they *have* been spotted using it a handful of times. It's always ended badly. Did someone make the connection between the strange youth with glowing tattoos and el Embrujado's only child?

El Capitán steps toward Mar, standing just a foot away from them. "Some whisper you might be cursed, like your father."

Mar lets out a held breath. He doesn't know. "And do you believe that?"

"I haven't decided yet." He pauses. "Curious that one of the most famous crews on these seas is defeated by a storm, of all things. And yet you survive, while they rest in the ocean."

Mar has nothing to say to that. They have no answer for why they survived, especially given that el Diablo himself told Mar no one would survive to see morning. Granted, it isn't morning yet, so maybe Mar *won't* survive; maybe this crew will decide the risk is too high to keep them alive.

But what would it mean if they did survive the longest night of their life? The one that was nearly their last?

"Do you know who I am, Mar León de la Rosa?" Though his words come out softly, there's something vaguely threatening about el Capitán's tone. Something that whispers Mar *should* know who he is, and fear him at that.

But the truth is Mar doesn't know. And after what they've survived so far tonight, they doubt there's much left that can scare them.

"No," Mar answers bluntly, and if that answer surprises el Capitán, he doesn't show it.

Instead, he just nods. "Your father did. Perhaps he told you about Alejandro Vega Torres."

And now Mar knows exactly who he is. Because Papá *did* warn Mar about el Pirata Vega—the only other well-known pirate left in the Caribbean. He told Mar that Vega Torres was an ally you held at arm's length. They had the same aim: returning the resources and gold the Spaniards have stolen to their rightful owners, and their methods were even similar enough, but Papá always said Vega Torres's recklessness would get him killed.

In hindsight, Mar isn't sure Papá really had much room to talk. Selling your soul to el Diablo for sixteen years of prosperity and a good legacy seems as reckless as it gets.

Now with el Embrujado and *La Catalina* at the bottom of the ocean, Vega and his crew are the only pirates of legend left.

"Well?" Vega asks, and Mar nods.

"I know who you are."

"Good." Vega steps toward Mar, standing only inches from them. But just as Mar braces themself for a threat, the man rests his hand on Mar's shoulder. "I'm sorry for what you've suffered. Your father was a good man."

Was. Mar struggles not to wince at the past tense. It's a reality they will have to accept—just . . . maybe not right this moment.

"Thank you," Mar mumbles.

Vega squeezes their shoulder lightly. "Bienvenido a *La Ana.*"

Mar tries to fake a smile, but it's like trying to carve into stone with their cheeks. Because this isn't an invitation, not really, not when the alternative is to jump back into the ocean.

So even as Bas laughs and claps Mar on the back, and the crew members nod and el Pirata Vega turns back to his navigating crew, Mar doesn't feel very welcome at all.

CHAPTER 5

When Mar was five years old, their magia was freedom.

They'd run around La Catalina shirtless to show off the magic painted on their skin, laughing as they pulled the chill from their bones to set their markings alight with a blue glow. Their magia made them special, and though they weren't allowed to use magia off La Catalina, their god-painted skin made them feel beautiful.

Or it did until a woman in Habana spotted Mar's markings. Mar had been preoccupied sucking the last of a freshly picked mango's sweet, tangy flesh off the pit. As sticky juice dribbled down Mar's chin and into the sand, the woman screamed so loudly, Mar thought she'd been stabbed. Until Papá whisked them away and Mar realized that the woman was screaming about them.

"¡Demonio!" her voice carried after them. "Where are the guards? ¡Monstruo!"

"Vámonos," Papá had said, carrying Mar close to his chest

as Mamá walked swiftly beside him. Neither of them so much
as glanced back.

"But we just got here," *a crew member protested.*

"It's not safe for Mar here. We'll head up the coast to
Matanzas." *Papá turned to Mamá.* "Mar can't walk around
shirtless off La Catalina. It's too dangerous."

"¡Demonio! ¡Monstruo!"

"Have I mentioned how pleased I am to finally have a re-
placement cabin boy?"

It is sometime in the afternoon when Mar returns to Bas's
cabin with his third cup of café of the day. Unlike the majority of the crew, Bas, like the captain and quartermaster, has
his own room—one that looks like a library vomited into it.
Maps are pinned to every inch of the walls—of countries
and islands around the Caribbean, but also the rest of the
Americas, Europe, even Asia. Paper is strewn all over Bas's
desk, and open books cover his bed. Mar can't help but be
a tiny bit jealous; they certainly didn't have their own room
back on *La Catalina*.

Helps explain Bas's superior attitude, though.

"Only about four times," Mar mumbles.

"I just want you to know you're appreciated." Bas sips the
steaming black liquid and sighs contentedly, propping his
bare feet up on the small desk. "And let myself know I'm appreciated, of course, as I'm the reason we have you on board

to begin with. Last time, it took us nearly six months to re-place our cabin boy, and let me tell you, the crew's morale was *not* at its best. But I've avoided all that! Not even three weeks and here you are. I should promote myself." Mar rolls their eyes, and Bas grins. "What? No thank-you?"

"Am I supposed to thank you for bringing you three cups of café?"

Bas laughs. "You're sharp. I like that."

Mar shoves their hands deep into their trouser pockets and turns back to the door, exhaustion heavy on their shoulders. It was the dark, ungodly hours of the morning when Tito had pulled them out of the ocean. They were given a chance to rest between then and now, sometime in the afternoon, but they were hardly able to sleep with the specter of smoke in their nose and the ocean on their tongue.

Every time they closed their eyes, all they heard was screaming.

"I don't care what you do or don't like," Mar says.

"You're very grumpy for someone who was just miraculously saved, then generously offered a place in a renowned crew."

Mar shouldn't take the bait. They should walk out of the cabin, shoulders back, ache buried deep in their throat. They should focus on the next task before the tempest of emotion brewing inside them pulls them under: getting three coils of rope for the boatswain before he becomes impatient, if it's not already too late. Then check the food stores for anything spoiled. Bring more mops to the deck for the swabbies. And probably something else Mar is inevitably forgetting and will undoubtedly be told off for missing.

Still, the implication that they should be anything but devastated twelve hours after losing their home, their crew, their papá—

Mar turns around, fists clenched, the weak buzz of magic humming under their skin. "Has it ever occurred to you I never *asked* to be saved?"

Bas arches an eyebrow. "Are you suggesting I should have waited for your unconscious corpse to call out for rescue?"

"I'm *suggesting* maybe you should have left me alone."

"In the ocean."

"Yes."

"About to die."

Mar stalls, words caught on their tongue, because the truth is they *don't* want to be dead, not now that they're alive. But did they really survive so much pain just to be a "cabin boy"? Just to be at the mercy of a ship full of strangers all too enthused to have someone at their beck and call again? It was hard enough waking up, choking on burning seawater and gasping for breath, just to realize they've lost absolutely everything.

Mar didn't want to die, not really; it just would have been so much easier if they had. And right now, easier sounds like sweet relief.

Mar doesn't have an answer for Bas. At least, not one they can very well say aloud, let alone to the arrogant boy sitting smugly in front of them. Bas seems aware that there's no way for Mar to win this argument, and he's probably enjoying that knowledge far too much. Instead, Mar turns back to the door, swallowing back the growing part of them that wants to wipe that smirk off Bas's infuriatingly handsome face.

"We'll be friends, you know," Bas says as Mar pushes open the door.

Mar doesn't even bother to look back. "Don't count on it."

A positive aspect of being *La Ana*'s new cabin person: the sheer magnitude of never-ending tasks assigned to Mar is so physically and mentally exhausting, they have little time or energy to dwell on their utterly bleak circumstances. It isn't until el Capitán intercepts Mar on their sixth café run down to Bas's quarters (carajo, who even needs that much café, anyway?) that Mar takes a moment to breathe.

But just a moment. Because Vega turning his attention to Mar isn't exactly an ideal situation either.

"For Sebas?" Vega asks, taking the mug from Mar.

Mar just nods.

"Interesting." Vega sniffs the mug for unfathomable reasons. "He doesn't even like café."

Mar stares. Bas doesn't even . . . ? "This is the sixth cup he's made me bring him today."

"Is it?" He brings the cup to his mouth and throws back

a gulp like it's hard alcohol, then smacks his lips and sighs contentedly. "Bueno. Dinner is ready." He gives Mar a long, hard look. His lip curls. "Are you wearing the same clothes you nearly died in?"

Mar glances at their dirty black shirt and soot-stained trousers. Their clothes look as though they smell like sweat and smoke and panic. Which they do.

"Tell Sebas I sent you to get some clothes. You're smaller than he is, but you'll still fit in some of his."

Mar's eyes widen. Ask Bas? For his clothes? "I don't think—"

"I wasn't asking. When you're done, I expect to see you both at dinner."

And with that he walks away, leaving Mar with a task that has them wondering if it might be best to just jump back into the ocean.

Bas's cabin door is shut, as it has been for the last five minutes Mar has stood there trying to come up with any excuse at all that el Capitán would accept. Of course there isn't one, and it's not like there's anywhere Mar could hide from his questions. So, that's it, then. Mar has to ask Bas for help.

Bas is going to love every second of it.

Mar steels their shoulders. Takes a deep breath. And raises their fist to knock.

Bas's door swings open so abruptly, Mar jumps. Bas raises his eyebrows and grins. "Miss me already?"

Mar scowls. "El Capitán sent me for clothes."

Bas's nose wrinkles. "I don't have any of his clothes."

"What? No—why would you have his clothes?"

"You tell me if he apparently sent you to get them."

Mar sighs and shoves their hands into their pockets. "No, not . . . *his* clothes." Bas tilts his head but for once stays quiet. They swallow a groan. So Mar's going to have to spell it out for him, then. "He said I'm smaller than you but I should still fit."

"Oh." Bas's face splits into a grin. "Sharing clothes already? I told you we'd be great friends."

Ten minutes later Mar stands with an armful of clothes, consisting of two fall-front trousers, one pair of breeches, and four white linen shirts. Mar holds back a grimace; white shirts are, of course, overwhelmingly common, but Mar has generally avoided them when possible. White shirts serve them as well as any other shirt, but only until they get wet—then it's easy to see the chest flattener they wear beneath. Not to mention it's much harder to hide the glowing of their markings when wearing a light-colored shirt.

Mar bites their lip. "Do you have any colored shirts? Or a serape or poncho or something?"

Bas grins and digs into his collection. "Hmm . . . not that

one . . . ah! Perfect." He tosses Mar three shirts: two black and one deep blue. It reminds them of the sea—or a storm—and they'll never admit it, but Bas is right. It's perfect.

"Thank you."

"Of course. We'll have to make sure to do this again before our first shore leave so we can get you some nice land clothes. I'll give you a moment to get changed." He waltzes out, humming happily as the door swings shut behind him.

Mar hesitates a moment to make sure the door is well and truly staying closed, then turns their back to it, just in case. They pull off their dirty shirt, letting it fall to their feet as they quickly shrug on the blue shirt. It smells salty, like the ocean, with a hint of something sweet Mar can't quite place—before it occurs to them it probably smells like Bas.

So. That's fine.

Mar rolls up the sleeves once, then runs their palms over their chest, reassuring themself that they still look flat. Even without anyone else in the cabin, the shape of their chest is a constant source of discomfort. Under cover of night, when Mar loosens the cloth to sleep and give their ribs a break, the raised softness of their chest still feels deeply wrong.

They wear the flattener so no one mistakes them for something they're not. But more importantly, they wear it because the shape of their chest doesn't fit them.

Thankfully, the ruffled collar of their borrowed shirt is high enough that you can't see the white cloth flattener beneath. They can even button it up to their neck if they want to.

But will it be thick enough to smother the glow of their markings? The fabric is light; ideal for the life of a pirate in the Caribbean but less so for hiding luminescent skin.

Only one way to find out. Mar closes their eyes, takes a breath, and relaxes their hold on their magia—just a bit. Just enough to let the warmth spread from that place in the center of their chest to their arms. As the familiar heat settles over them, they open their eyes.

Mar grimaces. While not as prominent as when they aren't wearing a shirt at all, the glow is still visible through the shirt. The only place they can't see it is where their chest is bound.

So they'll have to wrap their arms in cloth before raids, shore leave, and when their magia builds up and the glow becomes impossible to keep at bay. At least they're usually able to keep their hands from glowing when they need to.

Mar sighs, pushes their magia deep, and changes out their trousers as well. They have to admit it feels better to be in clean clothes, even if the clothes aren't theirs. They pick up their discarded shirt and trousers off the floor, and something clunks softly on the hardwood.

They blink at the crumpled bit of metal at their feet. Mar picks it up and turns it over in their fingers. A bullet, Mar realizes, holding it up to the lantern light; but squished like an accordion so it almost looks like a thick, misshapen coin. Mar's eyes widen and they shudder—el Diablo put the bullet he spit out into Mar's pocket. Which means it was their papá's bullet.

Their heart thumps loudly in their chest. This bullet is the only thing Mar has left of Papá. They push it into their pants pocket, rolling it in their fingers. *If there's any way at all to save you from el Diablo, Papá, I'll find it,* they silently swear. *Somehow.*

Like Mar's "invitation" to join the crew, taking part in their first dinner on *La Ana* isn't really up for debate, and to be honest, they entered well beyond hungry territory several hours ago, since they'd skipped breakfast. Mar follows Bas silently, rubbing their itchy palms together. Absurdly, Bas keeps going on about how good Mar looks in his clothes. Mar isn't really sure what Bas's motive is for going out of his way to compliment them, but they're too distracted to give it much thought. They pretend to listen with the occasional nod or shrug while trying to keep their mind—well, quiet.

Back on *La Catalina*, Mar used their magia daily to keep it from building up. It only required simple tasks, as long as Mar expelled the excess energy as soon as the itch of mounting magia developed—lighting a candle ten paces away here, cooling a glass of water with a frozen breath there. But that was where everyone knew what Mar could do, and what Mar had to do to keep under control. That was where no one thought of Mar differently for the very abilities that anywhere else could get them killed.

Now evening has fallen and it's been close to a full day

since *La Catalina* sank—since Mar unleashed magia like they hadn't dared to do in years, not since the accident. They hoped maybe using that kind of magia would drain them for longer, but the itch is already starting. Mar has never gone more than a couple of weeks without letting their magia loose, and even that was a struggle.

But that's a problem for later. They have some time to figure out how to discreetly release their magia on a ship full of strange eyes. Just not very much time.

Not for the first time, Mar wishes they could use their magia without lighting up like a firework.

Up on the deck, Vega hands Mar a bowl of what looks like paella—light on the rice, heavy on the fish—and nods to an empty space in the circle the crew has made sitting on the floor. Mar takes the space next to Tito, the quartermaster. Tito grunts at Mar in what they suppose is some kind of acknowledgment, and Mar just nods and shovels a handful of fish and yellow rice into their mouth.

Part of them wants the food to be just mediocre so it won't remind them of life back on *La Catalina*, but unfortunately the meal is halfway decent, and Mar finds themself making the comparison anyway. It was actually *La Catalina*'s quartermaster, Leo, who was the cook, and Leo's paella always managed to be perfect even when they were low on supplies.

The thought hits them like a boot to the stomach, and the food becomes a thick lump in their throat. Mar swallows hard and inhales deeply through their nose, giving their stomach a moment to settle. The loss washes over them like a wave, and it's all they can do to keep the tears at bay. It feels wrong being here, *enjoying food,* when everyone Mar has ever loved is de—gone.

Mar closes their eyes and takes another deep breath. The loss is too fresh—a wound with no time to heal. But Papá and Leo wouldn't want them to drown in their grief. They'd want Mar to heal. Live. And yes, maybe even enjoy food.

They look back at their food, blinking hard as they force their thoughts to stall. This paella isn't quite up to par with Leo's delicious creations, but the fish is fresh, and the balance of spices has that tang Mar expects in their food. They take one slow bite, then another. The crew laughs in an ever-increasing crescendo, and it isn't long before Mar's scraping the bottom of their bowl, picking up the stray grains of rice and sucking the spices off their fingers.

And then Bas squeezes between Mar and Tito—a space that certainly wasn't meant to contain the gangly limbs of another teen boy—and Mar grimaces as he shimmies next to them until they're shoulder to shoulder. He'd been chatting with Capitán Vega before but evidently decided not to sit with him.

"Hola, Mar." Bas's lopsided grin makes Mar want to shove the boy into the ocean.

Mar stands. "Adiós, Bas."

They half expect Bas to protest, or even try to get in their way or stop them somehow, but to their relief, he doesn't. Instead, Mar marches up to the growing pile of dirty dishes,

adds their bowl, and turns away from the increasingly excit-
able dinner circle.

"And where do you think you're going?"

Mar starts at the Capitán's voice cutting through the
noise. The conversation hushes in an instant, and chills creep
down the back of Mar's neck as the weight of the crew's gazes
settles on them. They turn around.

"I . . ." Mar's voice falters. They want nothing more than
to curl up in a corner and let sleep mute reality for a couple of
hours. Running around *La Ana* all day has made their bones
heavy enough that it might just happen without too much of
a fight.

But it seems Vega has other ideas. He nods to the mountain of dishes. "Who do you think cleans up after dinner?"

Mar bites back the answer gathering behind their lips:
*Whoever cleaned up after dinner before you dragged me from
the ocean.* Instead they swallow acid and say, "Perdóname. I
didn't know."

"Now you do." Vega turns back to his men, and the conversation resumes. Mar presses their lips tightly together, rolls
up their sleeves, and turns to the mess. They've just dunked
the first bowl into the bucket of cold, soapy water when Bas
sidles up next to them. But rather than say something that
makes Mar want to hit him, he picks up a cup and swishes it
in the water as well.

Mar focuses on the dishes. On the cold water pruning
their skin and making their fingers numb. On the rhythm of
grabbing a bowl, dunking, wiping, drying, and placing it back

in the padded crate it came from. On the laughter and song of conversation, flowing in and out, loud and quiet. On the warm, salty breeze pushing their hair out of their face.

When the dishes are clean, dry, and put away, Mar looks at Bas. "You're still a cabrón."

Bas grins. "Well, obviously."

"You won't change my mind about you."

But if Bas is concerned, he doesn't show it. Instead, he winks. "Don't count on it."

Mar sleeps on the floor, crowded in the belowdecks cabin with the majority of the sixty or so members of the crew. Well, "sleep" is relative, they suppose, as there hasn't *actually* been much sleeping, not tonight. Not for lack of trying, but sleep is a challenge when every time Mar closes their eyes, they're back in the ocean, clawing for the surface, flames dancing above them in the distance as the water drags them deeper.

Sometimes the heat of the fire still prickles on their cheeks, like an echo.

Sometimes the bone-jarring *crack* of *La Catalina*'s mast snapping—ready to cleave the ship in two—jars Mar awake again.

Sometimes just listening to the snores of the crew members around them is almost familiar enough to make Mar ache with loss. The emptiness is a physical thing, like someone carved out a space deep inside them with a spoon.

So Mar stares at the hardwood ceiling. Breathes in the salty night air. Takes note of who sleeps here and who, more notably, doesn't. Bas has his own room, of course. Tito shares el Capitán's cabin; they must be partners. Not the only ones on the ship, either, judging by how closely some of the crew members are huddled. The thought of it is the first thing that almost makes Mar smile, even if just softly, before they turn back to the shadows.

They reach under their shirt and unpin the chest flattener Leo made them, sighing as it releases the pressure on their chest. At least the darkness obscures the shape of their unbound chest.

Mar breathes deeply. And tries to ignore the chill on their skin of being watched.

They glance around the dark cabin, squinting through the shadows, trying to make out who, exactly, is keeping an eye on them. The cabin is decently large—Mar can't see the other side, not through the night—but they imagine anyone on that far side wouldn't be able to see them, either. So they scan their surroundings slowly, waiting until the dark lumps form recognizable shapes—barrels, used bedrolls, shelves and coils of rope and crates—until they've identified everything inhabiting the darkness around them.

As far as Mar can tell, everyone is sleeping save for them.

So why does it absolutely feel as though someone nearby is staring at them?

They're being paranoid. They're just too awake, too upset over the last day's events. Mar shifts on the bundle of folded clothes they're using as a pillow and pulls the light blanket covering them up to their neck.

They close their eyes. Breathe deep. But the breath catches—breaks—and Mar wraps their arms tight around their stomach, drawing their knees to their chest. Trying to hold together as they fall apart. As the tears they've been holding in burst out of them at once. As they bite their fist and try to muffle the spasming sobs demanding out.

It was all so unfair. They used their magia to try to save *La Catalina*—more magia than they'd used in years. They poured everything they had into the effort, but in the end it didn't matter. Absolutely everything and everyone was gone.

What's the point of having this godforsaken magia if they couldn't even use it to save the ones they love?

Of course, they should have known better. Nothing good comes of Mar's magia.

They're not sure how long they lie there, trying to muffle their sobs into the lumpy bedroll Bas has given them. Eventually, when they've run out of tears and the waves of unbearable loss calm, Mar stares dully into darkness once again.

They aren't going to sleep tonight; that much is obvious. Mar wipes their face with their palms, tightens their chest flattener again, then stands and tiptoes a careful path in the dark between sleeping sailors. When they reach the quiet deck, their feet carry them to the rail. Then, leaning against the railing, they watch the reflection of the silver crescent moon ripple in the water before closing their eyes as they breathe in the cool ocean breeze. The salt in the air and soft hush of wave upon wave.

With their eyes closed, Mar can almost pretend they're on *La Catalina*. Almost pretend nothing has changed and el Diablo didn't ruin their life. But of course, even with their eyes closed it's not the same. The railing presses against their forearms differently. The creaking and even rhythm of the rocking aren't quite the same either. And anyway, they can't keep their eyes closed and pretend forever.

Mar sighs and opens their eyes—then bites back a shriek. They stumble two steps back, away from a man who's silently joined them against the railing.

No, not a man. The edges of his black tailcoat shed wisps of smoke, and his heavy boots thud against the deck as he turns to Mar and smiles with eyes like coal.

"Ay, perdón," el Diablo says. "Did I startle you?"

CHAPTER 6

"You certainly are an enigma." El Diablo tilts his head, regarding Mar like some kind of curiosity. "You're supposed to be dead."

"And you're supposed to be fiction." Mar takes pride in the steadiness of their voice, even while their heart thrums unsteadily in their chest. They glance around, but as far as they can tell, they're alone with el Diablo.

"Most of the crew is asleep," el Diablo says, as if reading their mind. "And anyway, only those I want to see me will." He leans on the railing, pale, bonelike skin almost silver in the moonlight. "How did you escape?"

It's a question they don't know how to answer. They hadn't expected to survive, not after the ocean swallowed them whole. But they did, and Mar isn't sure if being the only survivor of devastation that wiped out an entire crew was better than dying alongside them.

It certainly wasn't less painful.

"You got what you wanted," Mar answers stiffly. "Papá and the rest of my familia are gone. So why are you here?"

El Diablo looks them over slowly, with an uncomfortably appraising eye. Mar resists the urge to cross their arms over their chest; even with the bindings keeping them flat, a part of Mar still worries their chest will give them away. When el Diablo's gaze meets Mar's, the ember-like glowing around his irises makes them shiver. "You'd do anything to get your papá back, wouldn't you?"

Mar's eyes narrow.

El Diablo pushes off the railing and walks around Mar, the sound of coins jingling in his pockets with every step. "The desperate are so . . . delicious."

They grimace. "What do you want?"

He rolls his eyes. "Where's the fire?" A wicked smile spreads across his face. "Shall I start another?"

Mar's heart stutters, but they keep their face blank. They can't let this cabrón scare them. "If you don't have anything important to say, then I'm going back to bed." They turn around and start back for the stairs.

"I can get your papá back."

Mar stops. They don't turn around. They try to keep their breaths even, but those words alone are enough to get their heart pounding anew. He's lying. He has to be. Papá is gone—he made a deal with el Diablo, and that deal is over now. Papá can't be saved.

But what if he can be?

"Even if you could get him back," Mar says to the darkness in front of them, "you wouldn't."

The jingle of coins and the heavy footsteps break through the quiet. El Diablo strolls casually in front of them, smiling. "I wouldn't be so sure if I were you. I might be persuaded with the right incentive."

Mar's lips press into a thin line. "Claro," they mumble.

El Diablo snorts. "I don't do anything out of the kindness of my heart, hije."

"Don't call me that."

El Diablo brings his hands together. Something about his clean, even nails and the plethora of shiny rings on his fingers makes Mar want to punch him. "Let's make a deal."

"Not interested."

"Not even to save your papá?" He steps closer, and Mar wrinkles their nose, resisting the urge to step back as the scent of smoke and sulfur fills the air. "I'm not asking for anything that would hurt anyone else. Consider it an even trade: your soul for your papá's."

Just their soul. Mar would laugh if el Diablo's appearance and "offer" weren't so cruel; dangling Papá's life in front of them just as Mar is trying to accept his loss and grieve. "Offering" as if it were a deal Mar could actually take. As if Papá would ever forgive them for throwing away their soul for his.

"No," Mar says.

"No?" El Diablo smirks. "How about now?"

Mar blinks, and Papá is standing beside el Diablo, hands

and feet in heavy chains, a black cloth tied around his mouth. His eyes are wide, breaths fast, sweat dripping down his face.

Mar chokes on their own scream. Tears flood their eyes, impossible to hold back. "Papá," they croak.

"Go ahead," el Diablo says. "Tell him to his face that you're too selfish to save him."

Mar clenches their fists, glaring at el Diablo through the hot blur of tears. "Vete al carajo."

El Diablo leans his head back and laughs loudly; Papá disappears in a cloud of black smoke. Was it really him, or was it just an illusion? Mar supposes it doesn't matter; the pain is fresh and raw all the same.

"Tell you what," el Diablo says. "There will be an especially large harvest moon on September 22—it'll be quite the spectacle. I'll give you until then—roughly two moon cycles—to change your mind and save your papá, hm? De nada."

Then he's gone. Just a lingering wisp of black smoke, the smell of sulfur, and Mar, shaking in the darkness until they sink to the ground, pull their knees to their chest, and muffle the sobs tearing them apart.

CHAPTER 7

Papá can be saved.

It's the only clear thought in Mar's mind for five days. The enduring, unreachable truth steadying them like a lantern in a storm, keeping their eyes forward as days blur to nights, and nights back to days. But the reality that he can be saved does nothing to answer the even more important question: How do you save a man's soul from el Diablo without giving up your own?

Mar doesn't even know where to begin. But it's a question that never leaves them through the smear of groggy mornings; endless sweaty afternoons with heat so thick it sticks to their skin, and the song of the sea: a hush, a spray, a sigh, again. After the first couple of days their magia begins buzzing unsteadily under their skin. On *La Catalina*, Mar had only once gone more than a handful of days without using their magia. They'd release it in small doses to keep it from building up dangerously. But now on *La Ana* it isn't safe to use it. Their magia seems to know that, at least—even five days after their encounter with el Diablo, Mar's markings don't glow.

They figure it's more than coincidence; it's self-preservation. Their magia may act out sometimes, but it hasn't ever acted out in a way that would give them away. Yet.

Of course, if they don't figure out how to release their magia in secret, it's only a matter of time before the buildup bursts out of them.

The days move quickly, at least. Mar is never still—as the only cabin person, they have an endless supply of work to do. And it suits them well enough; after all, it's in the still moments that they remember why they're aboard *La Ana* to begin with. And more than anything else, Mar just wants to forget.

It's also in the still moments that the prickle of being watched washes over them again, like charged air before a lightning strike. When they're looking for coiled rope below-decks. Or tying knots for the rigging. Or checking stock. It's the moments when they're alone that Mar is absolutely certain they aren't—and yet, whenever they whirl around, no one is there.

Days slide to a week. Then nearly two. Two weeks is the most Mar has ever gone without using their magia. Now just a day shy of that record, their bones are *vibrating* with pent-up energy, their skin hot to the touch. While the ice feels like a frozen block in the pit of Mar's stomach, it's the fire absolutely raging against the buildup, furious at the length of

Mar's suppression. Like an active, growing explosion pushing against their rib cage.

Though they've kept the magia overflow away from their hands for now, Mar had to start wrapping their arms to hide their markings burning with unshed power a day ago. The now-sweaty fabric is uncomfortable, to say the least, but it's working well to smother the light.

Mar shivers as they haul up a coil of heavy rope from below-decks, even as they emerge under the sun's heated glare, utterly sweat drenched. Tito catches their eyes, arching an eyebrow at them. Mar hadn't realized their trembling was that obvious.

But the warning is there, screaming in their bones. Their ears ring and the world is too bright, too sharp. They're on the edge of losing control. Mar dumps the rope on the deck and squeezes their eyes shut, filling their lungs with the salty ocean breeze. If they just focus on their breath—but carajo, even their bones hurt.

"Mar."

They force their eyes open, squinting in the bleached daylight. Tito is frowning deeply at them, and he's close. When did he get so close?

"¿Qué pasa?" he asks.

"No me siento bien," Mar mutters. "Might be getting sick."

"Then you should rest." Tito gently pats their shoulder. "Don't need you keeling over. I'll take care of this. Take the rest of the day off."

Mar almost wants to protest—after all, the work is a good distraction from the pounding in their ears and their uncontrollable trembling—but they can't go on like this. They need release. Before the magia says *enough* and lets loose in front of the whole damn crew.

With the growing, angry heat ready to erupt inside them, Mar is a slip away from incinerating everyone on board.

"Thanks," they force out, and Tito nods, humming as he walks away.

By the time Mar stumbles into an unoccupied stockroom, they're vibrating with so much energy, their teeth are chattering. It's too much. Their skin itches like hundreds of spiders crawling all over them. They can't hold it in anymore.

Given a quick shove, the door begrudgingly closes behind them. The stockroom is full of crates to the left and barrels to the right. The space in between leaves just enough room for one or two people.

All in all, the cramped space isn't exactly ideal for letting off some magic, but the larger storeroom is full of gunpowder, which is even less ideal given Mar's proclivity to fire. Small as it may be, this room fulfills Mar's requirements in their desperation: a place to hide where no one is likely to interrupt them.

Mar closes their eyes and sighs, relaxing their shoulders as they tap into that place in the center of their chest where their magia hums the loudest. Maybe if they hadn't waited so long, they'd be able to coax out the ice, but it's far too late for that now. *Bien,* they think. *Ahora.*

The heat consumes them in an instant. They open their eyes to the glowing fire-orange pathways blazing over their body, weaving over them from neck to fingertips to toes. They snap their fingers, and flames spring to life in their palms, burning, hungry. Mar focuses on the flames, letting them dance over their hands and up their arms, pouring their magic into them, resisting the urge to smile as the fire grows from candle flames to fireballs to fiery snakes slithering up and down their arms. They can't go too big, of course—don't want to set the stockroom on fire—but even just this controlled creation draws the trembling out of their bones.

Magia is a nuisance, dangerous, and has only ever brought pain to Mar's life; but the truth is that using it feels good. They sigh as the tension inside them—taut, like a rope drawing in an anchor—releases at last. It may not be the kind of explosive release of magic that they crave, but it's *something*, and finally, finally Mar can breathe easily.

For the first time since *La Catalina* sank, Mar smiles. Just a little.

Then the door opens behind them.

Mar gasps and whirls around, flames whipping up dangerously close to the crates.

Tito stares at them, wide-eyed and openmouthed, from the doorway. The bundle of canvas in his arms hits the floor with a thud.

"¡Maldita sea!" Tito whispers. "Mar?"

CHAPTER 8

Mar can't breathe. The flames die in their palms. Pinpricks of terror nip down their spine. The warmth of the magia lighting up their markings goes dull and cold, restoring them to normal black tattoos. But it's too late.

Tito has seen them using magia.

Seen the way their skin and eyes glow red, like a diablo.

The way they stand, unburned, when fire tasted their skin just moments earlier.

The door thumps closed behind Tito, and he flinches but doesn't reach for his gun. In fact, he doesn't move at all. Just stares at Mar with that wide-eyed expression they aren't sure how to decipher. Terror? Wonder? Uncertainty? All of the above?

"Tito," Mar chokes out. "I . . ."

But what is there to say? How do you explain the inexplicable?

"Please don't kill me," Mar whispers.

Tito's eyes widen just a little more; then he turns around. "Wait—"

He walks out without even glancing back, canvas forgotten. The door slams behind him—Mar jumps. Every racing heartbeat is a punch to Mar's chest. They scream. Cold explodes from them like a breath knocked out of them. Mar's eyes fly open, and they wipe their tears with the backs of their fists.

Dios.

Looking at the storage room is a kick in the stomach. Every crate, every barrel, every surface—even the bundle of canvas Tito dropped—is covered in frost and ice. The room is so cold, Mar's breaths gather in clouds in the air. They turned the storage room into an icebox. On a schooner. In the middle of the Caribbean.

How has everything gone so wrong in a matter of moments? Mar wants to chase after Tito, but they can't leave the storeroom like this—then *everyone* will know about Mar's magia. Even if Tito doesn't tell anyone, it won't matter.

Mar shoves their trembling fingers into their pocket, pulling the crumpled bullet into their fist, then presses their fist against their heart.

"Papá." Mar chokes on a sob, curling in on themself. "Tito's going to tell everyone. They'll kill me. I made a mistake. Papá, I need you."

"Not sure how a dead guy can help you, but okay."

Mar jerks back. A crew member Mar doesn't recognize is leaning against a frozen barrel. Was this person in here the whole time? But Mar swears they checked when they first entered the room—how did they miss them?

A wave of heat washes over them. They just can't win.

The person tilts their head to the side, smirking just slightly at Mar. They seem to be around Mar's age, and their long black hair is held back in a bun. Light skin, tall, all angles. Black kohl accentuates their dark eyes, and their short nails are painted black. But what gives them away is their clothes; they're immaculate and dressed like they're about to go on shore leave. Their black waistcoat is half-buttoned, revealing their black frilled shirt underneath. Their cravat, also black, is perfectly knotted, and even their dark trousers look like they've never been worn before. Over all that is a gorgeous black tailcoat patterned with embroidered silver roses and matching gleaming silver buttons.

Nobody who works on a ship is dressed like that. And they aren't covered in frost.

. . . *Are* they a crew member?

"Done staring?" the stranger says. "Not that I can blame you—I'd stare at me too. It's not often one encounters someone so stunning."

Even in the cold room, Mar's cheeks warm. "How'd you get in here? Who are you?"

"You can call me Dami." They push off the barrel and stretch their long arms over their head. "More important, I think, is: How are you going to clean up this mess? Not only did a prominent crew member see you use magia, but you turned this storage room into an icebox."

Mar's mouth opens and closes. How did they . . . ? "How long have you been here?"

"Oh, I saw everything." They smile. "I've been watching you for some time, Mar."

Mar stares at them for a moment, willing their heart to slow. "You're not a crew member."

Dami snorts. "Figure that out all by yourself, did you?"

"Then how did you get on *La Ana*? Are you—are you a stowaway?"

"Hmm." Dami tilts their head. "Not quite."

But if they aren't a stowaway and they aren't a crew member . . .

"You're asking the right questions," Dami says. "I bet you even know the answer."

That's when Mar notices it—the stranger's edges are . . . wispy. When Dami moves, they leave a thin trail of black smoke in the air, like they're moments away from bursting into flame.

"Diablo." The whisper creates a small white cloud in the frigid air; Mar shivers, but not from the cold.

Dami claps slowly. "Close—*demonio,* actually, but I'll give it to you. Well done. That didn't take long."

Mar's knowledge of diablos and demonios extends only to what Papá has told them—to what they once thought were just stories. Papá said both diablos and demonios made deals with humans, but only diablos were powerful enough to do the really *big* deals. Like ensuring Papá's legacy and saving Mar's life in the process.

Mar doesn't care to find out what demonios can do.

I've been watching you for some time, Mar, they said, which meant—what, exactly? Are they working for el Diablo? Spying on them for him? "Get out."

Dami arches an eyebrow. "You haven't even—"

Mar pulls their shoulders back and levels their most cutting glare onto the demonio. "I have no interest in anything you have to say. I'm not making any deals, not with you, not with el Diablo or any other diablo or demonio. Leave."

"I didn't say anything about a deal—"

Mar's clenched fists burst into flames. *"Leave!"*

Dami rolls their eyes and raises their hands defensively. "Fine, fine. But sooner or later you're going to need—"

Mar hurls a fireball at their face. Dami's eyes widen for just a second before they disappear in a cloud of smoke; the fireball slams into a block of ice. Mar takes a slow, full breath, wrinkling their nose at the reek of sulfur in the cold air.

"Que cabrón," they mutter. Mar closes their eyes and shakes their head. They can't make the same mistake as Papá. Nothing is worth losing their soul.

They glance around the ice-coated room and grimace. They can't focus on Papá right now; or even thawing this room out. They should have just gone after Tito to begin with, but Dami distracted them, and now . . . now they have to catch up to Tito first, whether he likes it or not—and beg him not to spill their secret. Not to get them killed.

If it isn't already too late.

Mar steels their shoulders, pushes through the door, and

walks directly into Bas. They stop short with a gasp, nearly smashing their face into his jaw as Bas grabs their shoulders to steady them.

He lets out a surprised laugh. "Oh, there you are! I suppose Tito was right."

Mar's heart gallops in their chest. "Tito?" their voice almost squeaks. They clear their throat at Bas's perplexed expression and try again. "You saw Tito?"

"Uh, yes," Bas says. "He said you were down here. He looked a bit pale—I don't think he's feeling well."

"Oh," Mar says lightly, choking back the panic clawing up their throat. "Do you know where he went? I need clarification on something he asked me to do."

Bas lifts a shoulder. "He said he was going to lie down, so I imagine he's with el Capitán in their shared quarters by now."

The room swims around Mar and they blink hard, fighting to stay grounded as their pulse roars in their ears. They can't breathe. It's too late. Tito is already with el Capitán, telling him everything. The crew will kill them—or at least maroon them. Not even Mar's magia can save them from a slow death on a sandbar with nothing but a gun and a single bullet.

They don't even realize they're crying until Bas's face breaks out in alarm. "What's wrong? Did something happen? Are you okay?"

For some reason, the questions just make them cry harder. Mar presses their palms against their face. They can't believe they've completely broken down in front of Bas like this, but they can't hold it back anymore. They made a mistake—they slipped up just once, and now it's over.

So when Bas wraps his arms around Mar, they can't help but sink into his embrace. And when he hushes them softly and says something about going to his cabin, they can't find it in them to refuse. It's been so long since anything has brought them comfort, since anyone has shown them warmth, and they need it like they need air.

Bas doesn't pry about Tito, and no one comes knocking at his door. Mar isn't sure how long they stay there with him, their head resting on his shoulder until the tears slow and the panicked haze in their mind clears. Eventually, they grow tired, and though the temptation to stay is there, they force themself to their feet.

"It's going to be okay, Mar," Bas says with a soft smile. "You'll see."

Bas can't know that—he doesn't even know what happened—but somehow, Mar manages to smile back.

They return to the storage room, praying no one else has found it. But when they push through the door, the room is, well, normal. The chill in the air and the ice are gone. Nothing is even damp.

As Mar stands there, alone, staring at the inexplicable room, they catch the faint smell of sulfur and a quiet laugh, like the fading memory of a dream.

CHAPTER 9

Suspiciously, the ship rolls on over the waves for five days as if nothing ever happened except for one thing: Tito's sudden absence.

In theory, getting ahold of *La Ana*'s quartermaster while out at sea should be relatively easy. After all, the quartermaster is essentially the crew's representative, so it's generally vital for Tito to be accessible, and it's not like there's anywhere to run; they're all stuck on the same ship until they dock somewhere.

And yet, for the five days between Tito's spying Mar with magia and *La Ana* reaching Playa del Carmen, Tito falls mysteriously and suddenly ill and doesn't leave el Capitán's quarters even for dinner.

Mar spends the first two days of his isolation wound so tight, they feel as though they might burst. Every time someone approaches them, Mar is absolutely convinced this is it. The moment the crew turns against them. The moment they see Mar for who they are—a monster.

By the fifth day, all Mar can think about is why Tito hasn't told anyone. Because that's the only explanation; it's been five days since he caught Mar using magia, but no one treats them differently. Bas orders café he won't drink and acts absolutely delighted every time Mar delivers. Mar doesn't tell him they know he doesn't even like the stuff.

Though of course, it's never just a cup of café—Bas loops them into conversations about clothing and personal style (Bas absurdly argues Mar could look good in a burlap sack), food (what kind of seafood is best, which Mar and Bas agree is obviously shrimp), and, most strangely, whether Mar would ever want to go to the edge of the world, if there is, indeed, an edge.

"I think, if it exists," Bas says, "I would want to see it."

Mar crinkles their nose. "Why? There'd be nothing to see."

"Exactly!" Bas beams and smells his cafecito before placing it on his small desk, where Mar imagines it will probably be ignored. "It would be fascinating to walk right up to the edge and stare into the end of everything. And so empowering to see it, then turn around and walk away, to continue on when everything else has stopped. Don't you think?"

Bas looks at Mar with a sort of wide-eyed curiosity that would be cute if he weren't such a callous bastard. But the truth is, Mar has already seen the end—looked into the glowing coal eyes of el Diablo himself—and walked away. And the experience didn't leave them powerful, just broken.

Mar shrugs and gets back to work.

The labor is different from what they did back on *La Catalina;* there, Mar worked with the sailing master and their papá to learn to navigate. They'd learned how to read the stars, the sea, the wind, and most complicated of all, navigational maps detailing currents and islands in addition to the skies.

But on *La Ana,* Mar is just a cabin person.

The boatswain, Joaquín, takes over Tito's duties of telling Mar and a third of the sixty-person crew what to do. Joaquín also seems to take personal offense at Mar's lack of muscle mass; he takes to calling Mar "Leoncito" as a play off their last name because he can carry a coil of rope around each large, toned shoulder, while they can only carry one.

At the end of the fifth day, Mar finally caves and asks Bas about Tito.

"What about him?" Bas responds with a frown.

"Isn't it odd that he hasn't left el Capitán's quarters in five days?"

Bas shrugs. "He must be ill. If anything, we should thank him when he's recovered for not spreading it to the rest of us."

Of course, Tito isn't ill—Mar is sure. It'd be far too much of a coincidence that Tito actually fell ill after catching Mar out the way he did. But they can't exactly tell Bas that.

At night, Mar lies awake on the floor, their arms crossed behind their head on their pillow of folded clothes as they listen to the sleep sounds of the crew. They fight to ignore the endless prickle of watching eyes, try to bury the knowledge that a demonio is watching them.

Tito still hasn't told anyone. Or at least he hasn't told the larger crew, which means, inexplicably, there's still time for Mar to corner him and beg for his discretion. Tito can't hide forever, and Mar keeps a constant watch.

With the crew asleep and the darkness complete, Mar silently makes their way onto the deck. It's there, under the bright stars with sea salt on the night breeze, that Mar can finally relax. Breathe. For a few minutes they don't have to worry about Tito, about the crew, about someone discovering their secret. They lean against the railing, look down at the gently rolling waves below, and sigh.

"Have you ever tried to freeze the ocean?"

Mar jumps and swears under their breath, glowering at the demonio suddenly beside them. And then Dami's words register.

"What?"

"Freeze the ocean," Dami repeats, as if there couldn't be a more normal suggestion. "I know you can create ice with your magia—I saw what you did to the storage room, remember?"

"What I accidentally did to the storage room is nothing like freezing *the entire ocean*."

"I didn't say the *entire* ocean. I just meant a part of it. Maybe turn a chunk into an iceberg—or even an ice *block*."

Mar frowns, peering once again at the waves below. "Moving water is a lot harder to freeze. And salt water needs to get even colder than fresh water to turn to ice."

Dami leans their back against the railing. "Sounds to me like the perfect way to practice using your magia on a ship, seeing how you only have just about a month left to practice before you're out of time to save your papá."

Mar whirls on them with a scowl, but Dami is gone—only wisps of black smoke remain.

Mar swears under their breath. As if they needed the reminder of how quickly time is slipping away from them. And they don't have to *practice* their magia—they're just forced to use it every so often to release excess energy. They don't want—or need—to become more adept at using it.

Then again, wouldn't using it be less risky if they had better control?

Mar shakes their head and sighs. As nice as it would be to live in a world where they could use their magia freely, that's just not their reality.

The ocean rolls beneath them, and Mar finds their gaze once again drawn to the waves. It's absurd to think any one person could have enough power to freeze the ocean, and yet . . . could a *portion* of the ocean be as feasible as Dami seems to think?

It has never occurred to Mar to try, but now the idea won't let them go. At the very least, trying would certainly expend more energy than dropping ice cubes into the water.

They glance around to check they're alone. Then, with a breath, Mar leans their forearms on the railing and closes their eyes.

When it comes to their magia, fire roars awake with the slightest thought, but ice takes a little more coaxing. Mar breathes steadily, a smile creeping onto their lips as coolness awakens in their chest and spreads to their fingertips. They open their eyes, homing in on a patch of water directly beneath them. *Just like cooling a glass of water without touching it,* they assure themself. *A really big glass of water without the glass.*

Steady breath in. Cold breath out. The bandage wrapping their right arm has loosened some, and their markings—glowing bright blue—peek between the cloth strips. Magia pours out of them, gathering on the surface of the water, but they have to go deeper. They push harder, sweat beading on their forehead. A huge ice cube, that's all they're doing. A giant block of frozen seawater, like—

"Mar?"

Mar jerks up with a gasp, snuffing out the flow of magia. A cold, violent chill makes their teeth chatter and body shake, but then their magia settles at last, their markings back to black. They spin around to Bas, staring at them wide-eyed.

"Are you okay?"

"Yes," Mar says, a little too quickly, a little too breathlessly.

"Are you sure?" Bas frowns and steps closer, just an arm span away. "You're sweating."

"I . . ." Mar can't think of an excuse fast enough. They shake their head. "No. I'm feeling a bit sick, but I'm sure I'll be fine. I just needed some air."

Bas nods. "Some rest should help too."

"I won't be out much longer. Why are you awake?"

"I was feeling a bit restless." He smiles softly. "But I'm going to head to bed. See you tomorrow?"

"Is that really a question?"

Bas laughs. "True. Okay. Buenas noches, Mar."

Mar nods and waits for him to disappear belowdecks before pressing their face into their hands. They nearly got caught—*again*. Serves them right for letting a demonio get to them.

A thunk behind them startles them from their thoughts. Mar turns with a frown and peers over the edge of the ship.

Below, bobbing in the ocean, as long and wide as Mar is tall, is a massive chunk of ice.

Later that night, Mar stares into the utter blackness of the enclosed cabin, breathing in the musty, sweaty air tinged with salt and sea.

Papá often told Mar they were capable of more than they realized. They'd like to think he and Leo would be proud of them, even if their little misadventure with their ice magia *did* almost get them caught. They turned some of the Caribbean Sea into a chunk of ice. Who else could say that?

Mar closes their eyes, imagining Papá's and Leo's smiles. On *La Catalina*, they slept most nights in the crow's nest, lulled to sleep by the sway of the ship and the warm sea breeze caressing their hair. Or sometimes tangled in the rigging, which made their papá nervous, so Mar didn't do it often even though it gave them a soft sense of security.

Like the ship was holding Mar in her arms—because, in a way, she was.

CHAPTER 10

When the crew docks the ship, Mar is ready. Tito may have stayed hidden in the last few days of their trip, but according to Bas, they've come to Playa del Carmen to connect with the leader of a local group of revolutionaries working with insurgency groups across la Nueva España to fight for independence.

This is a meeting Tito can't miss. All Mar has to do is corner him alone, even if just for five minutes. That's all they need, just a chance. Mar could grab Tito before they disembark—use the distraction of the preparing crew to pull him aside for a private conversation.

And if Tito refuses to keep their secret, well . . . at least they're on land. They'll have a chance to run before the rest of the crew finds out they're harboring a monster.

Mar continues slowly tying and untying the rigging, praying to whoever is listening that Joaquín is too distracted to notice Mar's taking ages to tie a couple of knots they know how to do in their sleep. But ducked down where they are, next to the mast, is the perfect place to keep an eye on el Capitán's quarters, where Tito's still hiding.

Mar is sure he'll emerge soon. He has to. They're all getting ready to leave, and Tito is too important to leave behind, even to keep an eye on things on *La Ana* while the rest of them are in town.

Unless, of course, he actually is sick.

The double doors to el Capitán's quarters swing open, and Mar jerks ramrod straight as Tito steps out, squinting a little in the bright sunlight. If he was ever truly ill—which Mar can't help but be skeptical about—he certainly doesn't look it anymore. Now Mar just has to approach him; maybe sneak up on him, as he seems to have been avoiding them.

Mar rubs the back of their hand, biting their lip. Sure would be nice if their magia let them turn invisible. Or appear and disappear anywhere at all, like el Diablo and Dami.

Mar stands and steps toward him, and Tito's gaze jumps to them. Mar holds back a cringe as Tito drills them with an even, passive stare before melting slowly into a soft frown.

Mar isn't sure what to make of that. Is he frowning because Mar is still here? Did he expect the crew to have already disposed of them? Is it too late to beg him to keep Mar's secret safe?

A clap on the back practically makes Mar jump out of their skin. They turn, startled, to Bas grinning obliviously at them. "Great news! El Capitán wants us to join the company ashore."

Mar frowns. "He . . . does?" It's not that they don't believe Bas would be invited—as la Pirata Vega's son, it makes sense that el Capitán would want Bas to learn every aspect of being a capitán if Bas ever hopes to vie for the position himself.

But why would el Capitán want Mar to join? They haven't really gotten the sense that la Pirata Vega is particularly impressed with them, not that they can blame him. Mar hasn't been trying to be impressive as much as forgettable. Unless . . .

Mar's stomach swoops nauseatingly. Unless Tito told el Capitán about Mar's magia. Would Vega expose them in front of everyone?

"¡Por supuesto!" Bas says, and it takes Mar a minute to remember their original question—and not that Bas is agreeing that el Capitán is about to reveal their secret to the whole crew. "Do you doubt me?"

Mar side-eyes Bas, pushing their clammy hands into their pockets. He has that lopsided grin that means he is, as usual, far too entertained over nothing at all. "Yes," they say. "I do."

Bas opens, then closes his mouth and frowns, evidently unprepared for that response. Mar steps past him—maybe if they catch Tito before . . . But Tito isn't standing by el Capitán's quarters anymore. They search the crew for Tito's large frame, but the man has somehow managed to disappear. Again.

"¡Mierda!" Mar swears under their breath. They looked away for barely two minutes. Where did he go?

Bas's cheek brushes Mar's and they jerk away, staring at him. Bas is hunching a bit, standing shoulder to shoulder with Mar, looking in the direction Mar was. He doesn't react to Mar's startled response; instead he continues staring off toward el Capitán's quarters.

"Hmm," Bas says. "Just as I suspected."

Mar doesn't want to take the bait, but Bas stands there, partially crouched, in silence, for an uncomfortably long time. Mar groans and sighs. "Fine. What?"

Bas shakes his head and stands up straight. "There isn't someone more interesting than me standing over there," he says somberly.

The laugh that bubbles out of them surprises Mar more than it probably does Bas. Bas's face lights up, and this time his grin is genuine. "Wow," he says, and something about the awe on his face and smile in his voice warms Mar's face.

Mar quickly looks away, scowling. They do *not* care if Bas has a nice smile or if the scar on his lip is endearing. He's an annoying child who lazes all day and takes nothing seriously—not even death.

They shake their head, clearing their thoughts. Another cursory glance at the busy crew confirms what they suspect: that Tito has managed to find another place to hide. Which leaves them with two possibilities for the path forward.

One: Tito told Vega about Mar's magia and will stick with him until el Capitán exposes them at the meeting. Or maybe shortly before. Maybe he just wants to get Mar off *La Ana* before attacking them.

Just the thought of it makes Mar ill. Even if they manage to fight off the whole crew without getting shot—which seems unlikely—Mar isn't sure they'd be able to protect themself without seriously injuring or killing the crew.

Of course, there's also possibility two: Maybe el Capitán really did pick them to be part of the team meeting without an underhanded motivation. This doesn't seem like a terribly likely scenario—Vega seems to generally tolerate Mar, but they certainly wouldn't go so far as to think Vega might like them.

But if el Capitán really *does* want Mar to join them, maybe getting inexplicably chosen can work to their advantage. Tito is bound to be part of that group as well, so all Mar has to do is follow along and wait for the opportune moment to pull Tito away.

Tito may have avoided Mar this long, but it ends today. One way or the other, Mar is going to get answers. Whether they run or stay is in Tito's hands.

Mar swallows their anxiety, takes a shaky breath, and turns back to Bas. "So. Who are we meeting?"

"Her name is Graciela," Bas begins. "She—"

"Hold on." Mar's eyes widen. "Graciela? As in . . . Graciela Soledad Ruiz Márquez?"

"That's the one," Bas says nonchalantly as a smile curls the corners of his lips. "I take it you've heard of her?"

"Only rumors and whispers," Mar answers. "I wasn't even sure if she was still alive."

It was Leo who told Mar stories about Doña Graciela,

alongside the legends like Gertrudis Bocanegra, La Corregidora, and Leona Vicario—women directly involved in la Nueva España's ongoing fight for independence. Mar was always inspired by the underground movement, and though *La Catalina*'s crew helped funnel them resources like *La Ana*'s crew was doing today, Mar had never had the opportunity to actually meet one of these revolutionaries.

Suddenly, their stomach is in knots again.

"Alive and well, though I'm sure the Spanish would prefer otherwise." Bas grins. "Exciting, isn't it?"

Mar swallows hard, forcing their face into a neutral expression. "Yeah. Exciting."

"And why are you here?" El Capitán looks at Mar with a combination of amusement and vexation, assessing them under the wide brim of his bolero. Like Mar and Bas, el Capitán has changed into his dressy shore leave clothes: a white silk shirt beneath a fitted navy tailcoat with gold buttons over tight tan pantaloons tucked into black riding boots. And, of course, a meticulously tied white cravat. It's odd seeing el Capitán out of his sailing clothes, but he certainly knows how to dress.

Mar's boot presses into the beach sand as they glance at Bas, who seems completely unsurprised by el Capitán's apparent lack of awareness of the invitation he supposedly extended them. Even Tito, standing beside el Pirata Vega, dressed in similar fashionable attire and facing Mar at last, seems confused.

So then . . . it's not a setup?

Now it all makes sense. Of course Vega didn't invite Mar along—why would he? Mar is the newest member of the crew, and the youngest, and it's not like they've gone out of their way to endear themself to el Capitán.

No, he didn't invite Mar along. Bas did.

The relief is so sudden, Mar almost laughs. The invitation isn't a trap. They still have time to bargain with Tito. Mar doesn't have to fight anyone. For the moment, at least, they're still safe.

"You invited me to be part of the team," Bas jumps in confidently. "And Mar is my assistant, so of course he has to come too."

Both Mar and el Capitán stare at Bas.

La Pirata Vega arches an eyebrow at him. "Your assistant, is he? And what do you need assistance with, hijo?"

"A capitán can't survive without the support of the crew. If I ever want to be selected as capitán myself, I need to learn how to work with even the most difficult crew members."

Mar's eyes narrow. Difficult? Mar isn't a difficult crew member! Sure, they haven't been the friendliest, but what does he expect after everything? They do what they're told, even when what they're told is to get someone who doesn't even like café un cafecito multiple times a day!

Tito laughs—loudly, Mar might add—and even el Capitán

smirks. But only for a moment, because his smile disappears the moment he turns back to Mar. "Let me be clear. If you betray us, I will kill you. Without hesitation. Understand?"

Mar glances at Tito. Given that the crew hasn't treated Mar any differently, they assume he hasn't told the larger crew yet . . . but has he not told el Capitán either? It's not like he didn't have ample opportunity, staying in el Capitán's quarters for five uninterrupted days.

Tito's blank face gives nothing away.

El Pirata Vega snaps his fingers. "Oye, what are you looking at Tito for? He's not going to save you."

"Perdón." Mar quickly turns back to el Capitán. "I—Yes, I understand." They hesitate. Would it be too much to add . . . ? Mar shakes their head. "You have nothing to worry about, anyway. The Spaniards killed my mamá. I would die before I helped them."

CHAPTER 11

The first and only time Mar completely lost control of their *magia*, they were eight years old. A child.

The child didn't know their *magia* was dangerous, at least not like this. Sure, they knew to be careful with fire, because though it didn't burn them, it could burn everyone—and everything—else. But until then, *magia* had been a friend. The child loved the way their body lit up as if stars sat packed under their skin; how fire whispered to them, always ready to play; how even on the hottest day a handful of ice or a cold drink was just a thought away.

One time, they thought they might have even made it rain.

But the child had grown careless. Sure, they'd known never to show their *magia* to a stranger—Mamá reminded them every single week and anytime they wanted to walk into town—but they'd forgotten that sometimes strangers appear where they aren't expected. They'd forgotten that the little strip of beach next to their small home was technically public land. And they'd forgotten that this little strip of technically public land was just picturesque enough that visitors sometimes strayed where they weren't wanted.

The child crouched, pushing the flame in their palm to the sand, grinning as the sand turned to glass. Then a scream shattered the night. They jolted up, snuffing the flame out in their fist, but it hardly mattered. Their markings were bright orange in the night, and there was nothing they could do to hide from the screaming woman and the man beside her, dressed in a fancy military uniform.

"¡Dios mío!" the woman shouted, hand over her heart, the words thick with a Spaniard's affectation. "¡Ay, es un diablo, un monstruo! Miguel, por favor, ¡protégeme!"

When the man pushed the woman behind him and stepped forward, his gun was outstretched. And that was when a second scream startled the child, a scream they knew all too well. But they didn't dare move, not even to look at Mamá. All they could see was that gun as cries of diablo and monstruo rang in their ears.

They barely flinched when the gun went off and Mamá was suddenly in front of them. Her eyes went wide as she cried out, then collapsed face-first in the sand.

She did not move again. And that's when things went blurry.

Mar didn't really remember the details. Their blood had turned white-iron hot, almost painful, as the heat of their magia consumed them. Then they screamed so loudly, they thought their lungs might burst.

No one expected the volcano to erupt—least of all Mar.

Later, they learned the smoke consumed the village just

before the lava did, swallowing everyone and everything, reducing Mar's home to thick black rock.

Papá found Mar in the chaos of the explosion, still clinging to Mamá on the beach. He ripped Mar away, chest heaving with sobs as he pulled the child into his arms and ran to La Catalina.

They never did return to their beachside home, because there was nothing to return to. Because the smoke had poisoned most, and the lava had taken the rest. Because Mar had lost control. Because maybe that woman was right.

Maybe Mar was a diablo, and maybe a devil's magic ran through their veins.

CHAPTER 12

The church is rotting. The concrete walls of the outside are absolutely moldered, the once-gray walls turned dingy black. Faded red paint peels off the massive double wooden doors. The glass window above the arched doorway is broken. The building doesn't look to have ever been grand, but what's left now is nothing but a husk.

"Sad, isn't it?" Tito pushes a large barrel next to them, and Mar practically jumps out of their skin. Tito is . . . talking to them? They open their mouth, but he cuts them off. "Help bring these inside. We have a lot to carry."

"Tito—"

"We'll talk later, Mar." He turns away. "We have much to discuss."

He walks away without looking back, and Mar can't help the sinking of their stomach. They've been desperate to talk to Tito, of course, but now the thought of what he might say is nauseating. If everything were fine, he could have just told them right there. But he didn't.

Inside is creaky and dusty, and they suspect it isn't more inviting in the daylight. The group selected to meet Graciela is composed of ten people, with six others joining Mar, Bas, Tito, and el Capitán. Together, the ten of them have rolled barrels and carried boxes down the dusty center aisle, resting them at the bottom of a massive crucifix, like an unholy offering.

El Capitán has reassured them that the church is long abandoned—evidently, a larger one was built on the other side of town. But that knowledge doesn't make them feel any better about standing in the building of an organization brought by the very colonizers who killed so many of Mar's ancestors and eradicated the acceptance of people like Mar. People who don't neatly fit in the category of man or woman.

They scowl and cross their arms over their chest, suddenly all too aware of the way the cloth binding their chest cuts into their sides beneath their white shirt, silk cravat, and blue tailcoat buttoned closed. Between the roiling of their anxious stomach and the way every glance at Tito sends a flash of panicked heat through their chest, the cloth feels tighter than usual. In a way, the pressure of the binding cloth is almost comforting. But mostly it's just an uncomfortable reminder of what they have to endure to feel like themself.

"Creepy," someone says next to them, and Mar turns, expecting it to be Bas.

It is not.

It's Dami. Again.

Mar's eyes widen as they glance around. Bas is talking to

Vega, and Tito and most of the others are sprawled out on the pews or leaning against the walls, murmuring in quiet conversation.

Certainly no one is reacting the way one would expect if a demonio appeared out of thin air in a church. So, then, no one else can see them.

Dami looks them over with an appraising eye. "You certainly clean up."

"What are you doing here?" Mar hisses. "Shouldn't you be banished from churches like this? I thought sacred places were supposed to be off-limits." Mar doesn't know much about Catholicism, but they *do* know churches are supposedly sacrosanct and Catholics aren't amenable to demonios. It's a huge part of the reason Mar has to hide their magia the way they do.

Dami snorts. "There is nothing holy about this building."

Mar grimaces, then does a double take. Dami looks . . . different. Their face is softer, lips fuller, their wavy black hair down to midback length. They're dressed much the same as before, but the shape of their chest has grown under their vest.

A pang of jealousy strikes Mar between the ribs. Can Dami just . . . change the shape of their chest at will? It feels weird to ask about their chest, though, so Mar says, "Can you change your appearance?"

Dami grins and winks at them. "Perks of being a demonio." They tilt their head. "You have some interesting perks with your magia too. You might want to consider actually using them."

Mar scowls. They'd hardly call *constant fear of persecution* a perk—

"Are you talking to someone?"

Mar whirls to Bas, trying to control their reaction but sure their eyes are far too wide to pass as composed and collected. "Uh," Mar says. "No."

"Convincing," Dami deadpans. "I'm sure he bought that."

Mar clenches their jaw, resisting the urge to snap at Dami while Bas apparently can't see them.

"Hmm." Dami circles Bas, trailing wispy black smoke, looking him over with a wicked smile. "Well, hello, handsome. I wouldn't mind having his soul for eternity."

Mar glares at them, but Dami's not wrong. In his deep green tailcoat, matching vest, and tight-fitting tan breeches, even Mar can't deny that Bas looks, well, excellent.

They will *never* admit that to him, though.

"I . . . take it you're not a Catholic?" Bas says with a slight laugh.

Mar blinks and wrenches their gaze away from his aforementioned tight breeches. "What do you mean?"

Bas lifts a shoulder. "You looked like you were trying to set the crucifix on fire with your eyes."

Dami cackles and disappears in a black cloud of sulfuric smoke. Mar wrinkles their nose at the smell and steps quickly down the aisle, relieved as Bas follows them. "Forget it. Is everything all right? I thought we were supposed to meet someone here."

"Graciela's not that late—no reason to panic yet," Bas says.

But Mar can't help wondering if something went wrong. They lie on the end of an empty pew, staring up at the moldering ceiling as the minutes tick by. There's a hole in the roof bigger than Mar, and the starry night sky peeks through it.

This late seems significant enough for at least a little concern. Were they caught? Did something happen? Mar's magia would normally warn them of danger, but as they watch dust gently fall from the rafters in small clumps, their magia is quiet.

Or at least as quiet as Mar would expect after a handful of days not using it, which means it's a constant annoying itch buzzing under their skin. But it hasn't morphed to the particular icy prickle down their back that indicates approaching danger.

Still. Just because Mar isn't in danger doesn't mean Graciela isn't.

Someone laughs on the other side of the church—Mar doesn't have to look to know it's Tito, which surprises them. The sounds of La Ana's crew have already become familiar to them, even comforting. Or they would be, if Mar weren't so nervous about what Tito has to say. Because even if Tito doesn't reveal their magia to the crew, he might tell them to leave.

The thought of losing their new home cuts deeper than Mar would like to admit.

They tilt their head back to peer at Bas, sitting beside Mar's head. He has his left leg slung over the back of the seat in front of him as he slouches in the pew, arms crossed over his chest. It doesn't look especially comfortable, but somehow he's managed to fall asleep. His face is soft and peaceful in a way Mar hasn't seen before. With sleep smoothing over his features and the quiet rise and fall of his chest, he looks even more handsome.

Mar's eyes widen and they quickly look away, glaring at the empty air in front of them. They can almost hear Dami laughing at them.

Bas is an obnoxious brat who takes nothing seriously, they remind themself, their face burning. There's nothing cute about that.

They reach up and punch the side of his leg. Hard.

Though they aren't looking, the gasp and scuffling of the startled boy gives Mar a picture clear enough.

"¿Qué?" Bas says, a little too loud. "Uh. Oh. Ow. How long have I been asleep?"

"How should I know?" Mar says, still not looking at him. "I haven't been watching you." Half an hour, they'd guess. He's been asleep for roughly half an hour, and Mar hates that they know that. They were a little astounded at how quickly the boy fell asleep after he sat near them; it seemed unfair, given that Mar can only fight their way to sleep after tossing and turning in place for a couple of hours. But never mind that.

They sit up and immediately spot Tito talking to el Capitán. Heat curls in their gut again.

"Who spit in your soup?" Bas asks.

Mar blinks and looks at him. "What?"

"You look upset."

"Oh." Mar frowns. They can't exactly tell Bas everything—and even if they could, they're not sure they'd want to. But maybe there wouldn't be any harm in sharing just a little. "I think Tito's angry with me."

Bas laughs but then stops at Mar's withering look. "Impossible," he says. "Tito isn't angry with you."

They shake their head. "You weren't there."

"Mar." Bas chuckles. "Tito doesn't do that."

"Do what?"

"Get angry. Trust me—even if he was upset with you, he never holds on to these things for long. Whatever happened, I promise, it's fine."

Mar frowns. Bas, of course, could never begin to imagine what it was, exactly, that happened. But on the other hand, he grew up with Tito, and he knows him much better than Mar does. Could he be right?

They shake their head and stretch their arms above their head, easing the tension in their chest. "Graciela must be at least an hour late now."

Bas frowns and pulls his leg off the seat in front of him, wincing slightly as it hits the ground a little too heavily. "Hmm. I'll see what el Capitán says." He starts to stand—then drops back to his seat, eyes wide.

Mar arches an eyebrow at him.

"Um," Bas says with a sheepish smile. "I'll go once I can feel my leg again."

The laugh that bursts out of Mar is so sudden, they can't fully cover it with a cough. Of course, that only makes Bas grin harder, which is completely unfair. No boy this annoying deserves to have a smile so stunning.

Mar clears their throat and looks away, but Bas, mercifully, doesn't call them out. A few quiet minutes later and he stands, sauntering over to el Pirata Vega and Tito, who have been huddled together in the corner the entire time. Mar knows, because they watched Tito for a solid half hour before giving up hope that he'd move away. It wasn't like they were going to vie for his attention in front of el Capitán.

The group talks for a few minutes, frowns deepening as Tito shoots glances at the sky through the hole in the roof. A couple of minutes more and Bas returns.

"We're going to wait a little longer before we haul all of this back to *La Ana*. El Capitán has scouts in town and no one's picked up any red flags, so he doesn't think we're in any danger, but Graciela might be."

Mar nods, then glances at Bas out of the corner of their eye. "Why do you call him that?"

Bas blinks and turns to Mar. "Call who what?"

"El Capitán. He's your padre, but you always refer to him so . . . formally."

"Oh." Bas shrugs. "I don't know. I thought it was impressive as a kid—you know, to call him Capitán when he was elected. Everyone knew he was my dad, of course, but I was so proud that the crew chose him that I wanted to use the title at every opportunity." He pauses, then smiles softly. "I guess it just stuck."

Mar nods, and this time they don't try to hide their faint smile. "That makes sense. Papá was already capitán when I was born, but I understand that pride. It feels good knowing your parent is well loved and respected."

Bas nods. "It always made me think maybe one day I could be the same, if I learn enough from him. But I know I can only do that if the crew likes me enough to choose me. It's not like we inherit the position, you know?"

Mar side-eyes him. "If you know that, then why don't you ever help? Doesn't seem like the crew is going to choose someone who doesn't hold their own on board."

Bas laughs. "You don't think I hold my own?"

"That surprises you?"

He smirks. "Who do you think charts the courses for our trips? Or makes the maps?"

Mar's mouth drops open—just for a second, though. They catch themself quickly. "You're the sailing master?"

"Mm-hmm." Bas's smirk widens as he leans back in the pew. "Pretty damn good one if I do say so myself."

Mar shakes their head. "But . . . how did you . . . ?" Cartography and navigation are complicated—even as a sailing master apprentice back on *La Catalina*, Mar was always mystified by the art of creating a map. They know how to read one well enough, of course, but actually charting out wide swaths of uncharted ocean—and doing so in ways the Spaniards can't read . . . It's not a trade that's easy to learn, both because of its secrecy and the required skill.

Bas nods back to el Pirata Vega. "El Capitán learned from the best. It was his job before he became capitán. He's been teaching me as long as I can remember, and when we lost our sailing master two years ago, I took over."

Wow. Mar eyes Bas with . . . well. They wouldn't say *respect*—that might be pushing it, given everything Mar has experienced with Bas thus far; but maybe he isn't as useless and spoiled as they originally wrote him off for.

"What did you think all the maps in my cabin were for?" Bas asks.

Mar's face warms. "I just thought . . . you liked them."

Bas laughs. "Well, that's true—I probably wouldn't collect them if I didn't enjoy it. But I don't keep them *just* for fun."

It's then that the squeal of rusty hinges and the beat of boots on wood make Mar and Bas turn to the door. Mar's heart all but leaps into their throat. A woman in a long, flowing red skirt and colorful top strides down the aisle, flanked by six treelike men. Her hip-length black hair is braided down her back, moving like a jaguar's tail as she walks. She looks like she could stab a man in the jugular without flinching; her sleeves are short enough to reveal leanly muscled arms, and beneath her low, wide-brimmed sombrero her brown face is stoic.

She needs no introduction as she whips past Mar without even a sideways glance in their direction. This is certainly a woman who inspires legends.

"Ay, Graciela, ¡por fin!" el Pirata Vega exclaims, throwing his arms into the air as he strides quickly down the center aisle to meet her. "We were worried you'd been found out."

"Close, but thankfully not." She embraces el Capitán, and they kiss cheeks before releasing. "I was worried we were being followed, so we had to split up and take a long way around to a new meeting point before coming here. But it's safe now. You've brought everything as promised?"

"And more." El Pirata Vega grins and gestures to the two barrels and twelve crates. "Pistols, ammunition, gunpowder, and rum."

She arches an eyebrow. "Rum?"

"Well, if you don't want it—"

"We'll take it."

Graciela moves to the far corner of the room with el Capitán and Tito, and they lower their voices, making it impossible for Mar and Bas to hear any more. Mar turns to him just as a shout echoes across the room.

"¡Oye, Sebas! Ven aquí." El Capitán gestures him forward.

Bas smiles apologetically at Mar and jogs across the room. El Capitán pats Bas's back as he turns to Graciela with a proud smile.

Something twists inside Mar—sharp and deep—and they shoulder past everyone at the door to the church to get outside so they can hide the stinging tears. They sit against a palm tree just outside the church, curling grass around their finger. It's not like they can't see Bas interact with his father; they see plenty of that all the time. But something about the pride in Vega's face as he undoubtedly introduced his son to Graciela was just far too familiar.

They press their palms against their closed eyes and inhale deeply through their nose. Every time they think it's getting easier to accept the loss of the crew, the loss of their papá, it all comes crashing back, fresh and raw, when they least expect it. And every time it hurts just as much, like opening a wound with a knife as it starts to heal over.

They don't know how, but they have to save Papá without making a deal with el Diablo. A quick glance at the sky shows the moon is already nearly full, which means the first moon cycle is almost over. Their time half-gone and they aren't any closer to figuring out how to save Papá without offering their own soul.

But still, they can't let go of the possibility. It doesn't matter how unlikely it is, or how impossible it seems—there's a chance, there's hope, and as long as that hope continues to burn like a candle flame, Mar has to try.

"Hold on, Papá," they whisper to the breeze. "Somehow I'll find a way. I promise."

"Mar?"

They snap their head up, more grateful than ever that they stopped themself from crying before it was too late. Bas is leaning out the front door, frowning just slightly.

Mar blinks and stands, brushing the dirt and grass from their trousers. "Done already? That wasn't very long."

"Uh, well, no. But Graciela wants to meet you." He smiles.

"Why?" they blurt out before they can stop themself.

Their cheeks warm at their outburst, and they quickly add, "I mean, not that I don't want to, but—why would she want to?"

"Because you're amazing, obviously." Bas grins. "¡Ven!"

Mar narrows their eyes at him as they hurry inside with him. "What did you tell her?"

"Nothing that isn't true," he says, far too smugly.

"Bas—"

"Relax, she's going to love you. Lo prometo."

Mar frowns, but they don't have any more time to argue. Graciela, Vega, and Tito watch them approach expectantly, Graciela smiling, Tito frowning, and Vega impossible to read as usual.

"I've heard a lot about you, Mar León de la Rosa," Graciela says as they approach. "Your father spoke very highly of you."

Mar's eyes widen. "You knew my father?"

"I met him once, yes. Five years ago in San Juan—I was visiting my cousin Eralia there, and he had some business with her. He said he'd never known someone full of so much spirit and potential."

Mar remembers that trip. They wanted to go into the city with Papá, but he insisted Mar stay on the ship because San Juan was so dangerous. Mar almost argued, but even at eleven they knew San Juan was a haven of sorts for the Spaniards. With the rest of Central America and the Caribbean fighting to shake free of their stronghold, Puerto Rico was a hold-out, and San Juan their fortress—literally. They had three different fortresses in the walled city: Castillo San Cristóbal, El Cañuelo, and the infamous El Morro, where García López presided. The last was known for being impregnable and a big part of the reason pirates didn't go to San Juan if they could avoid it. Mar never learned the details of the important mission that had merited such a risk, but now they have a good idea.

Graciela looks them over and adds, "Judging by what these three have told me, it sounds like your father was right."

Mar isn't entirely surprised Bas has talked them up but . . . el Capitán and Tito? Really? Mar glances at the older men, but Vega's gaze is as calculating and unreadable as always, and Tito keeps his eyes steady on Graciela.

If they've been speaking well of Mar . . . does that mean Tito doesn't plan to tell the others what he saw? It seems too good to be true. Why would Tito help them?

"Thank you," Mar finally says, turning back to Graciela. "It's an honor to meet you."

She nods. "I know you are under Capitán Vega's care, but it would be a great help to bring two strong young people onto my team."

Vega's eyes widen and Mar's mouth nearly falls open. Work with Graciela to directly aid Nueva España's fight against the Spanish? The idea is more than a little tempting, but could they ever leave the seas for good? They never feel more grounded, more at home, than when they're in the middle of the ocean with nothing but rolling waves in every direction as far as the eye can see.

Bas is the first to break the quiet. "Thank you for the generous offer, but my home is on *La Ana*."

Graciela nods and looks at Mar. "And you, hije? Has *La Ana* become your home as well?"

Mar isn't sure they know how to answer that question, but the thought of walking away from *La Ana*, from the crew, is inexplicably painful. Without really meaning to, they look at Tito, who finally meets their gaze. There's something sad in his deep brown eyes, but Mar can't begin to fathom why.

They wish more than anything that they could read his mind. If Tito intends to give Mar up, then maybe Graciela's offer is a way out. But if he doesn't . . . Mar doesn't want to leave.

Graciela is smiling softly at them when they turn back to her. "There's nothing wrong with wanting to stay, you know. You aren't replacing your lost familia by finding a new one."

Her words are a kick in the stomach, leaving them breathless. They quickly look away, blinking hard as they fight back the threatening tears. The last thing they need right now is to cry in front of el Capitán.

They scrub the back of their hand over their eyes and clear their throat before turning back. "I'd like to stay with the crew. But thank you."

She nods. "I understand you're headed to Puerto Rico— Vieques, was it? If either of you changes your mind, you can always reach out to my cousin Eralia in San Juan." She offers Mar a folded bit of paper. They take it and tuck it into their pocket, next to Papá's bullet.

They hope to never have to go to San Juan, but it couldn't hurt to hold on to it. Just in case.

"Unbelievable," el Capitán says with a laugh. "I bring you weapons and you try to poach my crew!"

She winks. "Only the special ones."

CHAPTER 13

After meeting with Graciela and successfully transferring the weapons and other supplies, the crew celebrates exactly as Mar expects: by making their way to the nearest bar. Mar is practically vibrating with nervous energy by the time the bar is in view. What better opportunity to corner Tito for a private conversation than when the crew is drunk and distracted?

Mar squares their shoulders as the group ahead of them enters the bar. A strong hand lightly squeezes Mar's shoulder just before they go in. They stutter to a stop.

It's Tito.

He jerks his head to the side, gesturing around the corner from the bar. Mar nods, heart in their throat. Tito wouldn't try to hurt them . . . right? They suppose it doesn't matter. Mar's magia could probably protect them, and they need to know where Tito stands one way or the other.

They really don't want to fight Tito, though.

Mar follows Tito down rickety wooden steps to the beach,

the moonlight painting the sand silver. They take slow, steadying breaths, but it does little to calm their panicked heart. The darkness of the night paints deep shadows on Tito's face, and his silence as they walk along the shoreline is difficult to read. Only the hush and sigh of the ocean interrupt the quiet as they walk away from the bar, away from the crew, away from *La Ana*, and past a small patch of overgrown tropical forest.

To a deserted stretch of beach littered with dry seaweed, shells, and the occasional coconut husk.

"Please don't kill me," Mar whispers into the night, repeating the last thing they said to Tito before he abruptly left the stockroom.

Tito stops and finally turns to Mar for the first time. But it isn't anger they find on his face—it's deep sadness. "Mar," he says, so gently Mar's heart aches with memories of Papá. "Could I even kill you if I wanted to?"

"I'm not immortal."

"Are you sure? You did survive that shipwreck." Somehow, Tito smiles, just a little. "And anyway, even if you aren't, you're certainly more powerful than anyone or anything on *La Ana*."

Mar shudders.

Tito takes a deep breath and wipes his hands against each other, as if brushing off dust. "Pues, I'm not interested in seeing you dead, so it doesn't matter anyway, does it?" And then he grins. "Where did that fire come from, anyway? Did you . . . make it?"

Mar pauses, but it's not like there's any sense in *not* telling

Tito, now that he's seen it for himself. "Yes," they say. "I can create and control fire and . . . turn things to ice. And I suppose my magia tells me when I'm about to be in danger. That's it, though."

Tito smirks. "Premonitions about danger, creating fire from nothing, and turning anything into ice. That's all."

Mar's face warms. "I meant it's not as if I can fly. Or turn rocks to gold." They shake their head. "There are limits—I can't turn fire into ice. The two don't mix, and fire doesn't stand still, not even for me."

Tito smiles and looks at Mar with something like pride. "I'm glad to know you, Mar," he says. "You're a very special person."

Mar's breath catches. It's the same thing Papá used to say about them, about their magia. Mar didn't believe it then, and they certainly don't believe it now, but the memory of Papá comes on so strongly, they can almost feel him touching their face.

"I'm—" Mar's voice comes out too tight, too full of anguish. They close their eyes and inhale the fresh, salty air before looking at Tito again. "You can't tell anyone." The words spill out of Mar in a rush. "If the rest of the crew finds out—"

"Some of the crew would want to kill you." Tito nods. "I'm not sure el Capitán would respond favorably either. There are many superstitious men aboard this ship. . . . No, better that no one knows." He frowns. "But you can't be using your magic like that on *La Ana*. What if someone else had walked in? You should have at the very least blocked the door."

Mar grimaces. "I wasn't thinking clearly that day—I was desperate. If I don't use my magia for too long, it makes me sick."

Tito slowly nods. "Next time you need to . . ." He gestures vaguely at Mar. "Let me know. I'll make sure you get the privacy you need."

Mar's racing pulse relaxes. And slowly they can breathe again. "Why are you helping me?" Their voice comes out small—the ocean breeze almost whisks it away.

Tito smiles so sadly, it almost hurts to look at.

"You aren't the first I've met gifted with magia."

CHAPTER 14

If the world flipped upside down and humans began walking on the sky while the moon shone from below, Mar would be less surprised than they are hearing Tito's words.

They must have misheard him. Because it sounded like Tito had said he'd met someone else with magia before.

Which would mean there are others out there, with magia they have to keep hidden. Just like Mar.

Which would mean maybe there are people out there who can teach Mar how to control their magia.

But that all just sounds too good, too incredible, so it has to be wrong. Doesn't it?

"What do you . . . what do you mean?" Mar sputters out. "You know someone else like me?"

Tito nods, running his thumb over one of the silver buttons of his black tailcoat. "I did, when I was a younger man. His gift was different from yours—he *could* fly. He came from an island called Isla Luceros, where everyone had similar gifts.

He told me stories of people who could predict the future, or turn to stone, or transform objects." He hesitates. "I take it by your obvious surprise you aren't from there."

Mar hadn't realized they were gaping until now. A whole *island* full of people with magia? Where anyone can use magia freely, and it's normal?

It sounds like paradise.

"No, I . . . I'd never even imagined . . ." There's an entire island out there where Mar could be themself. Where it wouldn't be dangerous to use their magia. Where there are others with their magia . . . maybe even someone with magia who could help them find Papá. "Where is it?"

Tito frowns. "No one knows, exactly. Carlos told me that once someone left, magia made it impossible to find your way back. All he knew is it's somewhere in the Caribbean Sea."

Mar grimaces. That doesn't really narrow things down. There are hundreds of islands in the Caribbean—and those don't have magical protection.

Tito hesitates. "Did your parents ever mention . . . ?"

They shake their head. "Papá was born in Havana and Mamá in a small coastal town in the Yucatán region . . . but there definitely weren't others like me there." Mar frowns, a spark of a memory lighting up in their mind. "But . . . Mamá mentioned Abuela came from an island we couldn't visit. She said Abuela left knowing she'd never be able to find her way back."

"Ah, sí. Just as Carlos said." Tito sighs and looks across the ocean. "He was . . . the most incredible man I've ever known." Tito's voice breaks, just a little, and Mar's stomach plummets to their toes.

Was.

Tito takes a deep, shaky breath. But then he clenches his fingers into fists, turns back to Mar, and speaks with steel. "I know all too well what happens when those who aren't ready learn about people gifted with magia. I'll protect you, Mar, because I wasn't able to save the man I loved from those who gave in to fear and violence when they learned what he could do. I won't let it happen again. Lo prometo."

Steaming cup of café in hand, Mar knocks on Bas's cabin door the next morning.

Bas opens the door and blinks in confusion. "I didn't order any—"

Mar passes him the café and slips past him. They've never paid much attention to the maps pinned to the walls in Bas's cabin, but now they eye them carefully. There's Puerto Rico, Cuba, Jamaica—

"This is a waste of time you don't have, you know."

Mar looks at Bas, but he's just watching them with a small, confounded smile. Next to him, however, is the last person in the world Mar wants to see.

Dami steps next to Mar, and it's all they can do to resist the urge to jerk away. "Even if you could find Isla Luceros, which you can't," Dami says, "the people there don't know any more about demonio and diablo magic than you do. You're focusing on the wrong kind of magia."

Mar scowls at the map wall. Of course Dami would want to discourage them from seeking out Isla Luceros. They're a demonio. They want Mar desperate—so they'll have no choice but to make a deal.

Bas steps through Dami, who gives an affronted huff before sliding out of the way. "Fine," the demonio says. "Ignore me and waste precious time. You realize you have less than five weeks until the harvest moon, right? You'll come crawling to me before the end."

The reminder is a punch in the stomach, but Mar steels their face. Dami waltzes through the map wall like a ghost. Mar hides their shaking fists in their pockets.

"So I take it you're *not* here to give me café." Bas smiles.

Mar takes a shaky breath and forces their shoulders to relax. "Not exactly. You're familiar with the region, right?"

"Around Playa del Carmen?"

Mar shakes their head. "The Caribbean in general."

Bas grins. "Oh. Well, I *did* draw half of these maps."

"Perfect. Have you ever heard of a place called Isla Luceros?"

"Sure."

Mar's eyes widen. They weren't actually expecting—"You have? Do you have a map?"

"I've never been, so I haven't drawn one, and I don't think I have one *of* the island, but . . ." Bas goes to his desk and starts riffling through the maps strewn over each other there. "I was just looking at . . . ," he mutters. "Ah! Here it is." He pulls out a map and smooths it out on top of the others. "If I remember correctly, Isla Lucero is . . . here."

Mar approaches his desk, heart in their throat. If Bas actually has a map with Isla Luceros on it . . . Wait. "Is that Argentina?"

Bas nods. "It's an Argentinean island."

Mar's shoulders droop. "That's not in the Caribbean." Tito had been sure Isla Luceros was in the Caribbean—but Argentina is decidedly not.

"Neither is Isla Lucero."

Mar frowns at the island Bas is pointing to. It's labeled *Isla Lucero*.

"Luce*ros*," Mar says with a sigh. "Not Lucero."

"Oh. In that case, no, I haven't heard of it. Sorry."

A dead end, then. The disappointment stings more than Mar expected. Of course, there was no guarantee they'd find someone there who could help them save Papá, but surely, in an entire population with unique magical abilities, *someone* would be able to do something.

But even entertaining that as a possibility is pointless if Isla Luceros is really as impossible to find as Carlos and Abuela said. They wish she were still alive so they could ask her all about the island. But why didn't Mamá ever mention that Abuela had magia? Maybe she didn't know. Abuela died before Mar was born, so it's not like it would have come up, since Mamá didn't have any.

"Are you okay?"

Mar's gaze snaps to Bas. His face is soft. Concerned. They quickly nod and force a small smile. "I'm fine. It's just a place I heard stories about. Don't worry about it—it probably isn't real."

It hurts to admit, but real or not, Isla Luceros can't help Mar if they can't find it. Which means even if there are others out there like Mar, it doesn't matter. They have no way to find the only people on the planet who could understand their struggle. Who could help them.

They'll have to save Papá on their own.

"This storm will kill us, you know."

The darkness is laughing at them.

Mar slips deeper into cold emptiness, an ocean of anguish. The screams of their crew members grate against them like saw on bone. The night's laughter is hollow, chillingly familiar.

"¡Papá!" The shadow smothers their voice to a choked whisper; though the scream is raw against their throat, it comes out barely a squeak.

The laughter grows louder. Mar whirls in the darkness. "¡Papá! ¿Dónde estás?"

El Diablo steps through the abyss, his eyes like glowing coals. "You have a month left, Mar. You still can save your papá." He smiles. "All you have to do is give me your soul."

Mar's eyes snap open to shadow. Their clothes are sweat-damp and stick to their skin. They shudder in the darkness and turn onto their side, wrapping their arms around their stomach.

Papá wouldn't want them to agree to el Diablo's deal—they know that. But a part of them still feels like they've done something wrong. For surviving. For refusing to trade their soul for Papá's. For every day that passes without a way to save him.

They close their eyes tight, ignoring the tears tracking down their cheeks.

They can still hear the night's laughter.

CHAPTER 15

Mar isn't sure if there is a worse smell than chicken, cow, and goat shit in a hot, enclosed space—like, say, belowdecks on *La Ana*. The stench is so powerful, they're a bit woozy as they scrub the deck of the animal pens, ignoring the angry squawking and bleating of the temporarily caged livestock.

Except for the cows. They are too big to be caged, so now they just stare at Mar with wide eyes, chewing hay open-mouthed as Mar scrubs the floor with a stiff-bristled scrub brush and a bucket of soapy water.

Mar swears under their breath as they try not to breathe through their nose, though that does little to save them from the nauseating fumes. Their sweat-drenched shirt sticks to their back. Their binding cloth, soaked through, clings uncomfortably tightly to their ribs. Tending to the animals is the kind of work they did as a child, when they were too small to help with much else. Even then someone else scrubbed the floors; Mar was just in charge of feeding and cleaning the animals.

It was about as glamorous as it sounded, but they were just a kid, and any amount of helping had made them feel grown up.

Now, not so much.

If only their magia could make the room immaculate with a snap of their fingers. That kind of magia Mar might not mind.

A freshly polished black boot steps next to Mar's hand. They close their eyes and suppress a groan—as if this disgusting situation weren't bad enough already.

"Sure is unbearably hot down here," Dami says.

"Remind you of home?" Mar asks, refusing to look up at them as they scrub.

Dami chuckles. "You don't really think the land of the dead is a lake of fire, do you?"

"How would I know? I've never been." *Papá has, though.* The thought makes them pause. "What's it like?"

The demonio crouches next to them. "You know, when I'm having a conversation with someone, I make an effort to acknowledge their presence."

Mar grits their teeth. "I'm speaking to you, aren't I?"

"If you scrub that spot of the floor any more, you'll start stripping the wood."

They groan and release the brush, turning to Dami at last. Their back aches from being hunched over so long; they grimace.

Dami flashes a perfect grin. "See? That wasn't so hard."

"What do you want, Dami?"

"Never mind what I want—don't *you* want it to be less like an oven down here?"

"Sure."

Dami stares at them. Mar holds their gaze. The demonio arches an eyebrow. Mar raises both of theirs. Dami rolls their eyes.

"If *only* you were able to do something about that—oh wait, you can."

"I can't control the weather."

"We both know you don't need to control the weather to cool down a room."

Mar's eyes narrow. Dami's right, of course, but—"Did you really come here to convince me to use my magia to cool down?"

The demonio grins. "Would you believe me if I said yes?"

"No."

"You suffer needlessly, you know. You have so many opportunities every day to make life easier for yourself, if you'd just stop running from your own magia."

Mar snorts. "You would say that."

Dami frowns. "What do you mean?"

"You use your magia all the time to make deals with no regard whatsoever to how you're ruining people's lives. You may not care about how you're hurting people, but I've already hurt too many people with my magia, and I do *everything* I can to make sure it never happens again."

Dami's face darkens. "Don't presume you know how I feel about my position, Mar León de la Rosa."

"I know that however you feel about it, it doesn't matter as long as you continue making deals with people. Because that's what you're after, isn't it? A deal with me?"

"Right now, all I'm after is getting you not to be so damn afraid of your own power."

"*Why?*"

The floor lurches beneath them and Mar stumbles forward, swearing as they trip over the broom and catching themself on the edge of a pen fence, just inches from a cow's stinking, chewing mouth. They grimace and right themself to face Dami—

But the demonio is gone.

Mar sighs, then pauses as a noise catches their attention. They can't make out the words, but there's yelling on deck—the kind of yelling that sets their heart pounding. The ship has slowed, and the rumble of fast feet tells them something is happening. Mar doesn't want to be cleaning cow shit while they could be getting in on the excitement.

It's been three weeks of dishes, scrubbing, hauling, and bringing Bas café since they left Playa del Carmen. They're not about to miss this.

They drop the scrub brush and bolt out the door, running past the storage rooms and skidding into the living quarters just as Joaquín descends the steps, knife in hand, and bellows, "BATTLE STATIONS!"

Mar grins as crew members jump up around them and rush to their stations. Finally, something familiar, something they're good at. Fighting is Mar's favorite place to subtly release some magia—in the chaos of everything, it always goes unnoticed by those it isn't intended for.

They take a step forward, then stop. A sinking feeling twists their stomach. They don't have a battle station. Because this isn't *La Catalina*, this is *La Ana*, and here they're just a cabin person no one takes seriously.

"Leoncito!" Joaquín yells, gesturing at them with his knife. "Don't just stand there! ¡Vamos!"

Mar blinks, but they don't need to be told twice. They rush over, and the man flips a gun into the air and offers it to Mar along with a leather holster.

"You're on the boarding party," he says. "Chance to work your way out of the shithouse, hm?"

Mar nods and reaches for the weapon, but Joaquín pulls it back. "Don't make el Capitán regret trusting you. He doesn't give second chances."

Mar shakes their head. "I may be new to *La Ana*, but I'm not new to this life. I know what I'm doing."

Joaquín nods and gives them the pistol. "Get on deck. This won't take long."

When Mar arrives on deck, arms freshly wrapped, *La Ana* is cruising at a nice, slow pace despite having full sails. On *La Catalina*, they would have kept the sails full and towed heavy things, like astern cables and heavy pots, behind them so as to appear to be a slow merchant ship. The crew of *La Ana* seems to be using the same tactic. Their typical black flag has been replaced with a British flag. Lumbering toward them is a ship flying Spanish colors, so weighed down with goods, it's practically crawling.

The perfect mark.

"Mar!" Bas bounds over to them, practically skipping with excitement. "Oh, good, so glad you're here—I was starting to worry you'd miss my favorite part."

"And what's that?" Mar asks with a smirk.

Bas nods to the approaching mark, now just a ship's length away. "Any moment now."

"¡Ahora!" el Capitán yells.

A roar of sixty voices fills the air as the black flag unfurls over the British one, and the false flag plummets like a rock in water. By now the merchant ship is far too close to turn around and run, and as *La Ana* comes to a stop, so does their mark.

"¡Hola!" el Capitán yells to the white-faced men on the Spanish vessel beside his ship. "Let us board or be destroyed."

The polished floorboards creak under Mar's feet. The dark, waxed boards gleam from the lantern in Mar's left hand; they hold a gun in their right. The Spaniards' ship is absurdly well organized, with meticulously carved and painted railings, and empty bedrolls bundled and stacked with military precision.

If Mar didn't know better, they would've guessed the ship was unused.

But while the lower decks, thus far, seem relatively untouched, the blood and bodies staining the top deck speak otherwise.

The Spaniards surrendered quickly, as most did. Merchant ships were always led by small, sparsely armed crews, usually no more than twelve or fifteen. Mar supposed that was, perhaps, the only good thing about nearing the end of the pirate age: The merchants had grown careless in their relative security. So when faced with a pirate crew of sixty, well . . .

The odds were obvious.

Mar had watched as el Capitán gathered those who surrendered. He lined them all up, then spoke individually to three Black sailors the Spaniards had enslaved. Out of *La Ana*'s sixty crew members, at least half of them are Black and likely joined the crew under similar circumstances. Thanks to the Spaniards and other imperialists, slavery is depressingly common in the Caribbean.

Because the disease, genocide, and oppression aren't horrifying enough, evidently.

La Catalina's crew had helped dozens over the years regain their freedom, but Papá told Mar that not all pirate crews were so humane. There were scores of pirates, especially during the Golden Age, who had profited from the horrific practice the colonizers had brought with them. Some of the most infamous pirates had even taken over slave ships without freeing a single soul.

Just thinking about it makes Mar's blood boil. A slaver is a slaver—pirate or not.

"I invite you to join my crew as free men," el Capitán said, "equal to every other member of our familia. Alternatively, if you so wish, you can join us until our next stop and part ways there. We're headed to Isla Mujeres next."

Mar grimaced. That isn't really much of an option when Isla Mujeres—like most of the Caribbean—is under Spanish rule. Papá sometimes took freed Black sailors to Haití, which had successfully revolted against its French colonizers, declaring independence the year Mar was born. But Haití isn't exactly on the way to Isla Mujeres, and it didn't sound like el Capitán planned to go there anytime soon, or he would have mentioned it.

"Isla Mujeres isn't exactly safe," one of the sailors answered in Spanish. He was the oldest of the three—silver hair peppered his beard and tied-back dreadlocks. "It'll only be a matter of time before the Spaniards capture us again if we go there."

The youngest of the trio, a tall boy not much older than Mar, with russet-brown skin, added, "It's not much of a choice if only one of the options guarantees our freedom."

El Capitán nodded slowly, considering. "That's true. How about this: You three join my crew, and if at any time you decide you'd like to make your home somewhere we make port, you're welcome to leave. Just like anyone else on *La Ana*."

The three turned to each other, speaking in hushed voices.

After a minute, they turned back to el Capitán, and the eldest said, "We accept."

The crew whooped in welcome. Joaquín told el Capitán he'd help them settle on *La Ana* before reboarding with them. Mar wasn't sure what el Capitán would do with the nine europeo sailors who weren't soldiers, but the three Spanish officers on board—the captain, first mate, and second mate—would surely be executed. Papá did the same during their dozens upon dozens of yearly ship raids—every one of those officers had committed atrocities of their own, not the least of which included the aforementioned enslavement of African people.

El Capitán sent Mar, the new crew members, and a handful of others to strip the rest of the ship. In addition to the resources that were stolen from the people, anything of use like weapons, food, drink, rope, sails—even pots, pans, and lanterns—was for the taking.

The sleeping quarters, while spacious, are deserted and uninteresting, though Mar makes a note to return for clothes, blankets, pillows, and candles. Maybe they even have soap!

A door on the far side of the room, however, catches Mar's interest. Not because the door itself is special—it's as absurdly ornate as every other door Mar has come across on the opulent ship—but because it's closed.

They cross the room, the warmth of the lantern flame reassuring even as the drumming in their ears sounds a little louder. The warning prickle of magic dances down their back, and Mar smiles: Someone is in there. Guarding? Or just hiding?

They kick the door open and crouch. It slams against the wall and bounces back. Mar's lantern light spills into the dark room. They wait a breath. Two. Three. Silence.

All right.

Gun ready, Mar stands and enters, pressing their back against the door as they check the cabin. Here there are walls of crates stacked high—filled with what, they aren't sure, but they intend to find out as soon as they find whoever is hiding here. The warning prickle is more intense now, buzzing endlessly at the base of their skull like icy pinpricks.

They turn the corner around a row of crates and process three things at once.

A man.

Gun extended.

A blast so loud that they're knocked onto their back.

"¡Carajo!" Mar hisses. Their heart is beating hard enough to hurt their chest. But nothing else does. And the man? Where is the man?

Mar swings the lantern and their gun forward, shaking with adrenaline, but the man is on the floor too. Choking on blood bubbling out of his mouth and down his chin, onto his red lapels. Crimson spreads over his chest, drowning the blue of his uniform in shiny scarlet. His eyes are wide, confused. "¿Cómo?" he sputters out, but Mar can't answer.

Mar turns in circles, looking for the person who shot the man. Because Mar never fired their own gun, so it must have been someone else, right? But there's no one here. The man on the ground fired his gun, and then Mar fell back, and somehow . . . somehow it's the man dying on the glossy hardwood and not Mar. Even for someone used to the inexplicable, it doesn't make any sense. They made a fatal error. The man acted faster. So how is Mar still alive?

Thick black smoke—far too present and dark to be from the lantern or gunfire—hangs in the air. It's familiar in a way that churns Mar's stomach.

The man stills, and his thick choking sounds fall silent.

Someone is watching them again.

They whirl around, but Dami isn't there—and neither is anyone else. Their magia has quieted, the man has died, and no one else is here. Mar's eyes tell them that they're alone, but the eerie sensation of being watched is so heavy, Mar could swear that someone is inches away. It has to be Dami, but why? And why don't they show themself?

"What do you want?" Mar whispers.

The room doesn't answer. But someone shouts their name—Bas—and then the boy is running around the corner, eyes wild. He jolts to a stop in front of Mar and sighs, hand over his heart. "You're alive!" Bas throws his arms around Mar and squeezes tight. "I heard a gunshot and I thought—"

"I'm fine," Mar says into Bas's shoulder, though their voice shakes. But something about Bas's warm, corded arms wrapped around them makes them melt. The shivering in their bones stills, and they breathe deeply.

Bas smells like sweat and ocean salt, and for some reason they don't want to examine, it's comforting.

Then Bas releases Mar, and the spell is broken. "It smells terrible in here," he says with a shaky laugh. "Like . . . sulfur? What's in these crates, anyway?"

CHAPTER 16

The dry white sand under Mar's toes is soft as silk, coating their brown skin in fine powder, while the cerulean sea laps at their toes. The water is so clear, it almost looks like Mar is standing on the ocean when the tide comes in. They've arrived on Isla Mujeres probably less than two miles from Punta Sur—the southernmost tip of the island and the highest point; it's a rocky coastline high above sea level, contrasting from the smooth, idyllic beach they're on now.

On this Isla Mujeres beach, *La Ana*'s crew laughs and opens up rum and unloads their spoils. Gold, jade, precious jewels—and weapons, and mountains of sugar, too—all reclaimed from the Spaniards and now to be distributed among the people here and across the bay on Playa Mujeres. The cabin Mar almost died in yesterday—Mar *should* have died in—had more sugar than Mar had ever seen in one place.

Extremely flammable sugar. Mar was lucky the room didn't explode when the gun went off. Unless Dami saved them from that, too. They grimace.

It should feel good, being part of a crew with the same aim as *La Catalina*'s, even returning to the same island Papá brought their spoils to. It should feel familiar. Comforting. A relief to know that even though everything has changed, some things haven't changed at all.

And yet, standing on a familiar beach with the tiny thatch-hut village in sight, one that Mar has always loved—standing here without Papá and Leo and their familia on *La Catalina*—aches in a way Mar hasn't let themself feel since they were ripped from the ocean some forty days ago.

How is it possible that they've gone over a month without their familia? Just the thought of them brings a fierce pain to the emptiness behind Mar's heart. Their vision blurs; they close their eyes and tilt their head back to the sun's warmth. Breathe in a lungful of the cool sea-breeze air.

It feels wrong, being here without them.

Mar takes another slow, shaky breath, shoving the pain deep as they wipe their eyes with the back of their hand.

It's then that a dark shadow swaying underwater, near *La Ana*'s hull, catches their eye. They crouch, peering into the clear blue water.

Seaweed. A large blanket of it, best Mar can tell, stuck to the bottom of the schooner. Mar frowns; come to think of it, in the time that Mar's been on board, they haven't stopped to careen the ship. Careening is a massive, grueling undertaking. First the crew has to beach the ship on her side at high tide somewhere isolated. Once the tide goes out, they scrape and burn the seaweed and barnacles and whatever else has gathered on the bottom, then finally replace rotted planks and coat it all. The task is usually only done once every couple of months, so Mar hasn't thought much of it before. But with this much buildup, there's no way *La Ana* is sailing at her full speed.

Mar stands and catches Joaquín's eye as he steps beside them, holding a large crate on his shoulder like it doesn't actually weigh fifty pounds. He raises a questioning eyebrow.

"When's the last time *La Ana* was careened?" they ask.

Joaquín hesitates. "Early July?"

Over two months, then; she's due for a scrape. "There's a lot of seaweed down there."

He nods. "Don't you worry, Leoncito. Capitán's already plotted out a course with Bas to handle that after we leave. It'll be easier to beach her without all this extra cargo. Speaking of which, why aren't you carrying anything?"

Twelve trips on and off *La Ana* later, after carrying crates and rolling barrels until their arms are numb with exhaustion, Mar sits on the sand and closes their eyes with their head tilted back to the sun. They open their eyes just in time to watch Bas launch himself back first onto the sand at Mar's feet, laughing as he creates an imprint in the beach and stretches his arms over his head. Mar imagines that throwing himself onto packed sand was probably somewhat painful, but if so, Bas doesn't show it. Instead, he grins up at Mar, eyes gleaming in the bright sun.

"Me encanta esta isla," he says with a contented sigh. "No

better place on earth. Well. Except *La Ana,* of course, but it *is* nice to stretch your legs for a couple days, wouldn't you say?"

Mar just shrugs and stuffs their trembling hands into their pockets. The shakes spread from their chest to their hands and legs this morning—they were mildly regretting not releasing some magia when they were exploring the merchant ship alone yesterday. It doesn't seem like anyone's noticed yet, but their bones are beginning to ache, and even their skin feels raw. It's been four days since they've released any magia. They were going to ask Tito for help finding some privacy, but Mar figured they could wait an extra day to find some relief on the island. It'd be easier, anyway, not being in such a contained space.

Another benefit of shore leave: Once they cross the bay to Playa Mujeres in the afternoon, they'll finally be able to buy some clothes of their own, hopefully more dark shirts to better hide their flattener and markings. Though they'd probably be more excited about it if the demanding heat of fire magia wasn't amplifying the already warm morning.

But if Bas notices their lack of enthusiasm, he certainly doesn't show it. Instead, he sits up and shakes sand out of his hair, then stands, somehow managing to look graceful in the process even as sand pours off him. "Pues, where do you think we should go first? I'd really like to eat something that isn't fish. There's a small taberna near here that makes the most incredible empanadas—ooh, I can almost taste them. . . ."

"Hold on." Mar lifts their hand. "What do you mean *we*?"

"Well, I mean, we don't *have* to get empanadas."

"You're doing it again."

"Doing what?" Bas grins and his eyes glimmer with laughter.

"I don't need a guide," Mar says. "This isn't my first time on Isla Mujeres."

"Well, I'd certainly hope not, you being a lifelong pirate and all." Bas smiles and shoves his hands into his pockets. "I was more thinking I'd enjoy your company off *La Ana* as much as I do on board. But of course, I can't force you to spend time with me if you don't want to—can't very well order you to bring me café four times a day on shore leave."

Bas's smile is sheepish in a way Mar suspects he probably perfected in a mirror. Mar rolls their eyes and looks away before it can have any detrimental effects on them, like making them actually sympathize with the boy, or worse, making them admit, even if just to themself, that if you get past the arrogant exterior, Bas is actually maybe not terribly unattractive.

Mar's thoughts are momentarily interrupted when they spy a bearded blond man roughly fifty feet away, leaning against a palm. Mar hasn't seen the man before, but he looks at them with a gaze that makes their stomach churn. The man doesn't look like a native—too pale, too europeo.

"Everything okay?" Bas asks. Mar glances at him—*is* everything okay?—but when they look back at the man, he's gone. Just an empty strip of beach with a happy palm tree fluttering in the light breeze.

They shake off the specter of the stranger's stare as they turn back to Bas. "I don't understand why you insist on bothering me all the time."

"Oh, that's easy," Bas answers without missing a beat. "I'm a sucker for cute boys."

Mar's face bursts with warmth and Bas grins, all too pleased with himself, and gestures to the scattered wooden thatch buildings and handfuls of wandering people. "So, what do you say? Get dressed, and then empanadas for two?"

The itch of barely contained magic is hot on Mar's skin when they take off their boots to step on the cool, grassy sand of Punta Sur. Bas, for his part, does the same, not that Mar is paying attention to him as they walk down the long stretch leading to the rocky cliff's edge. Up ahead, the remains of the ancient temple stand sentry; just one tall, half-crumbled lighthouse on the island's southernmost tip. Waves crash against the rocky shoreline to Mar's left and right; the cool, salty sea breeze is a relief against Mar's sweat-slick skin. They're glad they opted to wear a linen waistcoat and forgo the tailcoat entirely, even though Bas insisted it would look *excellent* on them.

"Admit it." Bas kicks a small rock into some green brush. "They were incredible empanadas."

Mar sighs. "Sure, they were good."

Bas makes an affronted noise like he's been personally insulted. "*Good?* No, no, that won't do. Coquito is good. Neatly coiled rigging is good. Those empanadas are *divine*."

But any semblance of an argument is long forgotten as they step up to the temple's base. The sun-bleached stone is white and gray, and though Mar imagines it was once much taller, the tallest wall of the remaining three walls is still twice as tall as they are. Mar smiles as they tilt their head back to see the top of the structure.

On their mamá's side, most of Mar's people lived on the other side of the bay not far from Playa Mujeres for hundreds of years, but they visited the island often. Mar's mamá brought them here as a child and told them how Mar's ancestors had helped build this temple, the lighthouse dedicated to the moon, love, and fertility goddess, Ixchel.

It's a sacred place, their mamá had said. *And it'll always be a part of your history.*

When they were young, Mar often closed their eyes to see if they could feel the goddess's presence. Once, they thought they did, though now they aren't sure it wasn't the sea breeze, or the hum of their own magia. Or even just the magic of this place, so deeply intertwined with a family history they can't access any other way. There was something special about seeing firsthand the mark on the world their ancestors had left behind.

But it wasn't just the proximity to their roots that drew Mar here every time they visited Isla Mujeres; they rest their palm on the partially collapsed stone wall of the temple, smiling as the hum in their blood becomes a roar.

It was here, at Temple Ixchel's steps, surrounded by the roar of the crashing sea and bathing in the sun's heat, that Mar first learned how to use their magia.

"It's been too long since I've visited this place," Bas says softly beside them.

Mar yanks their hand away, their eyes flying open as they shove their fists into their pockets again. They almost forgot Bas was there.

And so what if he is? So what if he sees Mar's magia—what can Bas do? Maybe he'll be in awe. Maybe he'll think it's impressive.

Or maybe he'll reveal their secret to the crew and have Mar killed.

"You know," Bas says, running his fingers lightly over the gray and white stone, "I've been to some of the other Mayan ruins. The markings etched into many of them look a lot like your tattoos."

Mar bites back a smirk. The likeness goes beyond the marks on Mar's arms; on their back is a profile of a jaguar that looks suspiciously similar to the guardians sculpted in relief at Chichén Itzá, except the one on Mar's back is rearing up, fanged mouth open and claws ready to strike. It's one of the reasons Mamá was sure Mar was blessed by the gods; the black jaguar is such an important symbol in Mayan culture that a coincidence seemed impossible.

Ixchel herself is a jaguar goddess. It was one of the reasons

Mamá had brought them here, specifically, to practice using their magia.

Mar doesn't know if the gods gave them magia, but if they did, Mar would ask the gods what they did to deserve such a punishment.

"Hmm" is all Mar says now.

"Is that on purpose?" Bas looks at them. "Did you get your tattoos designed to mirror them?"

Mar shrugs. "I did get them in the area," they say, which is only true because they were born not far from the coast, on *La Catalina*. "My mamá's people came here often."

"Oh, wow." Bas smiles. "I didn't know that. There's so much more I want to learn about you."

Mar's face warms. "Not my fault you spend too much time asking me to get you café you won't drink to actually get to know me."

Bas blinks. Then he laughs, abruptly, loudly. His laugh is so shocked and genuine that Mar can't help but laugh along. "All right," Bas says. "That's—fair, I can't argue with that. You're right. I'll have to do better. You're fun to be around, Mar, you know that?"

Mar isn't so sure about that—they've been pretty morose, grouchy, and *itchy* with magia overflow. But maybe spending time with Bas today hasn't been absolute torture.

Can't admit that out loud, though. The last thing Bas needs is a compliment.

With drunken Spanish sea chanteys and rum in the air, Mar takes steadying breaths while carefully chilling their coquito, much to their fire's chagrin. The laughter of the crew packing the small Playa Mujeres taberna around two tables shoved together is its own song as Bas challenges Tito to a drinking contest Bas is sure to lose. El Capitán watches his son with a bemused smirk, and other taberna patrons watch and cheer the two on, but most importantly, no one is looking at Mar.

Which means if Mar is exceptionally careful, maybe, just maybe, they can release trickles of magia a little at a time. Just enough to cool their drink, then warm it enough to melt the ice, then cool it over again. Once the crew crossed the bay from Isla Mujeres to the more populated Playa Mujeres, they were finally able to get some new, long-sleeved dark shirts. The one they're wearing now is blue like the sky at midnight. As long as they only release a little magia at a time, their markings won't glow through the fabric. All the while they're leaning back and trying to look as relaxed as possible, like they're just enjoying the fun, like they aren't boiling with pent-up power.

They cross their arms over their chest and focus on the drink. Casting their magia onto an object they aren't touching requires focus—and more magia. Ideal when they're trying to off-load excess magical energy. But even as Mar cools and warms and cools and warms their drink, they know it won't be enough. It's like releasing a small trickle from a flooded reservoir—the relief is so minuscule, it's barely worth noting at all.

But still. It's relief.

Mar has one boot on the edge of the wooden table as they tilt their weight to the back two legs of the chair. They breathe slowly, evenly, warming and cooling their drink, watching as Bas shouts about taking on Tito in a show of bravado. The warm lantern light gives a golden glow to his light brown skin, and his deep brown hair manages to look like an utter mess and intentional at the same time.

Mostly a mess, though. Almost like someone has just ruffled his hair, which, given the circumstances isn't unlikely. Or . . . like someone had been running their fingers through his hair, gently. Feathery short locks against rope-callused skin. Noses touching, limbs tangled, breathing each other's air.

What would it be like, being that comfortable with someone? Trusting someone so completely you could just . . . be?

"You can't take your eyes off him."

Mar startles at the light voice beside them, jerking so fast that their chair slips against the clay tile with a screech and drops back—but Dami catches it with an outstretched arm like they were expecting it. They smile almost apologetically as Mar scowls, face hot, heart crashing in their chest.

"Sorry," Dami says, and it almost sounds genuine. "I wasn't trying to startle you. You must have been more caught up in his eyes than I—"

"I was *not* caught up in his eyes." Mar's face is the molten center of a furnace. They blow a burst of cold through their drink with a quick exhale and take a big gulp, praying the near-frozen liquid will cool their cheeks.

Dami doesn't correct them, though Mar suspects the demonio knows Mar is walking the razor-thin edge of truth, because technically it was his hair they were looking at, not his eyes. As if that made any difference at all.

"I'm not judging you, you know," Dami says after a moment. "If I could be with someone . . . well. Bas certainly knows how to command a room."

"As if it concerns me what a demonio thinks of me," Mar snaps.

Dami frowns, and Mar examines them. They look different again; their face squarer, their neck thicker with corded muscle, black stubble darkening their sharp jaw. Glossy, straight black hair reaches their shoulders, and a dark kohl lining intensifies their deep eyes.

It's a little unnerving how attractive they are no matter how they present.

"You know," Mar says, "it's really unfair that you can do that."

Dami blinks and looks at them. "Do what?"

Mar gestures at them—then catches themself and puts their hand down. They don't need to draw attention to the fact that, to everyone else, they're having a conversation with an empty seat. "Look however you want," they say softly. "Like a boy, like a girl, or neither. And yet I can always tell it's you. Your face shifts so subtly, it's like different versions of you."

Dami tilts their head slightly. "Well . . . it *is* me. I've only ever presented as myself in front of you. I just feel more masculine, or feminine, or mixed, or something else from time to time."

Mar nods. "Yes, but . . . I just *wish* I could change my body to fit how I feel. And you get to do it every day, even as how you feel shifts." They stare into their glass and lower their voice. "If I could trade my magia for that, I would."

When they glance up again, Dami's face has softened. "You wouldn't be happy without your magia, though."

Mar snorts. "I'm certainly not happy *with* it."

"Why not? It's a part of you, just like your blood, or your soul. You don't want a life without your soul." Dami furrows their eyebrows. "Trust me, I would know."

"Magia has only ever brought me pain and heartache. If I didn't have it, I wouldn't have to hide all the time." Mar shakes their head and glances at the crew, still too mesmerized cheering Bas and Tito on to notice them. "It's a curse and I'd be better off without it."

"You're wrong." Dami rests their crossed arms on the table, leaning forward. "You have no idea, Mar León de la Rosa, how special you are. You have so much more power than you realize, if you just—"

"Is that why you won't leave me alone?" Mar interrupts. "Because of my magia? That really would just prove my point, you know."

"I— No," Dami says defensively. They lean away from the table and cross their arms over their chest, glancing away. "Not entirely, anyway," they mumble.

"Claro que no." Mar rolls their eyes. "What do you want with me, anyway? Why won't you just tell me?"

The demonio sighs and runs their hand through their long hair. "That's why I'm here. I think you're ready to hear it now." They square their shoulders and look Mar in the eye. "You only have ten days left until the harvest moon—but I can help you save your papá."

Ten days. The reminder is nauseating. Mar scowls. "Let me guess: for the low, low price of my soul."

Dami smirks. "If it was your soul I wanted, I would have let you get shot in that storeroom. I need your magia, not your soul."

So it *was* Dami who shot that man in the storeroom. They guessed as much, but the confirmation makes them shiver all the same. "If it's my magia you want, you can have it."

"Ah, pues, that's the thing. I can't *actually* just take it, because I couldn't use it, not myself. No demonio or diablo can—your magia is from the earth, and we aren't of the earth."

"I don't know what that means."

"It means I don't actually need to take anything from you as much as I need you to help me."

Mar shakes their head and looks away. "I don't make deals with diablos. It was the biggest mistake of Papá's life, and I won't repeat it."

"It's *also* what saved you," Dami says. "If he hadn't made that deal, you wouldn't be here."

Mar's eyes sting and the room blurs. "Well then, maybe I shouldn't be here," they croak.

The quiet that follows is so long that for a second Mar thinks Dami has left. But when they wipe their eyes with the back of their hand and glance at where the demonio was sitting, Dami is there, watching them. Mar can't hold their gaze, so instead they look back at the crew, who have finally started their countdown for Bas and Tito's drinking contest.

When Dami rests their hands on Mar's shoulders and leans down to their ear, Mar doesn't breathe.

"So many lives depend on you being here, Mar León de la Rosa," Dami says, their smoky breath hot on Mar's cheek. "You just don't know it yet."

And with that, the pressure on Mar's shoulders is gone. And so is Dami.

The cheers become a roar as Bas and Tito slam their glasses down, apparently having finished their drinks at the same time. But Bas doesn't seem bothered by the tie; he clambers onto the table unsteadily, then lifts his arms into the air as Tito laughs and the rest of the crew cheer.

"I would like to thank my inspiration!" Bas shouts over the crowd. Then Bas is inexplicably pointing at Mar, and Mar's heart leaps into their throat as the entire crew and half the taberna turns to look at them. "To the newest member of our familia, and the most beautiful boy I know, Mar León de la Rosa!"

Something about that combination of words, *beautiful boy,* feminine and masculine, curls up comfortably in the space behind Mar's heart. It's a nice enough—and fitting enough—compliment that Mar can almost forget the pressure of dozens upon dozens of gazes on them. The crew roars with cheers, and Tito wraps Mar in a one-armed hug, squishing them close to his soft chest in a way that makes a laugh burst out of them. Here, with Bas beaming at them, and Tito grinning at them, and the crew patting their back and cheering them on, Mar finally feels it. Familia.

Almost as soon as a smile ghosts over their lips, Mar's skin begins to prickle. It creeps up the back of their neck. Not in the magic overflow way that's become typical since the sinking of *La Catalina*, but a whisper of warning that has never led Mar astray. The whisper that says *look* and then *closer*.

As the warning grows from a whisper to a hum, as Mar glances around the taberna's warm, burnt-orange-painted room, past the sweaty, alcohol-flushed faces, they stop cold at a man walking through the door. The same bearded blond man who was staring at Mar on Isla Mujeres when they arrived earlier that day. The man whose stare made Mar's stomach churn in sickly waves.

Worse: Dami enters with him, whispering something in his ear. Did they bring him here? What are they telling him?

Then Bas sits on Mar's lap, breaking the spell.

"Hola," he says with a crooked grin. "You almost look like you've stopped enjoying yourself, you know."

"I . . ." Mar glances back at the door, but the blond man is gone.

Something isn't right.

Mar clears their throat. "I think we need to leave. Everyone. Right now."

Bas arches an eyebrow. "Leave? But we just started having fun!"

"I have a bad feeling," Mar says as the hum grows louder, colder, more insistent in their blood. Mar knows this warning: the *last chance to run* call. The *get as far away as possible* internal scream that Mar never ignores and has never regretted acting on.

It crawls up their throat. Suffocating. They have to leave *now*.

Mar jumps up, nearly knocking Bas onto the table, but they don't care. It doesn't matter. They turn to el Capitán, watching them now with narrowed eyes. "I can't explain it, but we need to leave immediately," Mar says. "Por favor, before it's too late."

Which is the moment the door bursts open and Spanish officers flood the taberna, a wave of blue, red-lapelled uniforms, pistols at the ready.

CHAPTER 17

For the briefest of moments no one moves. Caught in mid-blink. A held breath before—

Mar yanks Bas under the table as the taberna erupts. Roars of men and gunfire, breaking glass, steel on steel. The reek of blood is already thick in the air. Bas swears loudly beside Mar, reaching for his gun as Mar gestures the boy forward. They cross beneath the table, emerging on the other side—the side closest to the exit.

But Bas doesn't turn to the exit; he turns to the Spanish soldiers and fires. And Mar understands. If they'd been ambushed here with *La Catalina*'s crew, Mar wouldn't run either. Survival means little if you lose your familia in the process. Mar would've done anything to save them.

Mar could run. They could escape through the chaos and make their own way. And yet the thought of saying adiós to the sea—and yes, maybe the thought of turning their back on Bas, on Tito, on the rest of the crew—gives them pause.

They don't want to leave. Not when the crew needs them

to fight. *So many lives depend on you being here.* Mar isn't sure if this is what Dami meant, but it doesn't matter. *La Ana's* crew may not be blood, but Papá didn't teach Mar to run from a fight.

Mar grabs a beer bottle off the table. They've been holding their magia back for days, but now they let the hum in their bones go. Their markings light up under their shirt, but the fabric is thick enough to smother most of the glow—and the crew isn't looking at them anyway. *Ahora,* they think. Liquid fire rushes out of their chest, down their arms and into the beer bottle—hot and fast—until the glass is smarting in their palm. It takes all of a moment to heat the alcohol to boiling.

Mar grabs the bottle by the neck and hurls it at a mustached man aiming his pistol at them. A shot fires. Mar ducks under Bas's arm. Glass explodes. The mustached man drops his gun, claps his hands over his face, and screams. Broken glass clatters against the floor. Mar grabs a large, sharp shard and slams it home in the man's throat.

And here's the part Mar tries not to think about: Good people don't enjoy this. The blood, the screams, the gunpowder and chaos. But it's in the chaos of the fight that Mar can let their magia free. It's here that Mar can unleash the edges of their magia, because anyone they use it on isn't going to live to spread the word. After weeks of bottling their magia up, releasing only enough to keep it from spilling over, Mar is bursting at the seams.

A hand clenches a fistful of Mar's hair and yanks them back. They wince, lean back into the pull, snatch another beer bottle from the table, and shove it into their attacker's mouth, thrusting his chin up with their palm. The man takes a large, sputtering gulp of the beer, loosening his grip on Mar's hair. Mar twists out of his grip and grabs his throat with their free hand. They imagine their veins freezing over, and their blood hums with the release of magia—this time cold and sharp—freezing the beer in the man's throat.

The man's eyes widen as Mar breathes steadily, their blood singing as they keep their magia flowing. The man can't very well speak with ice jamming his throat closed, but the fear in his eyes is palpable. He must know this death is unnatural, but he can't cry out. Right now the man is the only one besides Tito who knows Mar isn't like any other young person.

Sometimes sharing the secret, even for just a moment, is a thrill.

Then the man slackens and drops to the floor, and Mar is nearly alone with the secret of who they are again.

The silence of the aftermath of battle is so loud, it startles them. Mar glances around, suddenly aware of *La Ana*'s crew finishing off the final scuffles and picking over the corpses. Mar knows all too well how this goes: The fine clothes are ruined with blood, but the weapons, gold, trinkets, jewelry—those can be sold or used. *It's a crime to leave it behind,* Papá used to say. *Not like they need it anymore, and we can't have it go to waste.*

Mar closes their eyes and inhales deeply, ignoring the thick stench of blood as they try to push the memory from their mind. Thinking of Papá hurts too much.

"Are you all right?" Bas is standing beside Mar, his face smeared with blood and his cheek swollen.

Mar nods at the boy and shoves their hands into their pockets. "You look worse than I do. Are you?"

Bas grins. "I think the bruises will look good on me."

Mar shakes their head, but a weak smile ghosts over their lips nevertheless.

"Well, it seems our shore leave has come to an early close," el Capitán announces to the ruined bar. "Time to go."

CHAPTER 18

"You!" El Capitán crosses the beach, murder in his eyes.

Mar jerks to a stop—they haven't stopped running since they left the bar with the crew, and now they're just fifteen feet from the dock. Most of the crew has continued on ahead to prepare *La Ana* for a speedy exit, but the rage on Vega's face turns Mar's blood to ice. They back directly into a palm tree.

Vega grabs the collar of Mar's shirt and shoves them hard against the tree trunk. "You knew! How did you know? Did you tell them where we'd be going? Are you working for García López?"

"What? No!" They're on the tips of their toes, their shirt bunched and pulling under their armpits as Vega holds them up. For a panicked moment they throw a glance at their chest, but the cloth isn't riding up enough to reveal their chest flattener wrapped tight around their upper ribs. The cover of night helps too.

Vega's face is red and twisted; a vein in his left temple visibly throbs. "Then how did you know!"

"I don't know!" Mar cries, because what else are they supposed to say? Revealing their magia will only get them killed—though if el Capitán decides Mar is actually a Spanish spy, they're sure to die anyway. "I saw this blond man who'd been staring at us at the beach when we docked. I just had a bad feeling!"

He snorts. "Get these *feelings* often, do you?"

Mar opens their mouth but quickly thinks better of answering. They suspect *Actually, yes* wouldn't be well received here. Instead, their heart lodges in their throat as they desperately search for answers.

"Papá!" Bas shoves his way between them, ripping Vega's hands off Mar. Mar's feet hit the sand hard, but they brace themself against the tree, ignoring their aching back. Bas stands wedged between them, physically blocking Mar from el Capitán's reach. "I was with Mar the entire time on Isla Mujeres. There's no way he could've worked with the Spaniards without my knowing. And anyway, we're wasting time. We need to focus on getting far away from here before they dispatch ships after us!"

"He's right, Ale," Tito interjects, stepping beside el Capitán. "Didn't Spaniards kill el Embrujado's wife?" His gaze softens as he turns to Mar. "That was Mar's mother."

Mar's vision goes fuzzy, and their throat aches as they hold back tears. Not trusting their voice, they just nod.

"See?" Tito looks at Vega. "Mar would never work for the Spaniards."

El Capitán scowls like he wants to say something, but

instead he makes a noise like a growl, throws his hands up, and storms off toward the docked schooner.

Tito sighs and runs his hand through his salt-and-pepper hair. "I'm sorry to bring that up," he says to Mar. "Are you all right? Did he hurt you?"

"I don't—" Their voice comes out quiet and scratchy. They clear their throat and try again. "I'm not hurt. Thank you."

Tito nods and smiles softly. "I'll remind him it's an advantage to have someone with strong instincts on the crew. Don't hesitate to tell me if you run into any trouble with the crew—I promise he won't go after you again."

Mar nods, and Tito goes after Vega. Bas turns to Mar, concern etched deep in his face. "Are you sure you're all right?"

Mar sniffs and wipes their eyes with the back of their hand. "My back hurts a little, but I'll be fine."

They walk with Bas onto *La Ana* and stand quietly for a moment as the crew moves around them, work resumed as if the captain hasn't just attacked one of their own. Joaquín nods at them from across the deck. "¿Estás bien, Leoncito?"

Mar nods, and Bas smiles, gently nudging their shoulder with his. "The crew cares about you, you know. Like it or not, you're one of us now."

A small smile cracks through Mar's stormy exterior. They might not have believed Bas even a few days ago, but it seems, maybe, he might be right. It's a comforting thought.

"Also," Bas adds, "you're absurdly brave. If el Capitán came charging at me looking like that, I would've jumped into the ocean."

Mar laughs.

The salty ocean breeze wicks the sweat off Mar's brow as they lean against *La Ana*'s railing, watching the ocean sway below them. It's been five days since they left Playa Mujeres, and four days since they've all relaxed after not seeing a Spanish ship for twenty-four hours. The itch of unspent magia has already returned, but if Mar is careful, they can drop little ice cubes, unnoticed, into the sea.

Not that ice cubes are anywhere near enough of a reprieve. Maybe they should ask Tito for help releasing some magia discreetly.

They tilt their head back with a sigh. With the sun high overhead, the ocean is painted in light. It's a clear day, and Mar longs to climb high into the rigging and watch from the crow's nest as the clouds slip away. But are they really ready to do something so familiar? Something that would feel so much like a home they can never return to?

Mar turns Papá's bullet in their fingers, running their thumb over the smoothing edges. Papá would want them to move on. To make a new home, whatever that means. He'd probably be nervous about Mar staying with Vega's crew, but is it really any more dangerous than sailing with Papá? Sure,

Vega is a little more arrogant, but the crew knows what they're doing. They aren't one of the last surviving pirate crews in the Caribbean by chance.

At least that's what Mar tells themself. It's easier to bear the long nights and days when they can conceive of a way Papá would approve of where Mar has ended up.

But how can they move on when there's still a chance—however small—of saving him?

"Have you ever been to Vieques?" Tito leans back against the railing next to Mar. Vieques is where they're sailing to now, to replenish their supplies before going back out on the merchant hunt. With the shore on the distant horizon, they're maybe an hour away from reaching land, with an additional couple of hours to sail around to the right part of the island.

Mar shakes their head. "No, but Papá loves . . ." They grimace. "Papá loved visiting Puerto Rico."

Tito smiles softly and nods. "There's a bay there that's my favorite place in all of the Caribbean. At night it glows blue, like magic. It's incredible. When I was a younger man, I used to go there with . . ." His face softens, and for a second, though Tito is looking at Mar, they suspect he isn't seeing them at all. But then he shakes his head with a small smile. "Well, you and Bas should go there together. I could show you both the way if you'd like. We'll have enough time for a short trip."

Mar has heard rumors of the glowing bay—even wondered if maybe it carried a magic like Mar's own—but they've never had the chance to visit. "I'd like that," they say.

Tito nods. "The crew likes you, you know."

Mar blinks, startled. "Oh." Their face warms. "That's . . . good to hear."

Tito's smile spreads, and something about the twinkle in his eye reminds Mar of Leo. "Joaquín doesn't nickname temporary stays Leoncito. As far as we're concerned, you're stuck with us now." He winks and Mar laughs.

"I could do a lot worse."

A call from above makes Mar squint up at the sky—and the lookout yelling down to el Capitán as he descends the rigging. "Spanish merchant ship ahead! Portside!"

Mar's heart skips a beat. They've been on *La Ana* long enough to know that spotting a merchant ship almost always means a battle—a battle *La Ana*'s crew is generally more equipped for than a ship full of goods would be.

Now, with the cry of *merchant* in the air, a stillness washes over the crew as they all turn to el Capitán, perched along the portside railing as he looks through his spyglass. The smile spilling over his lips says all Mar needs to know before Vega has spoken a word.

Bas nudges Mar and grins. El Capitán stands up straight and turns to the crew with exactly the same smile on his face. "It's a big one! What do we think, can we take on a big haul before Vieques?"

The crew erupts into cheers. From there: the turning ship, the snap of rope and sail, the packing of gunpowder and loading of cannons, the sharpening of swords and knives and checking bullet chambers. Mar keeps their hands busy tying rope, grabbing supplies, as *La Ana* nears the other ship, all the while ignoring the magia nipping their fingertips. They just have to wait until the battle. Then they can let go.

But the tingling of magia in Mar's fingertips grows to waves of sparks dancing up and down their back, a growing sense of unease in the pit of their stomach. They frown across the water at the towering merchant ship, now visible with the naked eye. *La Ana* is nearing quickly as the merchant ship sails lazily forward, seemingly unaware of *La Ana*'s presence. But how can that be? They've hardly taken a stealthy approach. Which means the Spaniards must not care about *La Ana* barreling toward them. . . .

Or.

The crew is a gathering storm around them, and Mar's voice would disappear in the tumult. Bas. Where is Bas? Bas will listen. Mar is sure of it, but everyone is in motion, and trying to find one boy—even a boy usually so good at making himself known—

Someone crashes into Mar's back, and they stumble several steps forward. "Don't just stand there, boy!" Tito yells. "Bring up more gunpowder!"

"Wait—"

But Tito moves too quickly for Mar to grab him, and if he hears them, he doesn't show it. The knot in Mar's stomach is tight and growing. *Run,* their magia screams, the urge to flee nearly as intense as that terrible night on *La Catalina.*

But once again, there's nowhere to run to. And this time, *La Ana* is racing toward the very thing that turns the prickling to full-on shivers.

Mar moves. Weaving between shouting crew members tossing weapons to each other, ducking beneath rope, and ignoring the calls for help, for Mar to aid them in rushing to the very thing they're increasingly sure will get them all killed.

And then Mar is standing in front of Capitán Vega, and they say, *"I don't think we should do this,"* as intensely as they can.

El Capitán just arches an eyebrow at them. "Sometimes a feeling is just a feeling, Mar." He slaps Mar's shoulder in a way they suppose is meant to be comforting but mostly just makes their already tingling skin smart more.

"No entiendes," Mar says. "We can't attack that ship. We need to turn around before—"

"Are you trying to give me orders on my own ship?"

Mar stills, eyes wide, heart in their throat. "I— No, I just—"

"You seem to be under the mistaken impression that because I've allowed you into this crew, you can become familiar with me. You can't." He nods back to the rest of the men racing to their stations as their target looms ever closer. "Go do your job before I decide you no longer need one aboard this ship."

He turns back to the crew, shouting orders. Mar is dismissed. Mar is dismissed, el Capitán isn't listening, and they're all going to die.

Run, Mar's magia hums, vibrating in their bones.

La Ana races forward: a thousand feet away.

Run. The warning is so strong, Mar feels as though their skeleton might grind down to dust under its weight. They crouch, wrapping their arms tight around their stomach.

Five hundred feet.

They've never ignored their magia like this. They've never raced stubbornly toward the very thing they know they must escape from. Blood bursts in their mouth—Mar bit their tongue—but the pain is distant and dull. What is present, what demands attention above all else, is the one thing Mar can't do. Their fate is anchored to *La Ana*.

They reach the merchant ship and the prey sits, unmoving, uncaring, unconcerned. The crew falls quiet as what is now obvious to them all sinks in: The ship is empty.

"A ghost ship?" someone mutters beside Mar, and with a start they realize they aren't alone. How long has Bas been crouched beside them?

"No," Mar whispers.

Bas looks at them, dark eyes wide. "Do you know something?"

"I tried to tell him." Mar's voice is scratchy, thin. "I tried to tell el Capitán we had to turn around, but he wouldn't—he didn't—"

"¡Capitán!" Eyes wide, Tito points out to sea behind them. "There are two more ships!"

"Carajo," Vega swears, turning to the merchant ship ahead of them. Then he slams his fist against the wheel. "¡Carajo! Where is that boy?"

"¿Capitán?" Tito asks at the same time Vega whirls around and zeroes in on Mar.

"You!" El Capitán crosses the deck, murder in his eyes. Mar scrambles to their feet, but there's nowhere to go on a ship about to be clobbered by two Spanish warships.

But instead of fury, he rips his spyglass from his pocket and offers it to them.

Mar blinks.

"Apparently," Vega bites out, "sometimes a feeling is more than just a feeling. What is it telling you now?"

Mar releases a shaky breath. Even without the spyglass Mar can spot the ships rapidly gaining on them on the horizon. They're large. Much larger than *La Ana*, Mar guesses. Which means *La Ana* is likely to be faster, but if those ships catch up with them . . .

"It doesn't work like that," Mar finally says. "I can't tell the future or anything like that, I just . . . know when we're about to be in danger."

El Capitán takes back the spyglass. "Like now."

Mar nods. "We can't take those ships."

Vega turns to the oncoming ships, looks through the glass, then lowers it, chewing his lip. "We can outrun them. *La Ana* is among the fastest on the seas."

Tito walks over, hands in his pockets. "We could have if we'd careened her, but we were sidetracked when we had to abruptly leave Playa Mujeres. We won't make it to Vieques before they catch up with us."

El Capitán swears again. He rolls his shoulders, collapses

his spyglass, and turns back to the crew, clapping his hands. "Well! Change of plans. What's the nearest port?"

"Guayama," Tito says automatically. "If we move quickly, we should be able to arrive there before the Spaniards catch up with us."

Vega nods. "¿Entonces? What are we waiting for? Full speed to Guayama!"

The crew moves without question—all except Bas and Mar, who stand sullenly by the wall.

"But what are we going to do when we get to Guayama?" Bas asks. "The Spaniards will just follow us there."

Vega's gaze pauses on Mar just long enough for them to understand the message left unsaid. That el Capitán may be done interrogating Mar for now, but the conversation isn't over. There's a gleam in his eye that makes Mar's stomach churn. Have they revealed too much with their "intuition"?

But then Vega turns to his son, and his face slackens just a little. "They very well might," he says with a sigh.

Bas frowns. "And if they do?"

"Then we run."

"And if they catch up to us?"

Vega turns back to the ocean, lightly trailing his fingertips over *La Ana*'s smooth railing. "Then we do the only thing we can: We fight."

CHAPTER 19

Of course, the Spaniards follow them to the island.

It's dark when the crew stumbles off *La Ana* and scatter across Guayama. They have to leave *La Ana* behind, even though the Spaniards will surely take it, but they're out of options. The only consolation is at least they recently left Isla Mujeres, so they don't have any loot on board.

Run today to fight tomorrow, Mar thinks, even as their heart twinges at the thought of losing yet another ship that has become their home.

El Capitán tells Bas and Tito to follow him, and Bas gestures for Mar to go with them. Mar doesn't love the thought of being anywhere enclosed with Vega. But they like the notion of hiding alone, speculating whether the Spaniards found Bas, even less.

So the four move along the outskirts of the sleepy port town with its dark stone streets of painted, flat-roofed stucco buildings and into the forest. As they move quickly between the densely packed trees, dodging low-hanging branches, the chitter of birds and the squeak of coquíes almost drown out the crunch of their boots on foliage and panicked breaths. A bat swoops low over Mar's head and they flinch, but they don't slow.

They can't slow.

By the time they break through into the swampy area of the mangrove forest, Mar is so sweaty, their clothes are practically pasted to them; they're silently glad they wore their black shirt today. Though the warm, clear green water reaches only partway up Vega's and Tito's chests, it reaches Bas's shoulders and Mar's neck; all four of them have to hold their guns above the water. Mar also has the paper Graciela gave them and the compressed bullet crumpled in their fist.

They step carefully, trying not to slip or trip over the slick sea grass and knots of roots. Thick silvery tree roots weave in and out of the water like paralyzed needle and thread, a complicated web that the group quietly ducks and slides around. Mar's arms burn from the strain of holding them up for so long. In the silence, their heavy breathing and the hush of moving water are explosive.

Deeper and deeper they go, embedding themselves into the complicated network of trees, along a progressively thinning pathway between interwoven mangroves until they hit a wall of silver roots knotted so tightly, it's impossible to go any farther. While Mar imagines they'll probably be difficult to find here—if only because the swamp is so expansive and the shadows cast by the endless roots make for easy concealment in the night—they can't help but think it'd be impossible to run if they're found. The tree roots are so thick around them, it'll be difficult to get out even if they aren't in a hurry.

El Capitán and Tito whisper quietly to each other and it's impossible to discern the conversation. Mar takes deep, steadying breaths, trying to keep their mind clear and the panic at bay. They and Bas have deposited their guns in the gnarled tree roots protruding above the water. Mar's magia has quieted, but only barely. They still feel the need to run, to move, to race to the other side of the large island and take another ship, maybe, in the opposite direction. Anything to get away from the Spaniards hunting them down.

Beside them, Bas is shivering.

"We'll be fine," Mar whispers, just as much for themself as for Bas. Because they want to believe they didn't survive something as entirely improbable as el Diablo himself dragging their home to the bottom of the ocean only to die six weeks later at the end of a Spaniard's rifle. They haven't even had the chance to do something significant with their borrowed time. They still have no idea how to save Papá; and anyway, how are they supposed to save Papá when they can barely save themself?

Mar squints up through the tree coverage above them to the slivers of moon visible through the leaves. Now in its second cycle, the moon is a little more than half-full. Mar's gut twists nauseatingly. How many days do they have left? It was ten when they last saw Dami at the taberna which was, what—five days ago?

Could they really have only five days left to save Papá?

"Bas," Mar whispers, "what's the date?"

Bas tilts his head and opens his mouth—

"Quiet," Vega whispers sharply.

Sea grass tickles Mar's leg, and it takes every ounce of their self-control not to jerk away. The pounding in Mar's ears drowns out any hint of whatever it was that alerted el Capitán. Their magia rushes back with a warning, their bones like tuning forks. Even their breath seems too loud; Mar presses their palm against their mouth to try to muffle the noise. With every passing second, the cold prickle of magia—of looming danger—becomes stronger. Mar and Bas lean into each other. Bas's eyes have snapped shut as his lips move in rapid, silent prayer.

Their magia is unbearable now. *Run,* Mar's magic screams, but there's nowhere to run to. *Hurry. Run.*

Mar bites their tongue. The hum in their bones has their teeth chattering. Their shoulder bumps Bas's. Neither of them moves.

And then the hush. The breath of a current, barely audible. Then a little louder, displaced water rushing and dipping back into the swamp. The smooth rhythm of oars slipping ever closer. Under the warm water, Bas's hand slips gently against Mar's, and before Mar can question it, their fingers are tangled together. Hands squeezed tight.

In any other situation Mar might wonder what it means to hang on to each other like this. To turn to each other for comfort, palm to palm, fingers interlaced, Bas's thumb lightly running back and forth over the back of Mar's hand. But right now, the tactile comfort is exactly what Mar needs. It's what they've missed since el Diablo threw them into the ocean to drown.

Lantern light splashes over them. "¡Aquí!" The voices of a dozen men, the barrels of a dozen pistols surrounding them.

Mar's stomach churns, and hot bile crawls up their throat as they squint through the glaring light. Mar's magia burns down to the tips of their fingers; they can't run, not anymore.

The only way to overpower the Spaniards would be to use their magia—and a lot of it. But after all was said and done, Vega and Bas and the rest of them would think Mar a demonio and have them killed.

The world isn't ready for Mar's magia. They know that.

Still—what if Mar is wrong? Tito trusted them. What if Vega and Bas would as well?

Before Mar can do anything, soldiers grab them roughly by the shoulders. They're hoisted out of the water and ripped away from Bas. Heavy manacles clamp onto their wrists. Too late to fight now. Too late to wonder what if.

Mar's hesitation may have just gotten them all killed.

CHAPTER 20

"¡Diablo! ¡Monstruo!"

The memory is paralyzing. Staring down the barrel of a gun, their breath trapped in their chest. Then the scream.

An explosion.

"¡Mamá!"

White-hot heat and pain like they've never felt before. The scream rips out of their throat. The rumble of the explosion is deafening; black smoke blots out the sun. Something has irrevocably broken in them. The agony, the heat, the fury—

It swallows them like the ocean would.

Mar startles awake, shivering and sweating in a dank, dark cell. Stone beneath their back. Only slats of moonlight peering into the barred window high above. The night air is sticky and still, in a way it never gets out on the ocean, where the winds dance with the waves. But Mar isn't out on the ocean, on *La Ana* or *La Catalina*. Mar is in a cell in San Juan, where they've been for three days.

Three days.

Though it was just a memory woven into a nightmarish dream, Mar can still taste the ash on their tongue. The echoes of screams ring hollow in their skull. At eight years old, Mar never meant to kill anyone, and they certainly never meant to decimate the coastal village that'd been their home. But what Mar wanted didn't matter to the magia that awakened inside them. The magia Mar is terrified they'll accidentally awaken again.

Still, not using their magia has made it harder, not easier, to keep control. And now, on the eve of their scheduled trial, it's becoming damn near impossible to keep it silent.

Their impending trial will be a mockery of justice, of course. Pirates are rarely found innocent, and there's only ever one end for a captured pirate. Over the last three days, the jeering jailkeepers have been all too happy to make sure they don't forget it.

As if lying on a cold stone floor for three days hasn't been uncomfortable enough, their ribs ache now too—a consequence of not loosening the binding cloth for more than seventy-two hours. But without any privacy whatsoever, what else are they supposed to do? Seeing—and feeling—the shape of their chest at night is bad enough. Doing so in front of others is unthinkable.

Not for the first time, they wish they didn't need the cloth to keep their chest flat.

The cells are small, really meant for one person, but the crew is split up among them in pairs. Mar supposes the only reason the Spaniards haven't stuffed more people into each cell is so the crew can't gang up on the guards—which they certainly would've attempted to do had there been more than two people per cell.

Mar's cellmate is Bas, currently sleeping. Across the aisle and down one cell to the right are Vega and Tito. Somewhere down at the end of the aisle is a locked door, and on the other side of that door are guards, always keeping watch. Every hour or so, two guards stroll down the aisle, shoulder to shoulder, peering into the cells, which seems to Mar a pointless exercise, because even if they *did* manage to get out of their cells, where would they go? The only way out is through that heavily guarded door.

Well. The heavily guarded door and—maybe—the barred windows. The ones in the cells are too small; even if Mar were able to get rid of the bars, there's no way they'd be able to fit through the narrow slit in the wall that barely qualifies as a window. But down the aisle, on the side opposite the door, is a slightly larger window. Also barred. Also small. But Mar could fit. And so could Bas.

Mar sits up. They just have to get out of the cell. And get rid of the iron bars blocking them in.

An impossible task without magia, of course.

"You know," Dami says next to them, "I've really underestimated your determination to not use your magia. If you're *that* insistent on ignoring the figurative key in your pocket to get out of here, you *do* know a magnanimous demonio who'd be delighted to make a deal with you."

Mar jumps and scowls at them. The silvery moonlight paints deep shadows on their soft face and glistens on their hip-length black hair. Dami is wearing silver earrings today, appropriately shaped like little keys.

"You have a lot of nerve showing up here after selling us out to the Spaniards," Mar whispers sharply.

Dami steps around Mar, their black skirt flowing around their ankles. For the first time, Mar realizes Dami's bare feet are floating just above the ground. Have they always done that? "Did I?" Dami asks.

"Do you deny it?"

"I do." Dami gives a grin like a machete. "Selling you out implies I got paid. I did that just for fun."

If looks could kill, the one Mar levels on Dami would send them back to the land of the dead.

"We are in *prison* because of you," Mar hisses. "The entire crew could *die*."

"No, you're in *prison* because of *you*," Dami shoots back. "If you weren't so afraid of your own power, you could have easily taken care of those soldiers at sea."

The charge hits deep; something inside them twists hot and sharp. "And if *you* hadn't told the Spaniards where we were, I wouldn't have been in that position to begin with."

Dami shrugs. "It's not my fault you refuse to practice using your magia unless your life is at stake."

"Leave," Mar says through gritted teeth, barely keeping

their voice down. "I already told you I'm not interested in making any deals with demonios—let alone traitorous ones."

"Not even if it would save your life?" Dami asks lightly.

Mar opens their mouth to say no, but the demonio continues. "Not even if it'd save the crew's life? Or your papá's? The moon sure is looking near full these days."

The mention of Papá—and their looming deadline—makes Mar's eyes sting all over again. Can they really trust a demonio to help them save Papá, especially after what Dami has done? It seems impossible, and Mar reminds themself that Dami will say or do anything to get them to make a deal. Even sell them out to the Spaniards. Even dangle Papá's life in front of them. Demonios are manipulative liars, and twisting words and pressuring weaknesses is exactly how Papá got caught up with them to begin with.

Mar stands, brushing their dirty hands off on their trousers. "I don't need your help," they whisper tightly. "Go away before you wake someone."

"Fine," Dami says. "But you know you can't save him without me. And you can't save your handsome friend without magia." They disappear in a cloud of putrid black smoke. Mar presses the heels of their palms into their closed eyes, fighting the tears threatening to bubble over. They have to focus. They can't think about Papá, or demonios, or diablos, not right now.

They're running out of time.

Mar drops their hands, blinking in the darkness as they

take a long, shaky breath. Bas—and the rest of the crew, as far as Mar can tell—is fast asleep, which makes this the perfect time. Mar scoots up to the bars, reaches through, and holds the cold iron padlock in their hands. The metal is a little sweaty from the humid air, in a way that's somewhat unsettling. Mar's palms go equally clammy in moments as they close their eyes and breathe deeply, settling their heart.

These are their options:

1. Do nothing and accept their sham trial and inevitable public execution.
2. Make a deal with a demonio and bind their soul for eternity.
3. Risk using their magia and pray no one wakes up and sees them.

It's not much of a decision. After the trial they'll likely be transported to El Morro, the heavily guarded Spanish fortress at the edge of the city. If it's difficult to break out of here unnoticed, it'll be impossible once they're imprisoned deep in the heart of the fortress.

Mar's been watching for three days, and the truth is undeniable: There's no way out without their magia. And if Mar doesn't act soon, they're all going to die. They've waited long enough. Too long.

Mar didn't survive an encounter with el Diablo himself just to die on a stage for the Spaniards.

Closing their eyes, Mar takes a breath and slowly relaxes their hold on their magia. It slips between their fingers, hesitantly at first, tasting the air. Then all at once, heat pours into iron so quickly, Mar's eyes snap open. Too fast. Too much. They snap their hold on their magia closed, a dam slamming shut.

This is what happens when you don't use your magia for so long, they think with a grimace. *The fire takes over and you can barely control it.*

The lock in Mar's palm is a puddle of molten red-hot metal dripping over their fingers and sizzling on stone. It all happened in seconds. Mar pulls their hand back into the cell, wiping the metal onto the stone, trembling like the earth during a quake.

But they did it. Sure, maybe it went faster than expected, but the lock is gone.

"How did you do that?"

Mar nearly jumps out of their skin at the whispered question. Across the aisle, el Capitán is watching them; still lying on the floor, up against the bars, but definitely not as asleep as Mar had assumed him to be. Which means he saw.... Oh, Dios.

How long has he been awake? Did he hear their conversation with Dami?

But Vega doesn't look angry. Or alarmed. Merely curious, and clearly expecting an answer.

"I . . ." Mar's voice falters. How are they supposed to

explain the inexplicable? It's not like Mar knows where their magia comes from—not really. And using it—how does one explain breathing? They just did.

"I should have listened to you," Vega says through the soft quiet. "Back on *La Ana,* when you told us not to attack. I regret it." He shakes his head. "A otra cosa, mariposa. I'll die for my mistake, but my boy won't. You'll take him with you."

It isn't a question—not that Mar planned to leave without Bas, anyway. They nod and turn to the sleeping boy.

"The guards will be returning soon," Vega says. "Hurry."

Mar wipes the cooling remnants of iron from their palms, pushes the cell door open, and nudges Bas awake. Bas squints blearily through the shadows, rubbing his eyes, his face set into a deep frown. "Something wrong?" he mumbles. "Besides everything?"

"Cell's open," Mar answers. "We're leaving."

Bas stares at Mar for several seconds, blinking sleep from his eyes. "What do you . . . What?"

Mar grabs Bas's hand and pulls him up. "I don't know how much time we have."

"I don't understand."

Mar groans and gestures to the open cell door. "*Now* do you?"

"Sebas," Vega hisses from across the aisle. "Corre, mijo. Before the Spaniards return."

"Papi," Bas's voice cracks. "I can't leave without you— without the crew."

Warm lantern light fills the aisle, filtered through the little barred window in the door at the end of the cellblock. Mar's blood runs cold. They're out of time. The guards have already returned to check on them, and Mar and Bas haven't even left their cell.

Mar bolts forward, grabs the cell door, and yanks it closed, cringing at the squeak of rusty hinges. There's no way for them to put the lock back together, and if the guards notice it's missing . . . Mar doesn't want to think about the consequences.

"Pretend to be asleep," Mar hisses at Bas, tossing themself onto the stone floor beside him. Bas stares at Mar wide-eyed but lies down and closes his eyes just as the door at the end of the cellblock creaks open. Slow, steady footsteps approach their cell, which is about halfway down the long aisle of cages.

Please don't notice the missing lock, Mar prays to no one in particular. To anyone who'll hear them. *Just keep walking. We're asleep. Just keep—*

A blood-curdling scream stops Mar's heart. Their eyes snap open, abandoning the pretense of sleep. Just down the hall, Vega has a guard yanked back against the bars at the far end of his cell, his arm around the soldier's neck and a knifepoint dug into the guard's side. Spaniards who've been standing at the end of the hall rush past Mar and Bas's cell, rifles pointed at el Capitán. But even as the guards crowd around the cell, screaming at Vega to release the guard, he looks calmly at Mar and jerks his head to the left. Toward the now-unguarded open door.

It's the opposite side from the window Mar wanted to go for. But it's an opening. A way out. And a chance they aren't going to have for much longer.

This time Mar doesn't need to tell Bas—they both jump up into a crouch as Mar approaches the cell door and carefully, slowly, opens it. The guards are all facing away from them—Tito has started fighting through the bars next to Vega too, effectively getting all six guards crowded in the aisle involved—but if any one of them turns around . . .

Mar opens the cell door just enough for them to slide through and slips out, keeping low to the ground, Bas on their heels. Then they move away from the noise—faster, sprinting until they're both through the door at the end of the cellblock. Bas hesitates, watching the guards scream at Vega and Tito, hand on the door.

Mar's heart beats in their skull, gasping for breath though they've barely run at all. Bas closes the door, effectively muffling the noise, but it's only a matter of time before the guards notice they've been locked into the cellblock and two prisoners are now missing.

"Bas," Mar begins, but he slides the deadbolt through with a satisfying thunk. He doesn't say anything, but his eyes are glassy when he meets Mar's gaze.

The room they're now in is small, more of a waiting area at the bottom of a short set of stairs that leads into an open archway. Mar can't see what's beyond the archway. Or how many guards may be waiting for them at the top of the stairs.

Trembling so violently they feel as though they might throw up, Mar takes a shaky step forward. Bas takes their hand and squeezes once. Then he smiles grimly at Mar through the shadows, and the two climb the steps together with shallow breaths.

CHAPTER 21

Mar and Bas peer around the corner. Even though it's night, the hallways are relatively well lit, and there's little place to hide. To the right, the hallway bends around another corner, from which comes boisterous laughter. To the left, rows of doors that lead to a dead end.

"The exit's probably somewhere to the right," Bas whispers.

"And so are the rest of the guards," Mar answers.

"But the other side doesn't look like a way out."

Mar grimaces. Bas isn't wrong, but they can't know for sure without trying, can they? On the other hand, the left side of the hall looks like the perfect place to end up cornered.

Still, there isn't anyone there, as far as they can tell. And that seems like a safer bet than trying to sneak past what sounds like another half-dozen guards waiting around the opposite corner.

"I think we should look," Mar says. "Maybe there's a side door or something."

Bas seems skeptical, but he lifts a shoulder nevertheless. "Worth trying if it means potentially avoiding an army of Spaniards."

They creep down the hall, the ruckus of laughter and conversation at their backs. Mar's heart is a drum against their rib cage; every breath shivers. How long do they have before the soldiers downstairs realize they've been locked in? How long until they find their way out? A thought hits them like a shot of ice to the chest: They likely have keys. Once the guards realize they've been tricked—and some prisoners escaped—it won't take them long to get out. And then what?

There are four doors in this hallway, two on each side. The first door is locked. So is the second. And the third. And the fourth.

"All right . . . ," Bas says evenly. "We probably should've guessed they'd be locked. Now what?"

Every heartbeat hammering in Mar's ears is a second less they have to figure out what to do. Mar closes their eyes. *Focus.*

"I don't suppose you have any lockpicks," Bas jokes. "That'd make things easier. Though I'd hope you wouldn't have let us sit in a cell for three days if you did."

He's trying to make light of the situation, but his voice trembles. Mar feels as though they've swallowed rocks. They didn't have lockpicks, of course, but they did have magia. And they did wait three days before finally trying to use it.

Mar bites their lip and glances at the taller boy. How would Bas react to their magia? They can't know without trusting him enough to use it in front of him. But even if he *were* inclined to react badly, would he really protest if it saved them?

Mar takes a deep breath and turns to him. "Bas—"

"¡Oye! ¿Qué haces?"

Mar and Bas spin to the guards at the opposite end of the hall.

They're out of time.

"Move!" Bas faces the door and rams his shoulder into it—the door miraculously swings open. Without thinking, Mar rushes into the room after him and slams the door shut behind them. The sound is a thunderclap, and the voices in the hallway aren't laughing anymore.

Mar and Bas are in a small office. A half-empty bookshelf sits beside the door, with a desk across from it. A large, barred window is on the far wall. Two chairs, an unlit lantern, stacks of paper on the desk. There's nothing of use. And nowhere to go.

"Help me move this bookshelf!" Bas says. "Quickly!"

Mar and Bas crash against it, grunting against the weight. But the shelf slides, screeching against the wooden floor until they press it flat against the door. Then they do the same to the desk, pushing that against the bookshelf.

"That's not going to hold them for long," Bas says, panting.

"No." Mar turns to the window and bites their lip. They haven't wanted to use their magia in front of Bas, but they're out of options. If they hide their magia now, both of them are going to die. "But it doesn't need to hold."

"What do you mean?"

Thunk. The slam against the door jars Mar's heart. Bas winces but looks at Mar hopefully.

"Don't panic," Mar says.

Bas laughs. "You mean more than I already am?"

Mar rubs their hands together, steps up to the window, and peers through the bars outside. They're on the ground level, facing the back of the building. It's dark, and as far as Mar can tell, no one is around. If they can get through, they'll be home free.

Mar rests their palms against the iron bottom ledge of the window, flattening their hands between the bars as much as possible. When they broke out of the cell, the fire inside them was a little *too* eager to surface. The last thing they need is to lose control and accidentally set the jailhouse aflame, killing the crew. They don't want to think about whether it'd be better to die by fire now or on the gallows in front of a crowd in a few days, but the thought of the crew slowly suffocating and burning in their cells by Mar's hand is too awful to comprehend.

Instead, they imagine their blood becoming frost. The frost moves through their body like an exhaled breath—then a rush. The magic responds quickly, shooting up Mar's spine and down their arms, cold, and exhilarating, and so fresh. The cloth wrapping their arms effectively dampens the glow, but beneath it their markings are undoubtedly bright blue.

The stone beneath Mar's palm goes so cold, it almost burns; frost races across the gray like an unfurled carpet. Then it climbs. Up the sides of the window and up the iron, weaving around like icy vine work until every centimeter is coated with rapidly thickening ice. But it's not enough. The iron itself has to change for Mar to be able to break it.

Another slam against the door almost bursts through Mar's carefully honed concentration. Mar doesn't know how long the bookshelf and desk will hold. But even as the shouts get louder and the slams against the door grow faster, the only thing that matters is funneling their magic into the iron.

Más, Mar demands, breathing evenly as the magia surges through them. For months, for years they've been saying *less,* they've been trying to fight the very blood in their veins. But now they need more, now it feels so good as the rush of energy lights up their every cell and the iron bars keeping them in the small room turn white, then clear.

Ice.

Mar gasps and yanks their hands away. Everything comes into crystal-like focus. Bas is staring at them, pale and wide-eyed. The bookshelf holding the door closed behind them is inching forward, and the thumps Mar has assumed were Spaniards trying to push the door open sound more like hacking. Like chipping away. Like their window of escape time shrinking.

There isn't any time. Mar turns to the window, punches through the ice, and clears it away. They have an exit.

"You first." Mar looks at Bas and gestures to the open window.

A crack like lightning rips through the room. And maybe it's the reminder of the ever-nearing Spaniards, or maybe it's the intensity in Mar's voice, but whatever it is, Bas snaps out of his openmouthed stupor. "But—"

"No." Mar pushes Bas toward the window. "I can fight them off better than you can if I need to. Go. Ahora."

Bas bites his lip but grabs the window ledge and hoists himself up and through.

A second deafening crack sends Mar's heart racing. They grab the ledge, pull themself through with burning arms and shoulders, and lean forward until they ungracefully topple out onto grass.

Grass! They're outside and clumsily get their feet beneath them. And with the shouts of Spaniards behind them and the crash of the door giving way, Mar and Bas race together into darkness.

CHAPTER 22

The rainstorm hits maybe ten minutes after Mar and Bas have escaped the prison, in the only way rain knows how in the Caribbean: the sky opening up all at once.

Now huddled under the awning of a quiet inn at the edge of the walled city of San Juan, at the farthest reaches of the famous shiny blue-cobblestone streets, Bas has gone exceptionally quiet. They're sitting shoulder to shoulder against the rough, incongruously bright yellow stucco exterior—the white-trimmed awning isn't that wide, and now that they're drenched, even the warm wind feels chilly—but beside Mar, Bas's silence is louder than any storm. Mar can only imagine what Bas might be thinking, and none of it is flattering.

Demonio. Monstruo. Diablo. All words strangers have spit at Mar, sometimes under their breath, other times right in their face. Bas hasn't left Mar, not yet, but what does that really mean? Maybe everything. Maybe nothing.

Finally, Mar can't handle it anymore. "Just say it," they blurt out over the roar of the storm.

Bas blinks and looks at them. His rain-drenched hair reaches into his eyes, and he runs the back of his hand over his forehead to wipe it out of the way. "Say . . . what?"

"I . . . you . . ." Mar frowns. After everything they've just experienced, Mar can't imagine Bas is actually sitting here not thinking about anything at all. The blank look Bas is giving them feels false—wrong, somehow, because it just isn't possible that the boy is completely apathetic about everything that just happened. Bas is theatrical about everything, down to the café he doesn't even like but pretends to.

This quiet boy isn't the Bas they know.

"Whatever you're thinking," Mar finally says, "I know you aren't just . . ." They gesture vaguely to Bas. "Whatever this is."

"This is exhaustion, Mar," Bas says flatly. "We got out, and I'm grateful and relieved, but we left everyone behind." He looks at Mar. "We have to go back and save them."

Mar stares at Bas. The rain slams down in sheets, spraying them both even beneath the protection of the awning. "We . . . Bas, we can't," Mar says. "You know we can't."

Bas frowns and shakes his head. "I know we don't have a choice. We can't just leave them to die—the trial is in the morning. And we both know what the sentence will be."

"I know, but—"

"Look." Bas raises his voice. "I know they aren't your familia, all right? I know it's not the same for you. But leaving them to die is not an option, not for me. And anyway, we took you in, didn't we? Doesn't that matter to you at all?"

Mar's face warms. "Of course it matters, but we have no way of saving them! This is San Juan. We're outnumbered. The Spaniards have an entire army and *three* fortresses here. I don't know how you can even think of going back when we barely escaped with our lives as it is!"

"Did we, though? Barely escape?"

Mar's eyes narrow. "What do you mean? You were there."

"Yeah, and we escaped, but you . . ." Bas's gaze drifts to Mar's hands; the very hands that turned iron to ice right in front of him. "Whatever you did back there. You can do it again, can't you? That's how we got out of the cell to begin with, right? You must have done that when I was sleeping."

Something of a warning trickles down the back of Mar's skull. Bas isn't afraid of Mar, at least he doesn't seem to be, but the place this is going doesn't seem much better. Something deep inside Mar whispers it might be worse.

"It's . . . not that simple," Mar says.

"How isn't it simple? I don't know how you can do what you do, Mar, but you can use it to defeat those cabrones. They don't stand a chance—you can just turn them all to ice!"

Something twists—hot and sharp and nauseating—in Mar's chest, all the way down to their stomach.

"No," Mar says firmly.

Bas stares at them, his mouth agape in something like disbelief. "What? Why not?"

"I can't take on an entire army, Bas," Mar says with a scowl. "I don't have that kind of control over the magia. And what I can do—it's dangerous. I've killed people before."

"Well, sure." Bas shrugs. "That's kind of the point. You kill the guards so they don't kill our crew."

Mar groans. "That's not what I meant! I've killed by accident, Bas. Because I lost control. Because I used my magia too much and it got away from me. I won't let that happen again."

"And it won't! You just need to free the crew—"

"Don't you think I would have if I could when we were in the prison? We ran out of time before the guards arrived. I can't just snap my fingers and *wish* them free!" They take a deep breath, cooling the heat in their chest. "Bas, believe me, I want to help them too. But it's not as easy as you think it is."

Bas scowls and glares into the pouring rain. Mar can practically see the steam rising from his shoulders, the anger radiating off him like a furnace. But the answer can't change. Mar won't go back, won't risk getting them all killed.

"El Capitán told me to run with you, you know," Mar mumbles.

Bas glances at them but says nothing.

"He saw me . . . break the lock of our cell. And he told me to take you and run."

They sit in silence for several minutes. The endless rumble of pounding rain would almost be soothing if they weren't sitting there shivering and angry and exhausted and scared. If the approaching dawn didn't also mean an approaching execution. If they weren't out of answers, and if the Spaniards weren't likely hunting them down, even now, looking to add them to the gallows.

How long will they be permitted to sit here, on the stoop of some inn, before the innkeeper notices and chases them off? And where will they go to next? They have no crew. No money. No home. They should leave the city, the sooner the better. It's only a matter of time before their descriptions will plaster wanted posters. Before someone recognizes them.

Mar closes their eyes. The sharp scent of fresh rain almost brings them back to their childhood home, back with their mamá. Before Mar's magia ruined everything. If they concentrate, really concentrate, they can just barely smell fresh tortillas cooking on the comal. Or maybe café, strong and black the way Mamá always liked it.

"You called it magia."

Mar's eyes snap open. The memory dissolves. They're sitting next to Bas, waiting for what feels like an endless storm to pass. And Bas just asked them a question—or maybe it wasn't a question really, but still. It begged for an answer.

Mar hesitates. "Yes."

Bas looks at them. "How did you learn it?"

"Oh." Mar frowns. "It wasn't— It's not something I learned. I just . . . always could."

Bas chews on his lip and taps his fingers on his knees. "Fine. But why? How?"

"I don't really know." Mar watches the rain blur the world into streaky, semitransparent sheets. "Papá used to say the gods of my mamá's people blessed me, but then Tito said he knew someone like me, who was from some magical island."

"What?"

Mar looks at Bas. The boy is watching them earnestly, with an intensity that sets Mar a little on edge, though they aren't quite sure why. They shrug it off and look away. "I don't know anything about that. It's just what Tito said."

Bas frowns, thoughtful. "Is that how you survived the wreck?"

It's a question that has crossed Mar's mind too. How *did* they survive the wreck? El Diablo was so sure they wouldn't—*Mar* was so sure they wouldn't. Last they remember was blacking out as the ocean pulled them deeper. It was the end.

But it wasn't, because they woke up on *La Ana*'s deck, with Bas and Tito and Joaquín looking at them.

"I don't know," Mar says at last. "El Diablo said I wouldn't live to see morning, but I did. I don't really know what happened between blacking out and waking up on *La Ana*."

"Wait, wait." Bas raises his hand. "*El Diablo* said you wouldn't live? What are you talking about?"

Mar watches him for a moment, biting their lip as the steady rainfall hisses around them. Bas didn't come unglued upon learning about Mar's magic. So maybe it'll be fine to tell him what happened.

"My papá made a deal with el Diablo for my life when I was born," Mar says. "I didn't believe him for a long time— I thought it was just a story. But then el Diablo came to collect, and . . . that's how *La Catalina* sank. It wasn't a normal storm—he used it to sink us."

Bas frowns. "A diablo was there? On *La Catalina*? As in . . . you *saw* him?"

Mar nods. "I know it sounds unbelievable, but—"

"Mar." Bas laughs weakly. "I watched you turn iron to ice. I'm ready to believe in the unbelievable."

Mar's smile is slight, but it's a smile nevertheless. They shrug and lightly rub their hands together. "Well. Now that I know his story about el Diablo is real, it does explain why, for as long as I was alive, no one on *La Catalina* ever got sick or injured. We never lost a single crew member until the end." They frown. "Except my mamá, but . . . she always said she wasn't part of the crew." The memory comes so fresh, Mar's eyes sting. "Just along for the ride," they finish softly.

Bas bumps their shoulder with his lightly. They sit quietly for a moment; then Bas says, "So your crew couldn't die because of a deal your papá made with el Diablo."

Mar hesitantly nods. "I never really thought about it before. I just thought the crew was skilled and we were lucky."

"Does that mean you've never been injured? Not even a paper cut?"

Mar laughs lightly. "I got plenty injured the night el Diablo came. Took weeks for my ribs to stop hurting."

"But before then?"

They lift a shoulder. "Not really. I mean, when I fell, or stubbed my toe, or smacked my shins, it hurt. But it never left a bruise."

They stare into the downpour for another minute or two, shoulders touching, breathing in each other's silence.

Then Bas says, "So how do I find him?"

Mar blinks. "Find . . . who?"

"El Diablo." Bas looks at Mar, and all at once the uncomfortable prickling in their stomach is back, because Bas looks entirely serious. "How do I find him so I can get some kind of protection deal too?"

Mar's heart beats a little harder. The rain's chill sinks a little deeper, into their very bones. "I . . . Bas, no. You can't—It doesn't work like that."

"Sure it does. Your papá found el Diablo and made a deal with him, and your whole crew was essentially undefeatable. I could do the same, but for myself, and then I could save the crew."

"It's not that easy—"

"Why not?" The words burst out of Bas and he jumps to his feet, suddenly towering over Mar. "Why do you have to complicate everything? If you won't use your magia to save my familia, fine, but *I* will. And I can—all I need to do is find el Diablo before they're killed. And you can tell me how."

Mar's dread is so palpable, a bitterness climbs up their throat. "I can't tell you how."

"Yes, you can! You can and you—"

"I can't because I don't *know*, Bas!" Now Mar is standing too, and though they're still shorter than the boy, at least he isn't towering over them anymore. "And honestly? Even if I *did* know where to find him, I wouldn't tell you. That deal got my papá and my entire crew *killed*. And it almost killed *me*! Doesn't that mean anything to you?"

"My familia is about to die!" Bas roars. "Doesn't *that* mean anything to you?"

But before Mar can even attempt to answer, Bas turns on his heel and marches into the rain. Mar could go after him. Mar *should* go after him. But they don't know what to even begin to say. They don't have any answers—all they know is they don't want to die, and they don't want Bas to die either, and going back to save the crew would kill everyone, and working with el Diablo would certainly mean the same end.

Not that Mar knows where to find el Diablo anyway. Which in a way is a sort of relief, because at least they don't have to lie.

But as they watch Bas disappear into the gray smudge of the storm, they can't help but think maybe honesty is what got them into this mess to begin with.

CHAPTER 23

Part of Mar knows they should leave San Juan, *La Ana*'s crew, the Spanish soldiers, and Bas, behind. Every minute they stay is another minute they might be recognized, might end up in a situation where they have to reveal their magia and run or end up in a cell again.

But as the night drags on, ever closer to the trial that will surely lead to the crew's execution, Mar can't bring themself to leave.

Only problem is they can't bring themself to watch the trial, either. They won't be able to stand there silently as el Capitán—who gave them a home when they didn't have any—and Tito—who swore to protect them with his secrecy—and Joaquín—who maybe was a little hard on Mar but somehow seemed to know that was the kind of distraction they needed to get through their grief-stricken day—are all sentenced to die. Smothering their magia deep beneath their skin is hard enough in normal circumstances, but when they're emotional, it's damn near impossible.

No, going to the trial is sure to end in magia-fueled disaster.

But they can find Bas. He, at least, can still be saved.

Reflecting on their argument has made them queasy. Mar understood his pain deeply, but they can't help thinking that they've only made it worse. The look on his face before he stormed off into the rain . . . they hadn't meant to, but Mar had really upset him.

They aren't sure how to fix that, but at the very least they can apologize when they find him. They just have no idea where to even begin looking. So they wander, letting the blue-cobblestone streets take them through the colorful city, searching around every corner and peering into every alley they pass. They try not to look at the walls of the city, closing them in like a prisoner even outside a cell. They watch their boots move over the glazed, cracked blue cobblestones beneath their feet. They pass white-trimmed stucco buildings of seafoam green, gentle lilac, pungent pink, and sky blue. Even in the narrowest alleyways, the city is a riot of color muted in the night, a curated cement garden.

If San Juan weren't a fortress holding the ever-looming specter of death, it would be indisputably beautiful.

A poster tacked to a building in a busy square catches their eye. Before they've even consciously decided to take a closer look, their feet carry them to it.

The chill that settles in their bones is unshakable.

The poster is a notice of an upcoming public trial. Not of the crew. Of a bruja.

To Mar's knowledge, brujes don't have the same kind of magia they do, but what they can do scares the Spaniards enough that even the accusation of using magic is enough to get someone killed.

Mar was barely ten years old when they learned how every brujes "trial" ends.

Leo rips the poster off the brick and crumples it in his fist with a scowl. "Trial," he snarls. "More like execution."

Mar frowns. "They'll kill the bruja during the trial?"

"No," Papá says softly. "But they'll sentence her to death. They always do, just like pirates."

"Then we should save her," Mar says. "I could save her."

"Absolutely not," Leo and Papá say together.

"It's too dangerous," Leo adds.

"You know what happens if someone sees you using magia." Papá takes the poster from Leo and smooths it out, holding it up for Mar to see. "This is what happens if you're lucky. A trial at least gives you time to escape. You must never put yourself in this position. No one but the crew can ever see you use your magia. ¿Entiendes?"

Mar looks at their boots. They understand, but part of them wishes they didn't.

Leo sighs and pulls them into a warm hug. "Your magia is special, Mar—you're special. But the world isn't ready for it, so you must be careful."

"What's the point of having magia if nothing good ever comes of it?" Mar mumbles into his chest.

Papá gently runs his fingers through Mar's hair. "The gods gave you this gift for a reason, tesoro. One day you'll understand."

Mar lets the streets take them without direction until they come across a beachside taberna, la Taberna Reyes. The coral-painted stucco building sitting on a street corner looks like a giant painted brick with dark wooden doors and windows. Their stomach is so empty it hurts. Bas must be as hungry as they are—would he have stopped at a taberna like this to try to get food? The doors open as a man exits, and the scent of fried plátanos makes Mar's stomach growl. They catch the door on the backswing and enter.

Food isn't free, but Mar has a handful of buttons and trinkets they swiped off unsuspecting people, so maybe they'll have enough to get some maduros. Or at least a drink. Or some pancito. Or something. Anything.

Even just a small snack will give them the energy they need to continue their search.

The windows behind them show nothing but large swaths of night, yet the copious lantern light glints off the coral tile floor and polished hardwood bar. The room is relatively small; Mar counts about a dozen tables crammed inside. No Bas, but the smell of food is so strong, their mouth waters.

Their boots clack on the tile as they waltz up to the bar, grab a stool, and dump three copper buttons, a single silver coin, and a small, half-used spool of fishing wire onto the clean counter. The bartender frowns, scratching his salt-and-pepper beard as Mar looks him in the eye and says, with all the confidence they can muster, "What food can I get for this?"

The bartender sighs and shakes his head, then pushes the trinkets back to Mar.

"Por favor," Mar starts, desperation leaking into their voice. "I just—even some pan—"

"Don't worry about it," the bartender says quietly. "I'll bring you some food. Just don't spread the word around." He smiles softly, wrinkles gathering around his eyes.

Mar relaxes at once, grateful for at least this one small turn of fortune. "Thank you."

The bartender nods and walks back into the kitchen. The wall behind the bar top is a floor-to-ceiling shelf, filled edge to edge with perfectly aligned bottles of alcohol, especially rum. Some of them Mar recognizes from Papá's collection; they try not to think about it too deeply.

As Mar scoops their mostly useless trinkets back into their pockets, a man sits next to them—wait, no, a boy. Roughly Mar's age, best they can tell from a quick glance. But the glance is all they apparently need to catch the boy's eye.

"Fancy meeting you here at this fine establishment."

Mar freezes. They know that voice.

Dami faces them with a grin. Today they have heavier

kohl around their eyes, rouge accentuating their sharp cheek-bones, and a knifelike smile. Black hair long enough to pull back into a knot, with long strands framing their face in a way that would be attractive if Dami weren't Dami.

The demonio smiles conspiratorially and leans closer to Mar. "Always nice to see another privateer here, especially one who seems to be as taken by me as I am by them." They wink.

Mar scowls. "You really won't leave me alone, will you?" they say, even as their cheeks prickle with warmth.

"Nope." Dami laughs, then tilts their head, looking Mar over with those dark eyes. "I see not making a deal with me is going well for you."

"I didn't need your help to get out of prison," they mutter.

"No," they acknowledge with a smile. "But we have so much more to talk about."

Mar glances at them. "You look different."

"Don't I always?"

"Yes, but . . ." Mar looks at them again, more carefully. They aren't quite sure what has changed, but it's almost as if the demonio is more . . . present. "You seem more . . . real."

"Oh, you mean this?" They rap their knuckles on the bar. "Yes, I'm fully here this time—everyone can see and hear me, so I'm not just a charming figment of your imagination."

Mar snorts. "You're never charming."

"No? Not even a little?" They bat their eyelashes and pout their soft-looking lips. "How about now?"

Mar laughs without meaning to—it just looks utterly ridiculous to see Dami *pout* and try to look *soft*—and Dami smiles triumphantly. "See? I'm plenty charming."

The bartender emerges from the kitchen with a plate and a mug, placing both in front of Mar. A mountain of arroz con habichuelas sits on the plate, with two slices of fresh bread. The aroma is so rich, Mar can almost taste it; their stomach grumbles. "Thank you," Mar says.

They dive into their food, barely suppressing a groan as the flavor of beans, sofrito, ham, and olives fills their mouth. Before they know it, there's nothing but bread left, which Mar uses to scoop up the last bits of tomato and spice-coated rice before devouring that too. When they're done, they sigh, satisfied at last. Much easier to think without the constant gnaw of hunger.

They glance at Dami, still beside them, now watching Mar with a smirk. They nod at Mar's plate. "Did you even taste it?"

Mar's face warms again. "I was hungry."

"So I gathered. Fair enough, I suppose privateering isn't as lucrative a field as it once was."

Mar stares at them. That's the second time the demonio's talked about pirating in the middle of a public space, as if that were a safe thing to talk about in San Juan, where the Spaniards regularly hunt down people like Mar.

"You're going to get me arrested again if you don't lower your voice," Mar mutters. "This isn't Playa Mujeres, you know."

Dami shrugs. "No one's paying me any attention. Except you, that is."

"You can't know that for sure," Mar says, though they probably aren't wrong. The taberna isn't packed, but there are certainly more than enough people that the drone of conversation has probably drowned out Mar and Dami's voices—but still. At the very least, the bartender could likely hear what they were talking about.

As if he could hear Mar's thoughts, the bartender glances over at them curiously. Mar just sips their water and pretends not to notice.

Dami crosses their arms over the bar top. Their loose wine-red shirtsleeves roll up, revealing edges of smokelike tattoos on both of their wrists, going up their forearms. Mar's never seen a tattoo that looked like smoke before, but somehow it suits them.

"Might want to be careful with those," Mar says, nodding at their tattooed arms. "Don't want the wrong person to see them."

"Or what? They'll *arrest* me?" Dami grins. "It's sweet that you care about me, though."

"Don't get excited. I just don't want to be arrested for associating with a pirate."

"Don't worry, I won't tell anyone."

Mar shakes their head and stands, but Dami rests their hand over Mar's. They startle but don't move, meeting Dami's gaze. They hadn't expected Dami to feel so . . . warm, though they're not sure why.

"I can only be fully present at night," Dami says, answering the question they haven't asked. During the day I'm not grounded—it takes a lot of concentration to manifest enough to be seen."

It doesn't sound like much of a way to live, but Dami is a demonio and Mar shouldn't care. Dami ruins peoples' lives just like el Diablo did to Papá. If the price for destroying the lives of others is living half a life for eternity . . . well. It doesn't seem unjustified.

Dami pulls their hand away and stands. "Before you leave, I said we have a lot to talk about and I meant it. I just need five minutes of your time—in private. There are empty rooms upstairs."

Mar presses their lips together and glances at the entrance. They should be out there, in the rain, looking for Bas, not wasting time with a demonio. But Dami is persistent, and Mar is tired of their constant visits, of the recurring reminder that they're being watched.

Going with Dami might be some kind of trap, but it might also be a chance to force the demonio to leave them alone, once and for all.

"Five minutes," Mar says. "Not a moment longer."

The door has barely closed before Mar shoves Dami against the wall, their forearm tight against the demonio's neck. They ease up on their magia with an exhale, familiar warmth rushing from their chest to the rest of their body. Mar's black sleeve and the cloth wrapping beneath are pushed up just enough for their tattoos to shine bright orange against Dami's pale skin.

"I'm done playing games," Mar says. "I already told you I'm not making a deal with you."

Dami rolls their eyes; then Mar falls forward into a cloud of black smoke. They catch themself on the wall and whirl around. The warm glow of the lantern light throws Dami's figure in sharp relief as they lounge casually on the bed pushed up against the wall.

"You know," Dami says, crossing their arms behind their head, "I realize the whole glowing thing is supposed to be intimidating, but it's actually incredible to look at. I don't think you realize how stunning you are."

Mar glowers, closes their eyes, and takes a sharp breath, snuffing their magia out like a fist crushing a lit candle. The magia protests with a crack of pain up their spine like a lightning strike, but by the time Mar has gasped, it's over.

"Doesn't seem healthy to suppress it like that," Dami says with a tilt of their head.

Mar scowls. "Still healthier than getting executed because the wrong person saw me use it." They shake their head. "This isn't about me."

"But that's just it, Mar." Dami sits up. With their back now to the lantern light, shadow falls over their face. "This is exactly about you. And as I told you, I need your help."

"And *I* told *you* I wasn't interested. You aren't going to change my mind."

"Maybe not." Dami shrugs. Then a sharp smile slices

across their face. "But there's nothing you can do to keep me from haunting you until you do."

Heat bursts out of Mar—their fists erupt in flames, but Dami just laughs. "What are you going to do? Burn down the bar? You can't touch me unless I want you to. And anyway, it's not that easy to kill what isn't living."

Mar practically growls as they shake their hands once, extinguishing the flames. Their magia wants nothing more than to burn, to show this infuriating demonio just how dangerous the magia they crave is. But Dami is right—there's little Mar can do to hurt them. All they'd do is hurt the innocent. Again. And with a population of over seven thousand in San Juan, there are significantly more people here at risk.

They can't let their magia get the better of them, no matter how tempting it sometimes seems.

"Can't you haunt someone else?" Mar snaps. "I haven't done anything to deserve this."

"You haven't," Dami agrees, "but neither have I. We don't always get what we deserve, do we?" They walk along the edge of the room, their hand trailing lightly against the bare wall. "Besides, it's not like it's easy to find people with magia as powerful as yours. Bas knows it—that's why he's so desperate for your help. It's too bad you're so afraid of your own power to even *try* to take a risk and save lives with it."

Dami might as well have punched them in the stomach. Mar's vision blurs; they quickly wipe their eyes with the back of their hand and glare at the demonio. "I've *tried* to save lives with my magia, and it didn't work!"

Dami tsk-tsks. "You tried *once* when you had literally no other option. That's not taking a risk, that's basic survival instinct."

"It's not like I don't *want* to help the crew—"

"Then what's stopping you? Stop running from your magia. Its power is yours. Take it."

Mar eyes the demonio as they slowly circle the room. "Go find someone else. Supposedly there's an entire island full of people with power just like me."

"So there is." Dami says it without hesitation, like it's such a simple, unexceptional thing to confirm. "But I can't go there—no demonio can. The magia that protects the island from gente sin magia also keeps those like me out."

Mar blinks. "Wait, so . . . it's true? That's where my magia is from?"

Dami wrinkles their nose. "The island exists, but your magia isn't *from* there. Magia is everywhere—it comes from the earth. Isla Luceros just has a population that can access it." They glance at Mar. "I don't know if that's why *you* have magia, though."

Of course not. Mar sighs and leans against the wall, watching the lantern light flicker against the wall. This was a waste of time. They should be out on the street looking for Bas, not arguing in the unholy hours of the night with a demonio who won't listen anyway.

Bas would probably want to hear Dami out. He'd probably agree to anything to get magia of his own if it meant saving his familia.

Mar grimaces, then looks at Dami, who has stopped cir-
cling the room and is leaning against the wall a couple of feet
away. "What does a demonio need my help for, anyway?"

Dami sighs unnecessarily loudly and pushes off the wall.
"*Finally.* I've been *waiting* for you to ask that question." They
brush off their hands. "Don't immediately react, okay? In
fact, take a moment to think about it before you say anything
at all."

Mar's eyes narrow. Whatever they're about to say, this
doesn't really seem to be a promising start. "You're already
making me regret asking."

"Just hear me out."

Dami's dark eyes meet Mar's, the flickering orange light
of the lantern flame dancing over their face. Something about
the intensity of their gaze makes Mar shiver; they feel as
though they're falling into a pool of black, and for a moment
all they have to ground them is their own breath. They've
never seen this side of the demonio, this part that makes it all
too obvious what Dami is.

Not an infuriating and distractingly attractive young person. A demonio.

And then Dami speaks, their words shattering the spell.

"I need you to kill el Diablo."

CHAPTER 24

"Excuse me?" Mar almost laughs at the absurdity of the request, but Dami seems deathly serious. "Kill el Diablo? You can't possibly think I can help you with that."

Dami groans. "Let me remind you I told you to take a moment before you react."

"Let me remind *you* it wasn't five minutes ago that you told me it's impossible to kill what isn't living!"

"Tch." Dami waves their hand. "I didn't say it was *impossible*. I said it wasn't *easy*. Diablos can be killed by other diablos or with very powerful magia. Like yours."

Mar crosses their arms. "Why would you want me to kill el Diablo anyway? Isn't he your . . ." They look the demonio over. "I don't know. Your father or something?"

Dami recoils, face aghast. "My *father*? You think— Oh no. Absolutely not. *Dios*, no." They shudder from head to toe. "My *father*, the *gall*, honestly—"

"All right, calm down." Mar rolls their eyes. "That still doesn't answer the question."

"He's . . . my boss. Essentially." Dami frowns. "Except it's more complicated than that. There's a hierarchy—he owns my soul and the soul of everyone who pledges their soul to *me*. And the soul of everyone else who's ever pledged their soul to *him*, and the soul of everyone who's pledged their soul to *them*, and so on. And that's not even getting into the power he gets from those he's killed, since he gets their souls too."

"That sounds like a lot of souls."

"It is. That's why he's so powerful and why no demonio can kill a diablo—he can draw on everyone's souls to augment his power and make his magic stronger. Unlike demonios, diablos can do magic outside of a deal—all I can do is transport myself and change how I look. A demonio who amasses enough souls eventually becomes a diablo, and if you thought a *demonio* was hard to beat . . ." Dami freezes—probably, Mar thinks, because they've realized they aren't really helping their case. Suddenly they smile and shrug. "And that's why I need you. I don't stand a chance against him. He's too powerful for me to take on alone."

Mar grimaces and shakes their head. "You're asking the wrong person."

"Mar"—Dami digs their fingers into their scalp before dropping their hands to their sides—"you're the only one I *can* ask. Please." They step closer, face imploring. "I'll give you anything within my power to give. You don't understand what this means to me—"

"I won't repeat Papá's mistake," Mar says firmly. "I'm not making any diablo deals—or demonio deals—*ever*."

"I can help you save your papá! We want the same thing!"

"Don't," Mar growls, tears rushing to their eyes. Dami is a demonio, they remind themself yet again. They'll say anything to get what they want. "Don't you dangle that in front of me. You have no idea what it's like to lose everything."

Dami opens their mouth.

"Even if I were willing to help you," Mar says before Dami can speak, "I don't have the power you think I do." They fight the tightness in their throat. "I can't control my magia well enough to survive a fight with el Diablo, let alone defeat him."

"You *could* defeat him if you weren't so afraid of your own power!" Dami throws their hands up. "You have so much potential, Mar. You can affect change like almost no one else, but you waste it because you're so damn afraid of who you are!"

"I *know* who I am!" Mar roars, nearly choking on the fire that rages inside them. Their magia rumbles just under the surface, so close to bubbling over. They have to calm down. They have to breathe. "If you knew what I've done—"

"I do, actually," Dami interrupts. "I've done my research."

"Then you know what happens when I lose control."

Dami sighs. "The volcano was *one* time."

Hearing it aloud makes them want to vomit. Mar stares at the demonio incredulously. "And how many times have *you* accidentally set off a volcano that obliterated an entire town?"

Dami grimaces. Mar turns to the door, wiping their teary eyes with the back of their hand. "If you truly understood who I am, you'd be afraid too."

"Mar, wait—"

But Mar is out the door before Dami can stop them. They never should have wasted their time with the demonio to begin with. Bas is out there, alone, and he needs Mar's help.

Mar knows what it's like to lose everything.

They won't let Bas learn it next.

CHAPTER 25

Retracing their steps back into the heart of the city is simple enough. Remaining unnoticed, on the other hand . . . maybe less so now that the rain has stopped. The good news, Mar supposes, is that most people in San Juan have no idea who Mar is. Plus, it's night, so no one's going to be looking at them too closely. It's mostly just the soldiers Mar has to be wary of—and anyway, isn't that always the case? So in a way, lurking around a city where getting spotted could mean trouble isn't actually anything out of the ordinary. But trying to track down an impulsive and emotional boy likely to be nearest the danger? That is.

Mar doesn't really know San Juan, which doesn't help matters. They wander the azure streets without a real destination, mostly keeping to what few shadows there are on a night with such a bright moon while trying to look—ordinary. They shove their marked hands into their pockets and keep their sleeves rolled down low, even though the humid night demands otherwise. Mar's never been ashamed of the markings people assume are tattoos, but tattoos are often the dressings of a pirate, and the last thing Mar needs is to draw attention to themself.

Wait. The moon.

Mar stifles the gasp in their chest as they stare wide-eyed at the sky. The moon is a sliver away from full, and unusually large. The harvest moon is coming, and Mar's quick calculation seizes their heart with a frozen grip.

Just under two days from their deadline, and the possibility of saving Papá has never felt farther.

Isla Luceros was a dead end. How on earth are they going to figure out how to save Papá on their own in less than two days?

Mar clenches their fists, burying their anxiety deep. One thing at a time. First, they have to find Bas before it's too late.

Though Mar has no desire to be anywhere near soldiers, especially right now, they also seem the most likely to have some proximity to Bas. Since Mar has no other ideas, they keep to the crowded night market, pretending to browse its wares—mangoes and coconuts, fishing rods and jewelry—while keeping an eye on the soldiers patrolling the streets. Though even then, they aren't entirely sure what to look for.

They stuff their hands into their pockets, their fingers brushing against the folded piece of paper Graciela gave them what feels like a lifetime ago.

"This way," someone whispers in Mar's ear.

They whirl. They've wandered close to the beach, under the cloud-breaking light of the moon, just past the night market.

There are fewer people here, and no one near Mar. And certainly no one near enough to have whispered in their ear.

Mar scowls. "I don't need your help, Dami," they whisper sharply, but it's entirely a lie and they know it. *Dami probably knows it too,* they think, which only makes them scowl more. "I'm not making any deals," they add.

Only silence answers.

The whisper came from their left, where a path runs along the edge of the night market and back into the vibrant town. And as much as they hate the idea of Dami helping them with anything, it'd be foolish not to listen when Bas's life could be at stake.

They swear under their breath and turn onto the path. Every movement, every shriek of laughter makes their heart race, but they keep moving forward, past the market, beyond scattered colorful tabernas and closed stalls, and it isn't until they break into a large square that a commotion catches Mar's eye. Three soldiers are huddled around—something (someone?)—on the ground. The disturbance is on the other side of the square, beyond an empty fountain near a shuttered fruit stand. And it could be nothing. A stray dog looking for scraps. An unskilled thief. It could be a thousand things of no concern to Mar, not worth getting near and endangering themself.

Or it could be something.

It could be Bas.

Only one way to find out.

Mar slips slowly around the fountain. It's at that moment,

standing just feet away from the three soldiers dragging what Mar can now see is certainly not a stray dog, that it occurs to them that maybe they should have some kind of disguise. What if the soldiers are the ones from the prison? What if they've seen Mar's face before? Or know of Mar's description?

But it doesn't matter; they'll just have to pray the darkness holds them close. Mar watches from their peripheral vision as the soldiers yank a boy off the ground. His face is bloodied and bruised, but it takes Mar all of a half second to recognize Bas's profile, even in the shadows.

So Mar has found him. Just a couple of minutes too late.

Bas doesn't seem to be that hurt, but he slumps almost comically forward, forcing the soldiers to carry his weight. They grunt and let his feet drag as two of them carry him out of the square and the third follows behind, gun ready. Not that Bas really seems to be putting up much of a fight. Or any fight at all, for that matter. It's almost like he wants to be caught.

Either that or he's passed out. Mar can't really get a good enough look at his face to know for sure.

As the men drag Bas away from the fruit stand and down the street, the boy begins singing. Loudly and off-key. So he's awake, then, and letting them take him. Mar can't imagine how getting arrested again and likely executed with the rest of the crew can possibly advance his plan to try to save his familia, but they also don't care to try to let it play out.

Whatever Bas is up to, it's a terrible idea that's sure to get him killed.

To complicate matters, it's incredibly early in the morning. This far from the market, there aren't that many people out, so getting near the soldiers unnoticed will be difficult. But just ahead of the soldiers is a bright orange inn with decorative white candles lit out front. And Mar doesn't necessarily need to touch any of them to, say, snag a sleeve on fire as long as they can get within a few feet of the group.

Mar carefully slips through the shadows, avoiding any step that might make a sound. The soldier holding Bas's right arm is closest to the inn—to the excuse they'll need to explain the inexplicable. Of course, it still won't really make sense; fire doesn't just leap out at someone's shoulder of its own accord, but people will go out of their way to accept nonsensical explanations if they have some kind of framework to cling to.

Mar focuses on the creamy white fabric of the soldier's shirt. As the magia awakens within them, singing in their veins, Mar imagines the energy building inside them gathering instead in the soldier's uniform. Gathering in the fibers, more and more until they turn from off-white to brown, then black, then—

"¡Dios mío!" the soldier yelps, dropping Bas and slapping his shoulder as the flames spread quickly down his sleeve. The acrid odor of burning fabric—and something else Mar doesn't want to think about—fills the air as the soldiers cry out in alarm, spurred into action to help their friend. His whole sleeve is on fire now, and he's screaming. His friend has dropped Bas entirely as he and the third soldier frantically try to put out the spreading flames.

Mar moves quickly, grabbing Bas's left arm and hoisting him to his feet. Bas shouts, spots Mar, and his eyes widen. "What—"

"Later," Mar says. "Keep moving."

They shove Bas forward into the shadows and around the corner. High-pitched screams pierce the air behind them. Mar isn't in control of the fire anymore, and part of them hopes the soldiers can put it out in time, though they aren't entirely sure why. This is the same army that was after Mar's own familia for as long as they can remember—and they're the same ones inevitably going to execute *La Ana*'s crew. And it's not like Mar hasn't maimed or killed before; in the heat of a battle they've left more bodies and scars behind them than they care to think about. Why should it bother Mar that one of them is suffering or may even die?

But of course, it's always been this way with Mar. In a fight the violence doesn't bother them—it's kill or be killed—but outside a fight, the death and suffering sit differently in their stomach. Even as the screams become more distant behind them, the sound is like nails raking down their spine.

It doesn't matter, though. They don't have to like it to do what they must to survive.

Mar and Bas walk in silence, following the sparse flow of the few pedestrians until the commotion is so far behind them, the sound dissipates into the calm noises of the nearby shore. Bas nods to an alley between two tabernas—one peach pink, the other deep red—and Mar follows him. They've no sooner turned into the alley than Bas shoves them against the red stucco wall, forearm jammed into Mar's throat.

Mar coughs and their magia rises up to defend them, ready to turn Bas into a pile of charred bones, but they push the instinct back down. And knee Bas between his legs.

Bas gasps and doubles over, and Mar stumbles two steps to the side, rubbing their aching neck. "What was that?" they shout. "Attacking me like—"

"Why do you have to ruin *everything*!" Bas yells, still bent over, tears streaming down his face. "I had it handled! And you just had to swoop in, acting like some kind of smug hero—"

"They were taking you back to prison, Bas! Do you *want* to die?"

"I can't save them from outside the prison!"

"You can't save them from inside the prison either!"

Bas stands up straight, face red and splotchy, fists clenched, breathing like he just swam for miles. "Did it ever occur to you," he hisses, "that maybe I didn't *want* to be saved?"

Mar crosses their arms over their chest. "I said that to you once, some time ago. Do you remember what you told me?"

Bas just glares. Mar takes a step toward him. "You reminded me I didn't want to die, not really. And even though I didn't want to admit it, you were right. My time wasn't up yet, Bas. And neither is yours."

Bas shoves past Mar, slamming his shoulder against theirs. "I'm not leaving this godforsaken city until the crew are free." He stops and turns back to Mar. "And if you try to stop me again, I'll kill you."

He spins away from them, but Mar catches his shoulder. "Wait—"

"I'm not joking, Mar." Bas rips their hand off his shoulder. "You don't want to be between me and my familia."

"You're right," Mar says quickly. "I don't. You were right before, too." Their voice shakes as Bas slowly turns back, facing them again. "I'm sorry. I should have done more earlier to try to save everyone. You have to understand, I . . . People have tried to kill me when they learned about my magia. My mamá died because of me, because of my magia, and I—"

Their voice cracks, a sob catching in their throat. They can't keep going—it's too painful to say the words aloud—but they want Bas to understand. They need him to understand.

Bas's face has softened, and when he speaks, the anger has evaporated from his voice. "Mar, you don't have to tell me."

"I do." Tears slip down their cheeks as they look Bas in the eyes. "I was careless with my magia when I was young. Someone saw me using it and they tried to shoot me, but Mamá jumped in front of me, and she died instead. Because of me. Because someone found out who I am." Their voice is trembling so hard, they can barely get the words out, but now that they've started, they have to finish. "When I realized she was dead, I lost control of my magia. I—I erupted a nearby volcano, and it decimated the town. There's nothing left of Mamá's home, of her familia, of the town she grew up in. I destroyed all of it because the magia took over and I lost control. And I can *never* let that happen again."

The tears are flowing freely now, but somehow they feel lighter for having said it aloud. They've never told anyone the full story—not even Papá. It was too painful to talk about, too painful to relive. They all just silently agreed it was better never to revisit that horrifying day.

But now someone else knows. And Bas isn't looking at them like a monster. His eyes are soft, sad, and Mar blinks and suddenly his arms are around them. Holding them tight. Caressing the back of their head while they sob into his shoulder.

"I'm so sorry," they say, over and over and over again. "I should have done more. I'm sorry. I'm sorry."

They aren't sure how long they stand there, leaning into his chest in an alley in San Juan. But eventually the tears run dry, and Mar's cheek is pressed against Bas's tear-drenched shirt.

"Thank you for telling me," Bas says softly, still gently touching their hair.

Mar could stay there forever in his arms, surrounded by his warmth and the strength of his embrace. But they aren't finished. There's more they need to say.

With a shuddering breath they pull away, wiping their face. "I didn't do enough before, but I want to fix it. I want to help you save them. I couldn't do it before the trial, but we can manage it before the execution. We know the layout of the prison, so it'll be easier this time."

Bas presses his lips together.

A sinking feeling tugs at Mar's stomach. "What's wrong?"

"I overheard the guards. They recognized me as part of the crew and said they were moved out of the regular prison after we escaped."

Oh no.

Bas's eyes reflect the silver moonlight as he meets their gaze. "Mar, the crew's in El Morro."

CHAPTER 26

The white sand is flour soft beneath Mar's feet as they look over the gentle waves, sun peeking over the horizon. The warm water laps at their toes, the rise and fall of the turquoise ocean sighing like the earth's lungs.

It'd all be very calming if they weren't desperately trying to figure out how to break into—and, more importantly, escape from—a fortress.

"Good news," Bas says, stepping beside them and offering them a banana. "I stole some food. And I didn't get caught on purpose this time." He winks, but Mar doesn't have the energy to smile.

They've barely slept. By the time they found Bas and the two made their way to a quiet stretch of beach where they rested under palm fronds, there were only a few hours until sunrise anyway. Bas seemed to pass out immediately, while Mar lay in the sand and tried to figure out a plan. It seems like they just closed their eyes when the first golden rays of morning light woke them up again.

Mar takes the banana and peels it. Bas flops in the sand next to them and drops a lumpy burlap bag at their feet as he rolls a mango between his hands, then rips the skin off the top. He hums as he eats, tracing shapes into the sand with his boot.

"You're awfully cheery," Mar says at last.

"I *am* in a good mood—thank you for noticing." Bas takes another large bite of mango. "And why shouldn't I be? With your help we can free my familia."

Mar grimaces. "You know I can't just . . . walk in, throw my magia around, and walk out, right?"

Bas slowly chews his mouthful of mango and swallows, juice dripping off his chin. "Why not?"

It takes a great deal of self-restraint not to groan aloud. "I can't use too much of my magia at once, or I lose control and innocent people get hurt. And anyway, there's an entire army in there. I'm not strong enough to take down a whole army."

Not without destroying another city. The thought hits Mar in the chest. They look back at the ocean, forcing themself to concentrate on the tide lapping at their feet like liquid aquamarine before the memory swallows them whole.

Bas finishes the rest of his mango in silence before tossing the pit into some grass behind them. He digs into the bag and pulls out another banana. "That's fine," he says. "We don't have to rely entirely on your magia—we're both good fighters and pretty smart, too." He smiles.

Mar wishes they had Bas's optimism. "We need a plan," they say. "And we can't be reckless about it or we'll just end up in prison again."

"And then you can break us out again."

"I doubt there are windows big enough to climb out of in El Morro. And I can't melt stone."

Bas grimaces. "Suppose you have a point." He scratches his chin with the stem of the still-unpeeled banana before placing it on his lap. "So do you have any ideas?"

This is the part Mar was thinking about all night. The part they still aren't sure will work, but then, when can anyone be completely sure of anything at all?

It *could* work. Maybe. And given their limited time, that's the best guarantee they're going to have.

Mar takes a deep breath. "One. But we need more information first. And if we get caught, we're dead."

"Great!" Bas claps his hands and grins. "Where do we start?"

The scrap of paper that's lived in Mar's pocket for weeks was folded into quarters. Mar holds it now, unfolded. On it is an address and one sentence:

dile que tu mamá te envió a recoger su vestido

"A secret password," Bas whispers, peering over their shoulder. "Neat."

Mar looks back at the building in front of them, craning their neck to squint at the top. The home is a massive rectangle with four columns running to the top and four street-facing windows with balconies on every floor except for the first. Painted pale blue with white columns, balconies, and windows, it looks vaguely skeletal. A huge, ornate, rectangular skeleton towering over the reasonably sized but equally colorful single-story homes on either side.

"Wow," Bas says, shading his eyes from the sun with his palm. "Three floors. Do you think people actually live here? Every day?"

Mar looks down at the crumpled paper in their hand, but they're unmistakably at the right address. The black iron letters nailed onto the building spelling out the street address make it impossible to miss.

They suddenly feel absurdly underdressed in just their black linen shirt, tan trousers, and boots. Bas is dressed similarly, except his shirt is white, but if he's equally uncomfortable, he doesn't show it.

"Do we just . . . knock?" Bas pokes the iron gate, which is closed over the huge double wooden doors.

Well, they've come this far. Mar shoves the paper into their pocket, reaches through the bars of the gate, and hits the knocker against the door three times.

Then they wait.

Mar scuffs their boot against the blue cobblestone, feeling out of place in front of such an elaborate building. They can only pray Graciela remembered her cousin's address correctly—something they hadn't thought to question until they arrived.

Mar doesn't want to say it aloud, but this looks more like a place a wealthy Spanish commander would live, not a revolutionary.

The right door opens and a stout abuelita in an ornate yellow dress peers stonily at Mar and Bas through the still-closed gate. "Well?" she says expectantly.

"Um." Mar scrambles to remember what they're supposed to say. "Mamá sent me to pick up her dress."

The ice in her expression melts into a warm smile, and the woman unlocks the gate and beckons them in. "Of course! You two must be Alicia's sons. I'm afraid it's not quite ready yet, but please, come in and I'll show you my progress."

Mar and Bas exchange a glance; then Bas shrugs and enters first. Mar enters behind him, blinking as the abuelita closes the door after them.

To say that Mar has never been in a more luxurious building is a laughable understatement. Colorful tile floors with woven bamboo rugs, painted stucco walls adorned with paintings, towering ceilings with dark wood paneling, and rooms opening up on every side. Large, shining, white ceramic vases house small palm trees and brightly colored flowers.

Is every room like this?

"This way," the señora says, and marches into the room to the left. This room is smaller, with a large, polished black piano at one end and two seats that look softer than any bed Mar has ever slept in. Then they're through an archway, down a step, into a room packed with so many books, the air smells like paper, ink, and glue; then around the corner into a small outdoor space between rooms.

It's an odd space; the home surrounds them on every side, with two gated archways built into tall stucco walls, and Mar can see right up to the sky. But the floor is tiled; there are three cushioned wicker chairs at a coffee table set with three place settings, and though there are plants, they're potted as well. It almost feels like another room, but someone forgot to put on a roof.

The señora gestures to two of the chairs. "You two can wait there. I'll tell doña Eralia you're here."

She turns around, and Mar starts. "Wait, you don't know our names. Won't she want to know who we are?"

The woman smiles at Mar over her shoulder and walks out of the room.

Behind Mar, Bas sighs contentedly. Mar turns to find him already lounging in one of the chairs, boots propped up on the table. They sigh and move around the table, shove Bas's feet off, and sit next to him.

Bas frowns at them, and Mar just mumbles, "Don't be rude."

"Is it really rude when you're a pirate?" Bas asks with a grin.

"Yes."

"Hmph."

The morning air is already warming quickly. Mar settles into the seat, glad to be sitting on something soft for once. If they lean their head back and close their eyes, they could fall asleep like this. Easily. All they're missing is a big sombrero to shield their eyes from the sun.

Bas picks up a spoon from the table and tilts it in the sunlight. "I think this is real silver."

"Not surprising, given . . ." They gesture vaguely around them.

"That's true." He stuffs it into his pocket.

Mar's eyes widen and they jerk up. "What are you doing?" they hiss.

Bas blinks at them; then a look of understanding washes over his face. "Ohhh, you're right, she'll notice if just one spoon is missing. Good thinking." He grabs the other two spoons from the place settings and tucks them away with the first.

"Stop that!" they whisper frantically. "Are you actually stealing from Graciela's *cousin*?"

Bas lifts a shoulder. "She can afford it."

"Bas!"

The clack of heels on tile is all the warning they have before a tall woman rounds the corner, skirt swishing at her ankles. Long, curly black hair streaked with gray reaches near her wide hips, and sparkling earrings catch the morning light. They look like crystal. Or maybe even diamond.

The abuelita walks in behind her, carrying a tray with two plates holding steaming bowls of golden broth and a round half ball of mashed fried plantains. Mar's eyes widen as she places the plates in front of them.

"¡Mofongo!" Bas exclaims, a grin splitting his face.

At the first whiff of the garlic and salty plantains, Mar's stomach grumbles. When they look up, the abuelita's eyes are gleaming with a smile. "Thank you," they say.

She waves her hand. "No one leaves my home with an empty stomach!" She looks at the woman and adds with a smile, "Don't scare them *too* much, Eralia. They're good boys." Then she turns and walks out of the room, leaving them with the much more intimidating woman.

Eralia's face is sharp, and her light brown eyes zero in on Mar's hands, where their markings are impossible to hide. Before Mar can think to shove their hands into their pockets, she says, "You must be Mar." Her gaze slides over to the boy beside him. "Which, then, would make you Bas."

Bas frowns, his mouth half-full of food as he says, "Were you expecting us?"

She smiles and sits in the remaining seat. "My cousin sent me a letter saying you might come by, though I didn't know when. I take it you've changed your minds about joining us?"

"Not . . . exactly," Mar says. They square their shoulders as they draw up the words they've been practicing in their mind all morning. "We aren't here to join, but we do want to do something that we think will help your cause."

Eralia examines her long nails. "I'm listening."

Now faced with the reality that if they can't persuade her to help them, Mar and Bas will probably never get into El Morro to begin with, their appetite shrivels. Depending on the graciousness of strangers hasn't always worked out for Mar. They can only hope this will prove to be one of the times it does.

"Bas and I need to get into El Morro—"

Eralia's gaze snaps up to them.

"—to free *La Ana*'s crew tonight. They're the last pirate legends on the seas, and they've provided vital resources to Graciela. I know if you help us free them, they'll do the same for you here in San Juan."

She purses her lips and lowers her hand. "I've heard rumors the crew was captured. When la suegra told me you were here, I hoped it meant the rumors weren't true." Eralia leans back in her seat and watches Mar and Bas for a long, uncomfortable minute. Finally she says, "Let's say we could get you into El Morro. What makes you think you could get to the crew unnoticed, free them, and escape?" She looks at Mar. "You're, what, twelve?"

Mar's face flames with the heat of the sun a hundred times over. "Si— Fifteen," they mumble.

She arches an eyebrow at them but doesn't push it further. "Both of you are young, and if you get caught—which as far as I can tell seems incredibly likely—you'll be killed. It's a fool's errand."

"Hold on," Bas begins, but Mar raises their hand, and for once the boy actually quiets.

"We have a way to free them and get out safely," Mar says. "But we need a way to get in quietly, and we need to get away quickly once we're out. That's all we're asking for, in exchange for a promise to help you."

Eralia taps her nails on her lap. "I have all the resources I need," she says. "But I know how much aid *La Ana*'s crew has provided for Graciela, and I think your time and energy is better spent there. There are some fighting here in Puerto Rico, but we have a long way to go, and sparse public support with such a high density of Spaniards here. But la Nueva España is close—your efforts will go a lot further there." She shakes her head. "Of course, none of that matters if you two are killed trying to do the impossible."

"None of it matters if you don't let us try," Mar counters, "because *La Ana*'s crew will be dead soon."

"Are your lives not important? I could get you safe passage back to Isla Mujeres with Graciela. If you really want to be in the center of something dangerous that actually has a chance of success, she could even get you to la Ciudad de México."

"We don't *need* safe passage to México," Bas says. "What we need is a way into El Morro tonight."

Eralia looks at Mar, and part of them wishes they were as committed to their answer as Bas is. Safe passage to Ciudad de México is an opportunity not only to survive but to make a difference. They could honor the lives they lost by helping the people force the Spaniards out of their country. Papá would be proud of them.

But they haven't lost *La Ana*'s crew, not yet. And as long as there's a chance to save them, to save Bas from the crippling pain of losing everyone he loves, Mar can't let it pass by.

They shake their head. "I know it doesn't seem likely to you that Bas and I will succeed, but you have to believe that we know what we're doing. I wouldn't have come here asking for your help if I didn't think we have a legitimate chance to save them."

Eralia sighs. "You're both certainly stubborn as pirates."

Mar smiles. "I like to think we're tenacious."

"You remind me of my hermana—young, brash, idealistic. She's currently locked up in El Morro with many other friends and fighters." She shakes her head and stands. "I won't help snuff out two more lives with so much potential. My answer is no."

"But we need your help!" Bas exclaims.

"I am helping you. One day you'll see that."

The crew is going to die. They don't have enough time to come up with another plan, and even if they had the time, Mar isn't sure it would matter. They spent hours turning over ideas in their head, but without a way to sneak in, their chances of success are next to none.

Eralia is trying to protect them. But in doing so, she's making it impossible to save their new familia.

"What if . . . ," Mar says as Eralia begins to turn, "what if I could prove to you we can protect ourselves inside El Morro?"

Eralia sighs and turns back to them. "You do realize there's an entire army inside that fortress, don't you? It's not a matter of a few soldiers."

"I know," Mar says, though that reality isn't one they want to dwell on.

"I don't doubt your skill as pirates—even as fighters. But

this is an entirely different animal. No number of guns or ammunition will allow you to overcome an entire army inside their own citadel."

"You're right." Mar takes a deep breath. "But we have more than guns and ammunition."

Bas's eyes widen, and Eralia arches an eyebrow. She doesn't sit, but she doesn't move to leave, either. It's now or never.

Sweat drips down Mar's back. This could go incredibly poorly. Showing any stranger their magia poses a great deal of risk, and though Mar doubts she'll try to have them arrested, she could certainly attack them. Or make them leave.

Of course, she's about to make them leave either way.

Before Mar can talk themself out of it, they exhale and loosen their hold. The heat responds instantly, like it always does, racing from their chest down their arms and bursting from their hands in twin fireballs.

Eralia gasps, then sits again, staring wide-eyed at Mar's hands. Mar rolls the flames over their fingers before bringing their hands together and closing their eyes, pressing the heat back as the ice takes its place. They focus on the space between their palms, smiling softly as ice builds against their skin more and more until Mar uncovers their palm and offers their hand to Eralia.

Sitting in their palm is a rosebud made of ice.

Eralia runs her fingers over the carved petals, then holds the ice in her hand. As their magia retreats into hiding, Mar holds their breath. Bas watches Eralia intently as she turns the rose over in her hand, shaking her head.

"This is incredible," she whispers at last. "It's real."

Mar finally breathes, though their exhalation shivers in their lungs. "It is. So trust me when I say I can protect us inside El Morro."

They hope they sound more confident than they feel.

"Hmm." She watches them for a moment, then puts the melting rose onto the table. "I can get you in and I can help you get away—"

Bas jolts up in his seat and sucks in a sharp, hissing breath.

"But I can't help you once you're in. And if you don't make it out of those walls, there's nothing anyone will be able to do to save you." Eralia pauses. "I really hope you two know what you're doing," she says, a hint of sadness in her voice. "You're both so young and so full of potential. I've seen too many revolutionaries die young because they took on more than they could handle."

Mar bites their lip. "Then why are you helping us?"

Bas's eyes widen, but Mar pretends not to notice. They imagine he's probably worried she'll change her mind, but this isn't the kind of deal they can make quickly and leave before second thoughts are had. There's too much at stake, and if they're going to entrust their lives to Eralia's hands, Mar wants to know why she'd help them when she doesn't seem to believe they can succeed.

"Because I'm selfish," Eralia says plainly. "I mentioned that my hermana is in El Morro. I also have close friends there right now, awaiting their trials and inevitable executions. They were working with me to organize outside the city, and they were caught."

Mar's eyes widen. "I'm sorry."

She sighs. "It's what will happen to us all, eventually, if we don't succeed. If I get you both into El Morro tonight, all I ask is that you free them and the other revolutionaries in addition to *La Ana*'s crew. You'll find my hermanita among them."

"Absolutely," Mar says at the same time Bas says, "Yes."

"Good." She sniffs and gestures to Mar's still untouched plate. "Now eat your food before it gets cold. La suegra will never let me hear the end of it if she learns I let you leave without eating. You'll need one of the spoons in your friend's pocket."

CHAPTER 27

It can't be later than eleven in the morning, but the Spanish soldier Eralia told Mar and Bas to follow is incredibly drunk. The kind of drunk that has led him to walk into an alley behind a strip of buildings, stumbling into the walls. It might have attracted attention, but it's raining sheets again, and the sky rumbles with thunder.

As much as Mar would prefer to be indoors while the rain is coming down like the clouds have a personal vendetta with San Juan, it discourages most from being outside. Which, given what they are about to do, is an advantage.

At least they've removed the cloth wraps from their arms, so they don't have to deal with an extra layer of drenched fabric stuck to their skin. Mar just hopes the soldier isn't too out of it to play his part.

"His name is Emilio Montoya Colón," Eralia told them. "He's one of the captains who preside over the prisons in El Morro, so he'll know exactly where they're being kept, to save you some time inside. He'll also know where they keep the keys

to the cells—and he's a drunkard, so it shouldn't be difficult to get it out of him. It's Thursday, so he'll be drinking at Taberna Rodrigo already. If you hurry, you'll catch him on his way back to the barracks."

"How do you know all this?" Bas asked.

Eralia forced a thin smile. "I told you there are people I care about in El Morro. We've been trying to figure out a way to break them free as well."

Mar bit their tongue and held in the words that swirled endlessly in their head: *They still weren't sure it was possible. But there was a chance, and a chance made it worth the risk.*

Now they nod at Bas, and the two of them close the distance. The man is humming quietly in the rain, dragging his boots through the puddles, running his hand through his short blond hair, when Bas slides up next to him and holds his foot out in the way.

The man splashes face-first on the blue-cobblestone street, his reflexes slowed too much by the alcohol to throw his hands out to catch himself. Mar cringes as the solider moans, then slowly, awkwardly rolls over to face the sky.

And them.

Face full of dirty water and blood leaking from his nose, the soldier blinks up at them. He doesn't seem to notice that his fancy blue, gold-trimmed uniform is now utterly filthy. "Oh," he says groggily. "Hola, niños."

Mar nods at Bas. He grabs the man's arms and pulls him up to a sitting position. The captain sits there, swaying slightly, as he slowly blinks through the rain. Blood from his nose drips onto the gold buttons of his uniform coat. Bas moves behind him, pulls out the burlap sack used to hold their food this morning, and looks at Mar.

They nod again.

Bas wrings the instantly drenched burlap sack as if fruit-lessly trying to squeeze the water out, then loops it in front of the captain's face and yanks it between the man's teeth. The soldier's eyes widen and he makes a protesting noise, jerking forward though Bas holds the ends of the sack firm.

And that's when Mar crouches in front of the Spaniard and ignites their right arm, from fingertip to elbow. They relax just a little, easing their hold on their magia, exhaling softly as warmth races across their body, setting their markings aglow.

The soldier goes utterly still. The fear in his wide, pale eyes is familiar. It's the way one looks at a wild animal poised to strike. The firing end of a gun.

A monster.

"Now that we understand each other," Mar says calmly, "my friend is going to lower the gag. And you're not going to scream, because you know what will happen if you scream, don't you, Emilio?"

The sky rumbles so loudly, Mar feels it in their bones. They smile.

The man nods frantically—or as best he can, with Bas holding the ends of the gag as tightly as he is.

"Good." Mar nods at Bas.

The boy eases the gag slowly, and when the soldier doesn't scream, Bas holds it taut against his neck. The man is breathing quickly, shivering in the rain. Some of his strawlike hair has fallen over his eyes, where it drips rainwater.

Mar rests their flaming arm on their knees, careful to keep the fire from eating at their clothes. Smoke rises from the flames as the rain tries to put it out, but Mar keeps it burning, fueling the fire with a steady stream of magia. It's not much—barely releasing the pressure of built-up energy—but the longer it burns, the better they feel.

As they hoped, the captain keeps his gaze steadily on the flames.

"You're going to tell us where in El Morro *La Ana*'s crew is imprisoned," Mar says.

The man keeps staring at the fire, growing paler by the second.

Mar snaps their fingers. The man's gaze jumps to their face. "Where—"

The man falls forward as much as possible with the gag holding him by the neck and throws up on Mar's boots.

It takes every ounce of Mar's willpower not to recoil; they're glad for the smoke and rain mostly overpowering the stench. Bas makes a disgusted noise but to his credit doesn't move. The man straightens again, a little less pale, but still looking at Mar like he might piss himself at any moment.

Mar waits, drilling the man with their coldest stare as the rain washes the bile off their boots. They can practically taste the tension in the air, but still, they sit in the silence, watching as it eats at him.

The man whimpers.

Mar smiles. "Let's try that again. Where in El Morro is *La Ana*'s crew imprisoned?"

The soldier's voice shakes. "Demonio. Y-you're a demonio."

Mar can practically see Dami rolling their eyes, but if the misconception helps them intimidate him, well . . . "Yes. And you're Emilio Montoya Colón, and if you don't want me to take your soul to the lake of fire right now, you're going to tell me where in El Morro *La Ana*'s crew is imprisoned." They throw in a grin just for fun.

"No!" The soldier cowers back into Bas. "Por favor, I'll tell you anything you want. But I—I don't know where they're keeping the pirates—"

Mar lets just a little more magia go, and the flames on their arm burst higher. The man screeches, pressing back against Bas's stomach. "¡Espera!" He squeals. "Espera, lo siento, por favor—they're keeping them with the rebels, on the sixth level! The soldier guarding the door to the prisons will have the keys." He whimpers, tears streaming down his cheeks. "Por favor, no me mates."

Mar smiles, and this time it's genuine. "That's good, Emilio. Now, you're going to stay home sick today. And you're never going to tell anyone what happened here. Do you know why?"

The man is trembling from head to toe, pale as a sheet of paper, but his eyes are glued to Mar's gaze. "You'll kill me?" he whimpers.

"Slowly," Mar answers without missing a beat. "I'll be watching you, Emilio. Don't disappoint me."

There's something intoxicating about letting people see

the monster. About feeling the hum of magia alive in their bones, warming them like a bonfire in their chest. The awe and fear they inspire—and it's all so easy.

They just have to let go.

Then, all at once, the man's eyes roll back, and he slumps forward in a way that must be choking him against the rolled-up sack. Bas's eyes widen, and he drops the gag. The man falls forward and hits the cobblestones face-first again, with a splat. Bas stares at him for a moment; then when the man doesn't move, he rolls Emilio over onto this back, grimacing at the man's vomit- and blood-drenched front.

Mar jerks to their feet and clenches their fist, extinguishing the flames. It's almost painful to pull the magia back, to lock it deep inside them again. Just as their markings dim to black, the fire reawakens in a rush and Mar grits their teeth, focusing on the flow of power flooding their veins.

¡Basta!

They clamp down hard, tensing as they force their magia back into that hidden part of their soul. No lock can hold it forever, but for the moment it's a reprieve.

Mar didn't realize they'd closed their eyes, but when they open them again, Bas is watching them like Mar might snap at any moment, which twists the wrong way in their gut.

The rain is cooling and comforting. Mar pushes their rain-drenched hair out of their eyes, then shoves their hands into their soaked pockets.

The thing is, Mar loves using their magia.

No matter how much pain and death it has brought them,

no matter all the ways it has made their life harder, none of that matters when it runs like liquid euphoria in their veins. Mar would give up their magia without hesitation, has wished it away every single day since Mamá was murdered, but no matter how much they wish it weren't true, using their magia makes them feel alive.

And they hate it.

They're watching the rise and fall of the soldier's chest when Bas steps next to them and nudges their shoulder. "You all right?" he says softly.

Thunder fills the air like the roar of a beast ready to swallow them whole.

Mar sets their shoulders and turns away from the soldier. "Let's go."

CHAPTER 28

The sun has just begun its descent below the horizon when Mar and Bas climb into a massive bin of laundered blue Spanish uniforms and blankets for the soldiers. Surrounded by cloth, their breath hot against their face, Mar can't help but think the fabric isn't going to be so clean by the time they get into El Morro. Not with the way they're sweating in the humid, stifling air, with the heat of Bas's body pressed tight to their side.

They try to lie as still and flat as possible, cringing at every bump and jerk of the wagon. The soft cloth smells surprisingly of soap, though, on reflection, Mar begrudgingly admits it shouldn't be much of a surprise; soap may be too expensive for most to use it on all their laundry, but this is the Spanish army. Of course they have the resources to buy it.

Now, tucked in the middle of a wagon packed full of supplies, Mar recites what they know endlessly in their mind.

Though only finished some thirty years ago, parts of El Morro are hundreds of years old. Built into the cliffside at the entrance to la Bahía de San Juan, the six-level-deep fort has made for dangerous waters for over two hundred years. Combined with the much smaller El Cañuelo fort on the western side of the bay, El Morro is one of the many reasons pirates avoid San Juan.

Except Mar and Bas, who are going out of their way to get inside.

Vincente, an older, balding man, is driving the bull-led wagon. In addition to the laundered uniforms and blankets, the wagon is also full of containers of food and water. El Morro receives at least one wagonload of supplies daily, and Eralia said that Vincente is the only civilian who can get into El Morro without any trouble. He makes trips like this a couple of times a week, so many of the guards know his face and his name.

This supply run is completely and utterly ordinary. They will suspect nothing.

Eralia said if Mar and Bas can get everyone outside the fort walls, she can provide a quick getaway. They don't think there's much chance they'll be able to sneak several dozen people out completely unnoticed, but Mar can take care of the small groups of guards they come across.

Provided they don't trigger an alarm that will alert the entire fortress.

Of course, long before they get to that, the tricky part will be getting out of the laundry bin unseen. Vincente always brings the food out first, because the soldiers love seeing what new food is coming in. Then he'll wheel out the laundry bin and push it close to the stairs that lead to the lower levels. While Vincente continues unloading and talking to the guards, Mar and Bas will climb out of the back end of the bin and hurry down the steps before they're seen.

If only Mar's magia could make them invisible. Staying out of the Spaniards' clutches would be so much easier if they could control who saw them and who didn't—like Dami.

Mar snaps their eyes closed and forces the thought out of their mind. They aren't sure that it matters, but the last thing they need is to summon Dami by thinking of them. Not that Dami has ever indicated that they can tell when Mar is thinking about them, but why take the risk?

They don't need a demonio distracting them while they attempt something likely to get them killed.

Mar bites their lip and slips their left hand in their pocket to roll the crushed bullet in their fingers. Enough is enough; they've lost too many already. There's no going back now. They'll either save *La Ana*'s crew or . . .

Mar's stomach flips, and they squeeze their eyes closed harder. No. Best not to think about the *or*.

Bas's hand slips into theirs, and Mar goes still. If they thought it was warm before, well, now they're a furnace. Their hands must be cold and clammy, but Bas gently squeezes their hand.

For some reason they don't care to think about, it makes them smile. Just a little.

Mar squeezes back, and Bas doesn't move his hand away. So neither does Mar.

They lie like that, side by side, hand in hand, buried in folded cloth and surrounded by the smell of soap and linen, the creaking and rumbling of the wheels beneath them, the uneven roads endlessly jostling them; and Mar tries not to think about how soft Bas's hands are.

The wagon jerks to a halt.

"¡Hola!" Vincente calls out, and Mar's heart all but jumps into their throat.

They must be here. Outside the gates.

There are voices, but Mar can't make out the words. The tone is light, though—Vincente even laughs. Then someone yells, "¡Ábrela!" and the unmistakable rattling of chains and grumbling of gears of a lifting gate make Mar forget how to breathe.

Bas squeezes their hand again, tighter this time, and Mar holds on like his hand is a cliffside and they're dangling off the edge. They don't let go as the wagon lurches forward. They don't let go as the clatter of wheels on cobblestones turns to the rumble of wheels on concrete and the cold warning prickle trickles down the back of their neck. They don't let go as the wagon comes to a shuddering halt again, and the decisive boom of a closing gate echoes like an explosion in their mind.

They don't let go.

Vincente is talking, but Mar can't make out his words until, all at once, his voice is louder. Closer. "Food, water, and clean clothes tonight," he says. "I may have even snuck some pastelitos in there."

The muffled cheers churn Mar's stomach, but they don't

move a muscle. They try not to breathe too hard, even though they know it's unlikely anyone will hear them breathing beneath two feet of cloth. But that knowledge doesn't matter. Not this close to people who want them dead.

Not inside the most dangerous place in the Caribbean for Mar to be.

They've never seen the commander of the Spanish army, García López. But Papá did, and they always thought he would be around to warn Mar if el Diablo incarnate was here.

But now Mar is surrounded by their enemies, and Papá isn't here. All at once the loss feels fresh again; they want nothing more than to press their face into Papá's chest and feel his arms squeeze them breathlessly tight one more time. They'd even let Papá tell them how special their magia is without arguing or brushing him off—anything to see him again, to hear his voice one more time.

I'll find a way, Papá. Somehow. And they'll figure it out without selling their soul. Just as soon as they've saved *La Ana*'s crew.

The laundry bin lurches forward on squeaky wheels, and Mar bites their lip to contain their gasp. The bin tilts backward, and they squeeze their eyes closed, holding Bas's hand so hard their fingers ache. The warning prickle becomes a storm, thousands of icy pinpricks dancing down their spine. This is the kind of warning Mar knows not to ignore, but right now they wish they could turn it off.

They don't need magia to be aware of how incredibly dangerous this mission is.

The laundry bin levels out, and it rumbles like a distant storm over the rough, hard ground, and then quiet. They've stopped moving, and Vincente's voice drifts away.

Ready or not, it's time.

The closest wall of the laundry bin is just a hand's breadth away from the top of Mar's head. They scooch back and sit up slowly, sliding their back against the wall, trying to jostle as few of the folded fabric bundles as possible. Bas does the same, and once they're both sitting up, Mar twists around and reaches their right arm above their head until their fingers touch the top edge of the bin, then slides over to the side wall like Eralia told them.

This is the riskiest part. There's no graceful way to climb out of a bin full of fabric, so Mar just has to trust that Vincente has the soldiers thoroughly distracted. It sounds like it, as best they can tell; uproarious laughter and happy shouts fill the night somewhere behind them, but it's impossible to know. And if Mar and Bas lean too heavily against the wall while they try to stand, they risk tipping the whole thing over, which most certainly will be noticed.

To whatever gods are out there . . . please.

Mar gets their feet under them, then stands, cringing as fabric falls off their head and back into the bin. The air is cooler out here, and darker, and the laughter seems so loud and there's no time to think. Mar kicks their leg over the side wall of the bin and climbs out, not breathing again until they're crouched by the outside of the bin.

No shouts of alarm.

Miraculously, Vincente has placed the bin well—the stairs are directly behind them. But everything is much more open than Mar had hoped. The bin is angled enough to shield them from the soldiers as long as they keep low to the ground: The barrier walls on either side of the stairs aren't more than a foot tall, so they'll have to move quickly if they don't want to risk someone spotting the top of their head.

Mar pats the bin three times so Bas knows it's safe to come out—though *safe* is truly a relative term here—and Mar starts down the stairs, crouching as low as possible. When they're four steps down and sufficiently blocked by the side walls, they dare a glance back. Bas is already scrambling after them.

They move quickly down the gray stone stairs and around the corner into a dark, arched tunnel. Once sufficiently bathed in shadow, Mar stops, heart so loud in their ears, they can barely hear anything else—problematic, given that they need to keep an ear out for any soldiers up ahead. Or behind them.

Soldiers could be anywhere.

"I feel like I'm going to throw up," Bas whispers.

"Perfect," Mar answers. "You can do that on the first soldier we come across."

The two share a nervous smile; then Mar reaches for their side, their heart calming just a little when their fingertips touch the holstered pistol Eralia gave them. Ideally, Mar won't have to use it, and logically, it probably won't be much use inside a fort full of soldiers, but having it feels better than walking in here defenseless.

Except you're never really defenseless, are you? Mar grimaces. Ideally, they won't have to use their magia either, but for once they maybe don't mind that they have it at their disposal.

"All right," Bas says. "Now . . . which way?"

Mar hesitates. It's not like Eralia had a map of the barracks, and of course Emilio Montoya Colón didn't provide one either. Unsurprisingly, the fortress is anything but straightforward. Just from where they're standing in this dingy tunnel, there are two different archways behind them, and back out by the stairs at least five more they can see. Any one of them could be a dead end or spit them out into a group of bored guards.

"Shame," a voice says behind them.

Mar whirls around, eyes wide. Bas, startled, does the same before squinting into shadow and peering side-eyed at Mar.

The demonio standing beside Bas, bored, examines their black-painted nails.

"If only you had an invisible guide," Dami says. "But sorry, I forgot, you don't need my help. Suppose I'll just go, then."

CHAPTER 29

"Wait!" Mar hisses into the darkness.

Dami's grin is sharp as a knife's edge, and Mar instantly regrets stopping them. Dami isn't going to do anything for free; they're a demonio, roping people into deals is what demonios and diablos do. They told Mar themself—it's how they get their power.

But they don't have time to waste wandering a Spanish stronghold. If Mar and Bas get lost, they'll be caught. Assuming they won't be shot on the spot.

"Mar," Bas says carefully, "I know we're both jumpy, but you know there's . . . no one there, right?"

Dami laughs. "Oh, he's precious."

"Hush," Mar says, not entirely sure if they mean Bas or Dami. "I'm not making a deal," they say to Dami.

"Okay, bye."

"No!"

Dami outright cackles. Mar would love nothing more in this moment than to punch them through their smug, attractive face. But Dami has them cornered, and they know it. If they leave, Mar and Bas have no way to find the crew. They'll have made it all the way into El Morro, a few floors away from the crew, just for their plan to fall apart before it ever had a chance.

Mar isn't sure why it hasn't occurred to them that it wouldn't be obvious which way is to the dungeons, but they suppose this is the consequence of putting together such a desperate, haphazard plan in a day.

"Okay, okay," Dami says, wiping tears of laughter from their eyes. "I'll even make it easy for you, start you off on a *baby* deal with absolutely no serious consequences whatsoever." They fold their hands behind their back and stand up straight, pushing their corseted chest out, their long black hair draping over their left shoulder. "I'll guide you down to your friends in the dungeons and give you the heads-up when soldiers are near, and in return you'll listen to the real deal I want you to make with me. The whole thing, without interrupting this time. And at the end of it, if you want to, you can say no. But you have to hear me out first."

Mar presses their lips together hard, biting their mouth closed. They look at Bas, who is staring at them wide-eyed and worried—probably because he still doesn't know who they're talking to—then back to Dami, who, judging by the smug look on their face, absolutely knows Mar has very little choice here.

"Fine," Mar snaps. "But if we don't get into the dungeons on the sixth level without raising the alarm, the deal is off."

Dami beams, practically radiating gloating waves of delight. "Deal." They step right up to Mar. "Dos besos make it official."

Mar scowls. "¿En serio?"

"Well, in America it's a handshake, and in Asian countries—"

Mar lurches forward, glaring as they bring their right cheek to Dami's, then touch their left cheeks together. They quickly rip away, then gasp as a rush of icelike cold flashes over them from the top of their head to their toes.

"Beautiful," Dami says, turning with a flourish of their black dress and hair. "Follow me."

"Santa María," Bas says. "What are you—"

Mar grabs his hand and pulls him forward. "I'll explain later, but I know where to go. Vamos."

And then they're moving. Under arch after arch, through shadows, as they weave around corners and avoid patches of lantern light spilling over. Dami moves quickly, their skirt billowing behind them and large silver earrings dangling soundlessly. They pause at each arch before beckoning Mar and Bas forward. Again and again, until they've reached a set of stairs plunging them deeper into the cliffside fortress.

Halfway down the chilly, narrow stairwell, Mar stops so suddenly that Bas runs into their back. They stumble a step forward and catch themself on the cool concrete wall.

"What is it?" Bas whispers at the same time as Dami hisses, "What are you doing?"

"It's just . . . we haven't seen any guards," Mar says softly.

Dami stares at them like they're thickskulled, and Bas squeezes next to Mar and frowns at them. "That's good, though," he says. "We should hope we keep getting lucky."

"Yeah, but . . . *is* it luck?" Mar whispers.

"No," Dami says. "It's me, diverting us away from the guards. Like I said I was going to."

Mar shakes their head and turns to Dami. "But have *you* sensed any guards even close to getting in our way?"

"There you go, talking to ghosts again," Bas mumbles.

But Dami frowns. "I mean . . . not *yet,* but we've only been through one floor."

The warning prickle hasn't let up for a second since Mar has entered the fortress. They've assumed it's because they're surrounded by Spanish soldiers—after all, that alone is a direct threat to their life.

But what if there's more to it?

Mar sighs and shakes their head. "We can't turn back now anyway."

Bas and Dami nod. And then they're off again.

When they reach the third level without a soul in sight, even Bas looks confused.

When they reach the fourth, then fifth, levels without having to pause once, Dami stops midway down the stairwell to the sixth.

"It's not me," Dami says suddenly. "The emptiness, I mean. Honestly, if you had a map, you probably could've made it down here on your own."

Which confirms exactly what they were worried about.

"It's been too easy," Bas whispers. "Do you think, maybe, they're all on the next level?"

Mar glances at Dami, who lifts a shoulder. "There *are* two in front of the door to the dungeon. But that's it."

"Not all of them, no," Mar says to Bas.

They stand in the quiet of the darkness for a moment.

Bas sighs. "Then . . . maybe we'll meet them on our way out."

It's possible, Mar supposes, that the Spaniards have focused their security on the entrance, as it's the only way in and out of the fortress. Or maybe they're just that confident in the security of their prison cells.

But somehow, those possibilities aren't the comfort Mar would like them to be.

And yet, once again, it doesn't matter. They're deep in the heart of El Morro now. No matter what happens from here, or what they face ahead, they can't turn back. And even if they could, Mar isn't sure that they would. Bas certainly wouldn't, and Mar can't stomach the idea of leaving without him.

Mar nods at Dami. They return the gesture, then say, "We're going to turn left, but they're at the end of the hall, so keep quiet and to the shadows. As soon as they see you, you'll need to take care of them."

Take care of them. Right. Mar steels themself, forcing a deep, slow breath over the racing of their heart. They relay the same information to Bas, who frowns.

"How do you know?"

"I'll explain later, I promise."

Bas's frown deepens, but he takes his pistol out and nods.

Mar places their hand over Bas's pistol and shakes their head. "It'd be best to avoid gunfire if we can—it's too loud. The others will hear it and come running."

Bas grimaces and puts it away. "Then . . . ?"

Mar looks at Dami, who lifts their hands. "I never said—"

"You agreed you'd get us *into* the dungeon unseen. Or the deal is off. Remember?"

Dami scowls. "You didn't say *unseen*. You said *without raising the alarm*."

"And what do you think is going to happen the moment they see us?" Mar asks lightly.

Dami stares at them for a solid ten seconds. Then they make a grumbling noise and disappear.

"A deal?" Bas says softly. "Are you . . . I thought you said—"

"It isn't el Diablo," Mar says quickly. "I promise I'll explain after this is over."

Bas looks away and stares into the shadows, his face too blank. Mar cringes, but they don't have time to fix Bas's hurt feelings, because a muffled thunk sounds down the hall, and then Dami reappears in front of them.

"Keys are on the wall," Dami says dryly. "You're welcome. But—"

"It's clear," Mar says to Bas. Then they sprint around the corner, Bas swearing as he follows behind. This deep into the cliffside, the chill is heavy and wet, the kind that sinks into your bones and holds on tight. Only two lanterns light the length of the dim stone hallway, but one is right beside the black iron dungeon gate, clearly illuminating two collapsed figures on the ground. On the wall beside the door, as promised, are keys hanging from a rusty hook.

"You're going to explain *all* of this, right?" Bas says, eyeing the unconscious Spaniards as he pokes one with the toe of his boot.

"Yes." Mar grabs the keys off the hook, smiling at the light jingle of metal against metal. They really made it all the way down. All that separates them from the crew now is a door. And Mar has the key.

It takes them three tries with three different keys, but finally one turns in the heavy iron gate. They push it open, cringing from head to toe at the loud, protesting screech it makes on its unoiled hinges.

"So much for being quiet," Bas whispers.

"Still quieter than gunfire," Mar shoots back. They grab the lantern hanging next to the gate and step into the narrow hallway, just wide enough for Mar and Bas to stand shoulder to shoulder.

On both sides, the walls are made up of cell after cell, each separated from the next by about a foot of concrete. Mar has taken all of five steps when the warning prickle on their back goes from thousands of icy pinpricks to an outright blizzard along the length of their spine.

The cells are empty.

Mar moves more quickly down the hall, heart pounding harder with every empty cell. By the time they've reached the end of the hall, they can barely breathe.

"I don't understand," Bas says. "Emilio said they'd be here. Is there another dungeon on this level?"

"No," Dami says, suddenly at Mar's other side in one of the cells. "Your information must have been wrong."

Mar whirls on them. "Couldn't you tell these cells were empty?"

"Not until I'd finished with the guards, no."

"But you can tell if guards are around—"

"I can tell if they're *near* us. I told you, Mar, I'm not a diablo. I don't have the kind of reach you think I do." Dami grimaces and glances past Mar's shoulder. "I can tell you they're coming down the hallway, though. A lot of them."

That's all the warning Mar and Bas get before a loud screech rakes down Mar's back and the clang of the iron gate against the concrete wall sends their pulse racing. They spin around and push Bas behind them as two guards fill the doorway, rifles extended. Crowding the doorway behind them are more guards. Mar knows without having to see them that the hallway beyond the dungeon is packed with them.

The only way out is through. And a glance back tells Mar everything they need to know: Dami is gone.

The deal—and the demonio's help—is over.

CHAPTER 30

Lantern light spills over the two guards leading the way. One of them Mar recognizes instantly.

"Coño," Bas mutters behind them. "Pinche Emilio."

If *pinche* Emilio is surprised to see Mar and Bas in an empty hallway of prison cells, he doesn't show it. But he does flinch when Mar levels their gaze on him.

Still, he's backed up by who knows how many soldiers. They may not all be able to fit into the narrow hallway, but they'll be able to keep pouring in endlessly until Mar makes a mistake—or runs out of magia.

A small part of Mar hoped they'd somehow be able to do this with minimal magia use, as unlikely as that was. But that isn't an option. Not anymore.

Ice magia fills their chest and rushes through the rest of them, cooling the hot panic clambering up their throat. Behind them, Bas gasps, and in front of them Emilio's eyes widen, but that's all they register before the magia's song drowns them out and Mar's bones hum with power.

Solo un poco. Por favor.

But even as Mar keeps their magia in check, time slows around them. Mar extends their glowing hands to the ground in front of them. Emilio turns slowly to his companion. Mar pulls their arms up as thick ice bursts from sweaty concrete. Shouts explode around them, but distant, a world away.

Mar is the ice filling the spaces between stone and concrete, building like a giant pushing up to stand. The ice throws their arms out wall to wall between cells, ballooning up and racing to the ceiling, separating soldiers from pirates. The ice wall is an extension of Mar, but they barely flinch as bullets smash into their barrier self.

Más. Mar pushes, even as a warning whispers, *But not too much.*

They don't stop. Not yet.

The winter in their veins sings. More ice over ice over ice, thickening from a hand's width to two until even the sound of gunfire is muffled into dull thumps. Until the chill turns Mar's breath to clouds.

Casi, casi . . . Mar fills their lungs with frozen, raw power, slams their hands into the wall and pushes it forward. Grating over concrete, muscles straining, pushing past iron bars, boots pressed hard against stone, forcing soldiers back, shaking with strain, sweat dripping down their temples, until the wall presses flush against the door and the dungeon is empty.

Only then do they release.

The quiet is almost surreal. Mar pants like they've run a

marathon, shaking with effort. Bas gapes wide-eyed at the icy barrier sealing them off from the soldiers, rubbing the goose-flesh on his arms.

"Wow," he whispers. Then he looks at Mar. "Can you turn the soldiers to ice too?"

Mar stares at him. "No."

"Why not? Have you ever tried?"

"Not to diminish how cool you are," Dami says, suddenly beside Mar again, "but how is a giant icy wall going to help you defeat an army of Spaniards and rescue your friends?"

Mar jumps and whirls on Dami, still glowing with unspent magia. "Where did you go? You just *left*!"

Dami arches an eyebrow. "What? Did you miss me?"

"You could have *helped*—"

"You know very well why I couldn't, actually. That wasn't part of our deal. And to answer your question, no, the Spaniards weren't my fault this time. I never double-cross a deal."

Bas clears his throat. "So. Are you a demonio?"

Mar's stomach plummets to their toes. Bas is staring right at Dami. Which means—

"Hello, handsome," Dami says, all too casually. "I most certainly am."

Bas's cheeks pinken.

Dami looks at Mar. "And if you must know, I was finding your friends out of the goodness of my black, hell-damned heart. So you're welcome."

Bas gasps, but Mar's eyes narrow. "You never do anything out of the goodness of your heart."

"I'm wounded," Dami says flatly. "Truly."

Bas says, "Where are they? Are they still alive?"

Mar scowls. "Dami's not going to just tell us—they'll want something first. It's their fault any of us are even here to begin with."

"The crew's a floor above us, and yes, they're alive. For now." Dami winks at Mar.

Mar just barely resists the urge to punch them.

"Then we can still get them!" Bas hesitates. "What do you mean, it's their fault we're here?"

Before Mar can explain, Dami casually says, "I told that Spaniard where to find some pirates on Playa Mujeres. Mar could have sunk the ship that followed you afterward, but they held back. As usual."

Mar glowers at the demonio. Bas's mouth drops open. "You *what*?"

"In my defense," Dami says, "I was sure Mar would help you all escape safely with their magia. I was just trying to push them to use it."

Bas pinches the bridge of his nose. "I . . . can't process this right now." He turns to Mar. "If the crew is still alive, then there's still a chance."

Mar shakes their head. "We're trapped. There's an army on the other side of this wall, and I don't know how long it'll hold."

"Holding back *agaiiin*," Dami singsongs.

To Bas's credit, he ignores them. "I say we go out guns blazing. Burst through the wall, and you can use your magia and I can take some down too— Wait." Bas turns to Dami with something like hope in his warm brown eyes. "Can't *you* give me magia?"

Dami laughs. Loudly. "No."

Bas's face falls. "No you can't, or no you don't want to?"

"Both," they say nonchalantly. "I can't because I'm a demonio—not a diablo—and I can't do that caliber of a deal. But also even if I could, no, I don't want to."

"Why not?" Bas demands.

Dami looks at Bas like they might an ugly bug. "I don't need to explain myself to you."

Bas scowls and steps forward, but Mar pushes him back with one hand and forces themself between them. "All right, *enough*. Bas, it doesn't matter what Dami does or doesn't want, because they're too weak to do it anyway."

Dami looks affronted. "I wouldn't say *weak*—"

"And *you*"—Mar turns on Dami—"you have no reason to be here anymore. The deal is over, and I know you're not going to fight alongside us."

"Absolutely not."

"So then you can go." Mar faces Bas, and behind them Dami tsk-tsks.

"Wrong on both points, actually." They move around Mar and sidle up next to Bas, as if the two weren't arguing thirty seconds ago. "One," they say, counting on their fingers, "the deal isn't over because I haven't gotten *my* end of it yet—the part where you hear me out, remember?"

Mar's eyes narrow. "Do you really think *now* is the time?"

"No, which brings me to two: I'm staying to watch. Because I *want* to." They flash Bas a grin. The boy glowers in return.

Mar shakes their head and focuses on Bas, trying to ignore Dami's smug face right next to him. "I can't beat a whole army. So we're clear. And not because I'm *holding back.*"

Bas sighs. "I know you don't think you can, but can you get us out of here any other way?"

They grimace. The only windows in these cells are barely tall enough to slide a coconut through, let alone a human. And even if they *did* somehow miraculously manage it, they're in the middle of a cliffside probably over twenty feet up with no safe way down to the shore.

So. No.

"That's what I thought," Bas says to their silence. "So either we try something that has a small chance of success or . . . what? We wait until we starve in here? Or until they figure out how to break down that wall and come crashing in here anyway?"

Mar doesn't want to admit it, but Bas is right. With their presence revealed, fighting their way out is their only chance. Even if that chance looks rather hopeless.

"Carajo," Mar whispers, and Bas grins.

"Still the long night."

And for some reason, those words from Bas are exactly what they need to hear. Mar inhales the cold air deeply, pulls their shoulders back, and loosens their hold on their magia, letting the glow come to their markings once more.

"Still the long night."

Blasting through a foot-thick wall of ice feels like smashing into a brick wall, but the ice breaks to Mar's will. Magia roars through them, so alive, demanding release, fueling every rapid pump of their heart. They race through the cloud of dustlike ice clinging to the air, ready to breathe fire on the first Spaniard who so much as looks at them.

But no one is there.

Mar staggers to a halt as Bas runs out from the dungeon screaming, guns drawn, before he too slows to a sudden stop, blinking in the empty darkness. "I'm . . . confused."

"So am I," Mar says. They turn around as Dami strolls casually out of the hallway, looking utterly unsurprised by their lack of an audience. And of course they wouldn't be. If the demonio can sense when guards are near, then they certainly can sense when they *aren't*.

"You could have told us the soldiers moved," Mar says flatly.

"I could have," Dami agrees with a smirk. "But watching you two burst out of there with so much enthusiasm was way more fun."

Mar scowls. "If you're going to insist on following us

around, you could at least make yourself useful and tell us where they went."

"Hmm. Don't know."

Mar steps toward them, fists bursting into flame. But Dami just rolls their eyes. "I already told you I can't sense the whole complex. All I can say for sure is they aren't near—so not on this floor." They pause, then frown. "And the crew aren't in the dungeons on the fifth floor anymore either."

The chill that rolls through Mar has nothing to do with their proximity to the cold dungeon they've just walked out of.

They look at Bas, not wanting to even suggest . . . what if? "You don't think—"

Bas takes off for the stairs. Mar swears and races after him, neither of them even pausing to breathe as they race through empty floor after empty floor, cold damp stairs and hallways and stairs again. They don't stop until they've burst back out into the cooling night air, at the bottom of the first set of stairs they took after crawling out of the laundry bin.

It's quiet here, too.

But at the top of the stairs, soldiers are standing. Waiting.

They've parted around the mouth of the stairs, to leave space for Mar and Bas to walk through. But lined along the walls, standing at attention not even a foot apart, are more blue-and-red-coated soldiers than Mar has ever seen at once. Possibly more than they've ever seen in their life, period, if they added them all up.

Mar isn't sure they want to know what's waiting for them at the top of the stairs. Why none of the soldiers have moved, even though the two of them are clearly in sight. Why it's so quiet, even the crash of the ocean against the cliffs feels muted.

But their choices dissolved the moment they set upon this path. And even as they force themself up one step, then another, heart in their throat and stomach twisted in a knot, all they can do is hope Papá is proud of them.

Hope that by some miracle they'll get out of here alive so they can still figure out how to save him.

Mar and Bas climb the steps together, but when they make it to the top, it's Bas who reacts first.

"No!" he screams, lurching forward.

Mar throws their arms around his middle, barely moving fast enough to hold him back as soldiers close off the stairs behind them. Not that going back was an option. Not that going back was ever an option, not as soon as they swore to save the crew.

The very crew on their knees in four long lines, hands shackled behind them.

Behind each one, a soldier holding them at gunpoint.

El Capitán and Tito in the front row.

"The execution isn't until tomorrow!" Bas screams, fighting to break free of Mar's tight grip. "You can't!" His voice breaks and catches on a sob.

A Spaniard is standing in front of the firing squad, and with a start Mar recognizes Emilio.

Mar can't say they've ever regretted *not* killing someone before, but they suppose there really is a first for everything.

"Surrender," Emilio says. "Both of you. Weapons on the ground, on your knees, hands behind your heads."

Mar doesn't move, but Bas stops struggling.

"Surrender and your crew will see another sunrise before attending the *public* execution they deserve." Emilio smiles. "And you will join them."

"I liked him better drunk," Dami mutters beside them.

Bas drops to his knees like a rock in the ocean. He throws his pistols on the ground, out of reach. And he doesn't even look at Mar as he raises his hands behind his head.

Bas may not be looking at them, but over two hundred soldiers are. Mar has given themself away. The Spaniards know they can do magia, but they also know they can't do magia fast enough to save the crew. And it's no coincidence that they're standing *behind* the crew members; even if Mar were strong enough to defeat them all, which is questionable to begin with, they aren't sure they'd be able to hit the soldiers without hurting *La Ana*'s crew.

At least if they surrender, the crew has more time. So, then. It's over.

When they lower to their knees, Mar is shaking so hard their teeth chatter. They throw their gun beside Bas's, but of course no one there is under any illusion that a pistol is their true weapon. The one time their magia could make a positive difference, it's not enough to save the people they care about. Again.

As the shuffle of movement behind Mar makes them flinch, Dami crouches in front of them. Inexplicably, terribly, the demonio is smiling at them.

"Good night," Dami says with a fluttery little wave. "We'll talk soon."

Stars burst across their vision.

A crack of hot pain that steals their breath.

And Mar is falling with only the darkness to catch them.

CHAPTER 31

Mar wakes to a throbbing in their skull so violent, they immediately curse their consciousness. The low rumble of thunder and hiss of rain wash through the darkness. Mar blinks, slowly, wincing as they roll to the side and touch the tender spot on the back of their head. Even just a delicate brush of their fingers against it makes them grit their teeth. They lower their hand and take in the cool, wet darkness.

Cheek against cold concrete. A quiet broken only by a distant storm. The dank smell of mildew. The hollow reality of death creeping toward them. And absolutely no one to share the dread with.

Mar moves slowly, pushing up onto their hands and knees and closing their eyes when the room rocks nauseatingly beneath them. After a few slow, careful breaths they open their eyes again and peer cautiously into the shadows.

The cell is small; just wide enough for Mar to lie across with their arms extended over their head and their legs outstretched. Maybe twice that in length, probably a little less.

A small window near the ceiling too far up for Mar to peer through and barely more than a slit anyway.

But the most unnerving thing isn't the size of the room, the lack of accessible windows, the darkness, the chill, the loneliness, or the smell. No, the most unnerving thing is the four stone walls and windowless stone door.

No iron bars for Mar to melt. No chance to even entertain the idea of escape.

A cold numbness settles over them. They failed. Not only did they not rescue the crew, not only did they not even *see* any revolutionaries to free, but now Bas and Mar will be executed with the rest of the crew.

Because they failed.

Mar slowly lowers themself onto their stomach, then tucks their face into their crossed arms. It doesn't do much for the throbbing in their head, or the disappointing numbness, but at least here on the floor they aren't risking another dizzy spell.

"Oh no," an all-too-familiar voice says. "You aren't *crying*, are you?"

Mar doesn't bother moving. "Would you leave if I were?" they say into their arms.

"I don't do . . . that."

"Leave?"

"Emotions."

Mar snorts. They slowly, carefully, lift their head just enough to peer over their arms. Dami is standing directly beneath the useless window, wrapped in darkness. The sharpness in their gaze has softened somewhat—not that Mar believes for a second that the demonio cares beyond what Mar can do for them.

"Well," Mar says flatly, "you got what you wanted."

Dami arches an eyebrow. "Did I?"

"A captive audience. I agreed to listen. Now's your chance."

"Hmm. Well, that's true." They step into the strip of thin moonlight provided by the window and sit in front of Mar, their black dress settling around them like liquid shadow. Mar didn't notice it earlier, but their nails are a little longer than usual—painted black as expected—and their hair . . .

Mar squints. "Did you shave the side of your head?"

Dami grins. "What do you think? Striking, right?"

"You didn't come here to talk to me about your hair."

"No, but I never pass up a chance to be admired." Mar opens their mouth, but Dami continues before Mar can deflate their ego. "Anyway, you're right about being a captive audience, and I *am* here to relish every second of it, so let's jump right in, shall we?"

Dami looks at them expectantly, but Mar doesn't answer. The demonio keeps staring at them until Mar finally says, "I'm listening."

"You could at least pretend to be enthusiastic."

"That wasn't part of the deal."

Dami sighs and drums the nails of their left hand against the concrete floor. "Fine. Where did we leave off? Oh, right, killing el Diablo."

"Which we agreed was impossible."

"We did no such thing. Impossible for *me*, but not impossible for *you*—"

"Debatable."

"Regardless"—Dami huffs impatiently—"I was about to tell you why this benefits you before you rudely stormed out on me like a jilted lover."

"Like a *what*?"

"This is the part where you can't interrupt me," Dami says firmly. "No speaking until I tell you I've finished. That's the deal."

Mar rests their cheek against their arm. The true genius of Dami insisting they have this conversation *now* is that even if there *were* somewhere for Mar to go, they'd be far too exhausted to leave.

Dami must take their silence for agreement, because, as promised, they jump right in. "El Diablo owns your papá's soul. That was the trade-off of their deal, and why it was such a powerful exchange. Not only did it save your life, but arguably it saved the life of every crew member until it ended the way all his deals do: terribly.

"So—what does this mean? I'm glad you asked. It means if you kill el Diablo, your papá's soul will be freed along with everyone else's that el Diablo has acquired in a deal. I wasn't bullshitting you when I said our interests align—especially since now you only have, what, a day left to save him? The harvest moon is tomorrow night. If you help me, you really can free him. I'm literally handing you the solution to your monthslong question of how to get him back. You're welcome, by the way."

Mar opens their mouth, but no sound comes out—not even a squeak. Their face falls and Dami grins.

"I really do love this," they say. "You not being able to interrupt me. It's nice. We should do this again sometime."

Mar glowers at them and Dami outright beams.

"Okay, okay, I'll stop teasing you. My proposed deal is this: You agree to kill el Diablo *now*—not next year, or in twenty years, or whenever—and I will give you anything in my power to give. I'm done—you can speak now."

"Save the crew and revolutionaries," Mar says quickly. "If you save them all right now, then I'll agree."

Dami cringes. "That's . . . a diablo-sized deal. I'm sorry, I can't affect the course of more than a couple of lives per deal. That requires magia I don't have."

Mar looks away as hopelessness settles in their stomach like an anchor. If they can't save Bas, the crew, and the revolutionaries, then what's the point? They'll still have to live with that failure, with the knowledge that they took an escape and left the rest of them behind.

"Okay," Dami says, "I can see you're giving up on this, so here's what I *can* do. Bas is in the cell next to yours. I can get you both out of here safely, and I can . . ." They pause, frown, then nod. "I can delay the execution. It's not a guarantee that they'll be saved, but it gives you a chance to try again after el Diablo is dead."

"And I want a flat chest." The words tumble out of Mar before they've even processed them. Mar's eyes widen at the same time as Dami's.

"I— Well, okay." A warmth washes over Dami's face that feels unexpectedly genuine. "Body modification is easy."

Dami can do that? Easily? Their heart pounds at the thought; if they never have to bind their chest with tight cloth ever again . . .

Dami smiles. "So you and Bas get out of here safely, the execution gets delayed, and as a bonus you'll have the flat chest of your dreams. Just because I like you. What do you say?"

"You don't like me."

"This is the part where you say yes, Mar."

The quiet settles around them as Mar's mind races with possibilities. They can't see a scenario where they face el Diablo and survive. But they also can't begin to imagine how they'd manage to save themself, and Bas, the crew, *and* the revolutionaries before tomorrow's execution. They can't even get out of this cell on their own—worse, right now they can barely *stand* on their own.

"I need to know something first," they say, meeting Dami's gaze. "And I won't even consider this unless you tell me the truth."

Dami frowns a little but nods. "Then you'll have the truth. What do you need to know?"

"Why do you want this so badly? Why does it mean so much to you?"

"Oh," Dami says, so softly Mar almost doesn't hear them over the distant thunder and rain. "I guess I . . . never really told you that part, did I? Hmm." They lean back on their hands and look away, searching the shadows for something Mar can't begin to guess at.

Dami doesn't look at Mar when they speak again. "Well, I told you diablos get their power from amassing souls. He got mine before I was born. He made a deal with my mother before she knew she was with child. She'd tried to have children for many years, and it had always failed. Doctors had told her it was impossible, so when she made a deal with el Diablo and he asked for her firstborn, she thought she was fooling him when she said yes."

Mar's stomach sinks. All this time they had assumed Dami had made a deal of their own and was suffering the consequences, but they'd never even had the chance to save their own soul.

Dami finally meets Mar's gaze again. "My mother barely had time to hold me. As soon as I was born, he came and took me away.

"When a diablo owns your soul, you become one of their demonios for eternity. You live half a life, unable to connect, to taste, to feel. Even as I got stronger, I could only ever interact with the world at night, and even then not fully. Being a demonio is its own kind of torture, living in the shadows of a world that you can't be a part of, knowing the only thing you can do to grasp at a better chance of a life means making other people just as miserable as you.

"I've spent years earning his trust, helping him grow more powerful, but I've been waiting my whole life for a chance to be free, and you're it, Mar. You're my chance."

Mar bites their lip. Evidently, they badly misjudged Dami. All this time they assumed Dami was as evil and twisted as el Diablo himself, but Dami just wanted what Mar did.

A chance to fully live.

"I don't know anything about el Diablo," Mar says softly. "I wouldn't even know where to start. Or how I'm supposed to even *try* to kill him."

"I can help you with that part. I'm somewhat of an expert on that subject." Dami smirks.

Mar runs their fingers over the markings on the back of their hand. "I really don't think I can kill el Diablo," they whisper.

"Then you'll die trying to save everyone you love," Dami says without missing a beat. "Seems better than doing nothing and getting a personal experience with the gallows, don't you think?"

Dami's right. Mar can't deny it anymore.

A devil's magic may have gotten them into this mess, but a demonio's magic might just get them out of it.

Or, more probably, they'll die trying. But at least they'll have tried.

And so even though they swore they wouldn't, even though they never wanted to make a deal with a diablo, not after what it did to Papá, to *La Catalina,* even though it seems utterly impossible, Mar does what would've been unthinkable just yesterday.

"All right," they say. "You have a deal."

CHAPTER 32

Beneath the tiny window in Mar's cell, the wall collapses like a giant invisible hand scooped it out. The hole is as tall as Mar and as wide as they are tall, and it extends into the cell next to theirs, knocking down a chunk of the dividing wall between them too. It all happens in seconds, and more quietly than Mar would have expected—just the tumble of debris down the cliffside, but even that is muted by the roar of stormy sea and rumble of thunder.

Bas peers around the edge of the broken dividing wall, mouth agape. Mar almost cries with relief to see him alive and not seriously injured.

"Did you . . . ?" He gestures to the gaping hole.

Mar shakes their head and staggers to their feet, cringing as the room rocks around them like a ship on angry waters. "Dami did," they say, pressing their palm into their throbbing temple. "We need to get out of here."

"Preferably quickly," Dami adds, eyeing Mar. "You two

need to climb down and get away from here before the next round of patrols strolls along the beach."

Bas clambers over the rubble and rushes over to Mar, gently touching their shoulder. "Are you all right?"

"Yes," they say at the same time Dami says, "No."

Bas frowns and Dami rolls their eyes. "Mar has a concussion. You can play worried boyfriend later, okay? I'm not kidding about that patrol."

Mar grimaces and nods to the hole in the wall. "They're right. We need to go."

"But what about—"

"Dami's delaying the execution. We're not giving up on them," Mar says, their voice cracking. "Lo prometo. Por favor."

Bas purses his lips but nods. He slides his arm under theirs and behind their back, gripping their side as he helps support them. Together they hobble to the edge of the cell, peering over the end to the rocks and sand below.

It's actually not as big a drop as Mar expected, though they suppose that makes sense given that they assumed they were being held on the sixth, and lowest, level. If they dangle over the edge and let go, it'll probably only be a two- or three-foot drop.

"All right," Bas says. "I'll go first; then I can help you if you need it. How does that sound?"

"I'm so sorry," Mar blurts out.

Bas stares at them. "What could you possibly be sorry for? I don't know if you noticed, but you're helping me escape here."

"I know but, I should've . . ." They aren't even sure how to finish that sentence. Should've what? Tried to take on the entire Spanish army with the crew at gunpoint? Even if the crew *hadn't* been on the firing end of a line of guns, Mar couldn't have taken them all on their own. There were just too many of them. They aren't strong enough.

. . . right?

"Not to ruin the moment," Dami says dryly, "but time is literally ticking away, and I, for one, would like to see you *not* in a heavily guarded fortress. There will be plenty of time for an internal crisis later."

Mar glares at them, but as much as they hate to admit it, the demonio is right. Again. Every second is a moment closer to the Spaniards discovering their escape attempt.

"Here." Bas helps Mar sit at the edge of the cell, their legs dangling over the end. Then he effortlessly climbs over the edge, lowering himself until his arms are fully outstretched and just his fingertips hold on to the concrete. Bas looks up at Mar, squinting through the rain pelting his face, and his mouth moves, but whatever he says is lost in the wind.

Then he lets go and lands in a crouch on the rocks below. He stands, grins, and says something again, but there isn't a chance Mar can catch it. They don't have to, though—Bas extends his arms over his head and gestures Mar forward, which is all the information they need.

Mar turns onto their belly, breathing deeply through their nose as the motion churns their stomach dangerously. They hold on to the edge of the cell and try to grip the outer wall with their boots, but they slide right off the rain-slick stones and yelp as their body weight yanks them down. Their fingers grip the concrete so hard it bites, and their shoulders burn as they come to a jarring halt. Mar's heart thunders in their chest, and the cool rain drenches them instantly, and now they really *do* think they're going to throw up.

"Let go!" Bas's voice just barely carries distantly over the raging storm. "I'll catch you!"

Mar closes their eyes, the tip of their nose pressed against cold wet stone. They take another deep breath. Bend their knees just a bit. And release.

Their boots hit stones hard—the world tilts violently backward—and Bas's arms wrap around them, his chest against their back. Steadying them.

"See?" Bas says, a smile in his voice. "I caught you."

Mar bends over and vomits at their feet. They groan, spit, and wipe their mouth with the wet back of their hand. The pouring rain washes the vomit quickly away, and the world, at least, is a little less tilty.

Bas gently rubs their back as they force themself upright again. "All things considered, I think that went pretty well," he says.

Mar doesn't have it in them to smile.

"It'll be going better when you aren't directly on the patrol path," Dami says. "I've closed up the wall, but the guards aren't far off. You need to move."

Bas side-eyes them. "If you wanted us to move quickly, maybe you should have included magically healing Mar's concussion in whatever deal you made."

Dami opens their mouth, closes it, then says, "Okay. Fair point. I just did a huge deal, though, so if you give me a few minutes—"

"I can walk," Mar says. "At least . . . I can with Bas's help. Dami, you can tell us if any soldiers are getting close, right?"

"Obviously."

"Then let's go."

It's slow going, but the storm helps. The rain comes down so heavily, Mar and Bas can barely see in front of them, which makes trying to move with any direction difficult but also means the Spaniards won't easily spot them. They walk along the shore, from rocks to sand, the crashing waves rushing up to their ankles and washing their footprints away.

With El Morro behind them, they move away from the shore to get back within the city walls. They walk slowly, staying close to the barricade to avoid Calle del Morro, where they'd be easily spotted.

When Mar's limbs feel as heavy as their waterlogged clothes, they reach the edge of the city again. Through a blur of rain and thunder and exhaustion and darkness, they end up on the steps of a small mint-green boardinghouse.

"I can handle this one," Dami says. Black smoke whirls up around them, obscuring them completely, and when it disappears again, a richly dressed man in a black-and-gold pin-striped silk waistcoat beneath a trim black tailcoat, with a curled mustache and tall black top hat, stands in their place.

It's a true testament to their exhaustion that neither Mar nor Bas laughs.

Dami grins at them, smooths down their elegant waistcoat, then enters the boardinghouse.

Mar and Bas huddle against the building on the stoop—not that being against the painted stucco does much to protect them from the downpour that still hasn't let up. Bas's arm is still around their shoulder, and Mar lets themself lean against him. They rest their ear against his shoulder and close their eyes, not moving when their forehead touches the side of his neck. Bas's skin is chilled and slick with rain, but the spot where Mar's forehead meets his neck slowly warms.

"Mar," Bas whispers, so softly they almost miss it.

Mar goes utterly still. Their heart pounds. Is he going to tell them to move? Is this too much? Are they making him uncomfortable? Not trusting themself to speak, they go with a noncommittal "Hm?"

"Can you make it not rain on us?"

Oh. Mar blinks water from their eyes and peers up at Bas. "Don't you think I would have done that earlier if I could?"

A small, sheepish smile curls the corner of Bas's lips. "Well, yes, but you can create and manipulate ice, right? And ice is a form of water, so . . ."

"It doesn't work like that." Mar closes their eyes again. "I can't control water."

"But have you ever *tried?*" Bas presses.

"I'd rather we didn't do this right now. I'm exhausted, and I still feel like my brain is trying to hammer its way out of my skull."

Bas goes quiet. After a moment, he whispers, "Sorry." Then he doesn't speak again, but he also doesn't let go of them.

It's enough.

The door opens and Dami beckons them inside. They lead Mar and Bas up a creaky set of narrow steps. They climb two flights, then turn left into a closet-sized room with one bed.

"This is the only room they had left," Dami says after closing the door behind them. "You have it for the night."

"That's— Thank you." Bas helps Mar onto the bed. "The room is dry and out of sight. That's all we need."

Dami nods. "The sun's coming up soon, so I'm going to go. But I'll be back to talk over the plan."

"Wait," Mar says, cringing at the loudness of their own voice. "Can you . . . fix my head first?"

Dami smiles. "Well, well, well, you make two deals and now you want more, huh?"

Both Mar and Bas skewer them with heated glares.

"Okay, okay." Dami lifts their hands. "But you have to give me something—that's how this works."

"I can give you a soggy boot," Bas says helpfully.

Dami snorts. "Generous, but no. And anyway it has to come from Mar. Another demonio-diablo distinction, I'm afraid."

Mar barely has the energy to keep their eyes open, let alone try to think of a deal they can actually agree to. "What do you want?"

"Hmm . . ." Dami strokes their mustache. Then they break into a wide grin. "Oh! I've got it. Tell me I'm the greatest, most generous, and most attractive demonio to ever exist. Those words exactly."

Bas chokes down a laugh while Mar stares at them. "*That's* what you want?"

"Yes. And before you ask, no, I won't settle for anything else. Agree to the deal and say those words, and you'll be completely healed."

Mar can think of a lot of things they'd like to call Dami in that moment, but on the other hand, they *did* help them escape. And find shelter. Even if it was absolutely just because they want Mar to kill el Diablo.

Bas gently nudges Mar and arches an eyebrow at them. It's obvious that this is an easy deal. Even if it's going to make Dami disproportionately smug.

"Fine," they grumble. "It's a deal."

Mar would've thought it impossible, but somehow Dami's grin widens. "Excellent! Now go ahead."

Mar's eyes narrow. "Hold on, you said you have to do dos besos to make it official."

"I did say that, yes."

Mar and Dami stare at each other. Bas bites their lip, and Mar can't help but think he's trying not to laugh again.

"You made me do it twice," Mar says.

Dami flashes them a smile that would be charming on anyone else. "I did."

"And?"

"And you're a delight to irritate," Dami says. "Now go ahead. Tell me how incredible I am."

If they had the energy, and their skull didn't feel like it was lined with red-hot iron, Mar would scream. They might even throw a fireball at them—futilely, of course, but it would feel good.

Instead, they bury those feelings and grind out, "Dami is the greatest, most generous demonio to ever exist."

"Hmm. Pretty sure you're missing an important adjective in there. Why don't you try again?"

Bas presses his fist against his mouth. Mar isn't sure if it's possible to actually begin smoking from rage, but they suspect if they weren't concussed and they hadn't just used magia earlier, they would be in danger of accidentally setting the bed on fire.

"Dami is the greatest, most generous, and"—Mar reminds themself to breathe as they force the words out—*"most attractive* demonio to ever exist."

They've barely finished the sentence when their headache disappears midthrob. They blink and gingerly touch the back of their head; their hair is still soaked, but it doesn't hurt to touch. Just like that.

Huh.

"Bueno, señores, it's been a delight." Dami stands, utterly beaming. "Mar, thank you for those kind words. I'll treasure them always." Dami winks at them, and Mar rolls their eyes.

The demonio turns to the door, then pauses and glances back. "Oh, and Mar . . ." This time, Dami's face has softened again, and when they smile, there's nothing smug about it. "You won't need your wrap anymore. Just saying."

When the black smoke takes them, an echo of their laughter lingers in the room.

CHAPTER 33

Mar is too afraid to hope.

When Bas asked them what Dami had meant about the wrap, they shrugged and said they weren't sure, even as their pulse pounded in their ears. Now he's gone down the hall to relieve himself and Mar has their chance.

Their hands shake as they lift their soaked shirt off and unravel the cold, dripping fabric around their arms. It plops with a wet splat on the floor as Mar then grabs the end of the drenched cloth wrap around their chest and unpins it.

Mar closes their eyes, takes a shaky breath, then unravels it. Only when the cloth falls to their feet do they open their eyes. With one more trembling breath, they look at their chest.

Tears blur their vision and they blink hard to clear it. They run their hand down the smooth, flat expanse of their chest, grinning as nothing obstructs the path of their palm running down and up and down and up again. Unmarred brown skin, small nipples—their chest looks exactly like it did before Mar's body began to change in ways they never wanted.

It's perfect.

Even as they grin down at their own skin, their face is wet with tears. They've never imagined they could get this again, never thought for even a moment it would be possible. But it's here like a dream Mar never wants to wake from.

They take a long, deep breath and laugh at the lightness of their ribs. There's no tight cloth constricting the movement of Mar's chest, and there never will be again.

"Gracias, Dami," they whisper, wiping their wet eyes.

The door opens and Mar jumps, covering their chest for a second before forcing their hands back to their sides. Bas waltzes into the room and stops short when he sees Mar. His face pinks, just a little, and he clears his throat.

"Getting comfortable, I see."

Mar shrugs and smiles. They still want to cover their chest out of instinct—protect what once would have made people think Mar was something they aren't—but they don't have to anymore. They keep their hands at their sides and show their chest proudly. They can be as loose and free with it as they want.

That thought alone is intoxicating.

Bas turns to close the door behind him and Mar kicks the wet binding cloth beneath the bed. When Bas turns around again, he smiles just slightly at Mar, tilting his head. "You seem uncharacteristically upbeat given the circumstances."

Mar scrambles for an explanation that doesn't sound utterly ridiculous and goes with the first thing they can slap together. "I'm just . . . happy we're alive."

"Right." Bas peels his soaked shirt off, and Mar's eyes widen. His light brown skin looks pearl smooth save for a dusting of hair below his navel; Mar has the sudden mortifying urge to run their hands down his chest, too. "And how is that again?"

Mar's gaze snaps to his face. "What?"

Bas smirks, and Mar's face warms. He's absolutely caught them gawking at his unfairly beautiful torso.

"How did we get out of there alive?" Bas looks at them pointedly, his tone a little sharp. Irritated.

"Oh." All at once the heat in their face drains away. They promised to explain to Bas, and of course they would have to whether they'd promised it or not; but thinking on the deal they've made with Dami that the demonio will absolutely cash in on . . . well. They can't think of much else they'd want to think about less.

The way Bas is eyeing them, though, Mar suspects he may have already figured it out.

Mar sighs and sits on the edge of the bed, running their hands over the itchy blanket draped beneath them. "Well. Dami is a demonio."

"Yes, we established that much." Bas crosses his arms across his chest. "But you *said* you didn't know how to find el Diablo."

"I don't. Dami isn't el Diablo. Or a diablo at all." Bas rolls his eyes, but Mar presses forward. "*And* when we last talked about it, I was adamant about not making any demonio deals either. I thought— It's how I lost my familia and nearly died, Bas. I never wanted to go that far."

"And now?"

Mar bites their lip. "I haven't changed my mind. I still think it's a terrible idea that's likely to backfire, but . . . if I didn't accept their deal, we'd still be in prison. And tonight probably would be our last night alive."

Bas shakes his head and sits next to Mar. "You still could have told me you were speaking to a demonio days ago."

"I wasn't *speaking* to Dami—they just wouldn't leave me alone."

"That doesn't change that you could have told me. You said you didn't know how to find el Diablo, but you had a demonio visiting you!"

Mar jumps to their feet, turning on Bas with a scowl. "I was trying to protect you! I *told* you how that diablo deal destroyed my life. I wasn't about to let you run off and destroy yours."

"And what do you think losing my familia will do to me?"

"I'm trying to help you save them, aren't I?"

"Nevertheless, you could have told me about Dami—it might have given us more options."

"I could have, but I didn't." Mar shoves their hands in their pockets. "And I don't regret it. Dami's the reason the crew is in danger to begin with."

Bas presses his face into his hands and sighs heavily. They stew in silence for a moment before, finally, Bas glances up at them. He looks exhausted. "So what was the deal that you agreed to?"

Mar grimaces and relaxes their stance. Thinking about it is unpleasant enough, but saying it aloud? It makes it all the more real. They run their hand down their flat chest as they worry their lip.

Their chest is proof enough that this deal is absolutely real.

But finally, reluctantly, Mar says it aloud. They tell him everything. Well, everything except the part about their chest, because he doesn't need to know that. When they're done, Bas leans back on his arms and whistles.

"So you can't find el Diablo, but now you're going to kill him."

Mar groans. "You're really not going to let that go, are you?"

"Nope." Bas glances at them. "But how *are* you going to do it?"

They shake their head. "I have no idea. Dami said they'd help with that part, but I'm not who Dami thinks I am. I'm not strong enough to kill him."

"I bet you're stronger than you think. You limit yourself."

"Knowing what I can and can't do isn't limiting myself."

"It is when you refuse to use your magia unless you're absolutely desperate."

Mar scowls. "You don't understand."

"No, I don't." Bas stands and paces across the room. "If I could do what you can do, I wouldn't hide it away. I'd use it to help people, and to make my life easier—but you insist on only ever letting it make your life more difficult than it needs to be."

"I don't *let* it do anything," Mar snaps. "You have no idea what it's like to have to constantly fight yourself so you don't become a target. I *wish* I could use my magia freely, but I can't, because people would try to kill me and my familia if they knew what I could do, *and* because this magia is dangerous! When I make a mistake with it, innocent people die!" The room blurs alarmingly quickly, and before Mar can stop them, hot tears spill down their cheeks. "I'm a *monster,* Bas. I'm no better than Dami or el Diablo—this magia is *poison.*"

Bas has frozen across the room, mouth slightly open. He reaches for Mar, but they duck out of the way. "Don't."

Bas crosses the distance between them anyway, but this time he doesn't reach for their shoulders. Instead, he gently touches their hands, searching their face. When Mar doesn't pull away, he slips their hands into his. "Mar," he says, so, so gently. "I've met a lot of monsters in my life, but I promise, you aren't one of them. You're the most incredible person I've ever met, and you're devastatingly beautiful."

If there was any chance of controlling the tears before, it's gone now, and Mar doesn't even bother trying. A sob bursts out of them—they pull their hands away from Bas and wrap their arms around their middle, squeezing tight.

"I—I'm not," they insist. "You've *seen* me use my magia—"

"Yes. And you're breathtaking."

Those are the words that break Mar. They're out the door and down the stairs, with Bas calling their name after them. Mar runs, their mind a hurricane no shelter can weather.

CHAPTER 34

By the time the tears have slowed and Mar can breathe without gasping through sobs, they have no idea where they've whirled to. Bas didn't try to follow them, which for some reason hurts almost as much as their conversation did.

They lean against the side of a bright blue building, peering up at the looming city walls, as slowly, finally, their breaths slow. Then they realize three things:

1. They stormed out without their shirt or arm wraps, which means they've been wandering San Juan covered in tattoos—not exactly subtle about their status as a pirate.
2. It's stopped raining.
3. Improbably, the air smells like smoke.

The night sky is shifting to a dusky gray with the soon-to-be-rising sun. Mar sniffs again—definitely smoke—and ... is that yelling?

They move toward the sound, down long, quiet blue-cobblestone streets, as the smell of smoke becomes unmistakable and the yells grow louder. Then Mar spots it: a hellish glow at the end of a row of homes. The fire is out of control, flames licking the air and spreading from one home to the next as people back away in horror.

Mar moves forward automatically, the hum of magia awakening in their bones. The heat is palpable against their face; if the sun breathed, it would feel like this. Three connected homes are already engulfed, and men are desperately throwing sand and water at the edges nearest the closest unburned building. Though dozens of people have come out to try to help their neighbors, the fire is too large, too powerful. Those flames won't stop until they've eaten the entire row of eight connected homes.

A soot-covered woman to Mar's right is absolutely distraught, sobbing and reaching for the middle building as two men hold her back, one of them crying. She's coughing so hard, she's near impossible to understand, but then Mar catches two words: *¡Mi bebé!*

Mar goes rigid and steps in front of her. "Where?"

"Upstairs!" She points at a flame-engulfed window.

You can do this, hije. The memory of Leo's voice comes to life so quickly, so strongly, that tears prick their eyes again. For just a second he's holding their shoulders again, like he did the last time Mar saw him. For just a second his warm brown eyes are peering into theirs, afraid and sad, but undeniably proud.

¡Vaya!

And then Mar is running. Toward the crackling flames, pushing past people and into the building, ignoring the panicked shouts of strangers after them.

If it was hot outside, inside is a furnace. The heat is so thick, so overwhelming, it feels like the air itself is cooking their lungs. But the flames won't hurt them. Fire has always been a friend to Mar, and when they extend their arms, the flames leap onto their bare chest, welcoming them in.

They take the stairs two at a time, even as their reach expands, even as the fire on the banister, the floors, the ceilings, the buildings next to them, fills their consciousness. Mar is the fire eating the curtains and rugs and clothes and blankets; Mar is the flame laughing at the futile attempts to smother them with buckets of water and sand. They see every crevice of each burning building—and it's how they instantly know where to find the screaming toddler.

Mar exhales, clearing the flames from their skin. They cradle the baby to their chest, wishing they had a wet cloth to drape over them to block out some of the smoke. They grab a small, mostly unburned blanket crumpled at the edge of the child's bed and throw it over the baby's head. Mar can't create water, but they hold the edge of the cloth and try to quiet the raging heat inside them.

The problem is Mar has never been good at balancing both sides of their magia at the same time. It was always too risky to call on both—they were asking for trouble trying to loosen their control without losing it entirely. But as Mar holds their control over the flames close, they run their thumb over the warm fibers of the blanket and breathe in deep, calling winter to the smoky air in their lungs, their throat, their mouth.

The cold rushes through them so quickly, Mar yanks it back before they turn the whole blanket to ice. But when they breathe out, a frost races over the cloth—then instantly melts in the heat. Mar keeps their hand on the cloth, holding it to the baby's head, breathing steadily to keep it cold as they let their magia trickle out.

A crack like a thunderclap nearly breaks their concentration. A supporting beam crashes from the ceiling through the floor on the far end of the room. Mar's heart gallops in their chest.

The fire may not kill them, but the collapsing building certainly will.

They move quickly, whipping out of the room and down the stairs, pulling on the far edges of the flames to slow the spread. But as they do, the blanket warms beneath them. Mar swears under their breath and forces a chill through the water again, but with both edges of their magia pulling them in opposite directions, they can't fully grasp either one.

Mar barely registers running out of the building, so focused are they on chilling the blanket and holding the child and pushing the flames back. But it's impossible to miss the people rushing toward them, the mother shoving people aside and throwing her arms out to hold the crying baby.

It's not a simple thing telling their body what to do while trying to hold so much magia at once. Mar's fingers are numb when they push the blanket off the child's head and hand the baby to the mother. She's speaking through her tears, caressing the baby's dark hair and looking at them, but it's all so far away. Their work isn't done. The fire knows it doesn't have Mar's full attention, and it's starting to catch on the fourth home.

They turn back to the inferno and close their eyes.

In their mind's eye, all they see is flame. They breathe in deep, locking the ice away to grasp the flames with everything they have.

The last time they handled a fire this big, *La Catalina* was minutes away from sinking. The flame is familiar in a way that hurts; once a friend, perhaps, but one that has betrayed them in the most unforgivable way.

And yet, as they pull the flames toward them, they can't help but feel so, so alive.

The first time Mar fills their lungs with smoke-choked air, the fire shrinks away from the edges, touching only what has already kissed flame.

The second time, it races back to the center building where the first spark began.

The third time, fire explodes from every window of the center home and pours into Mar so quickly, they stagger back. Vibrating with an inferno they have nowhere safe to place. Their markings glowing so brightly, it hurts their eyes in the night. Fire rages inside them, demanding release. Mar can barely breathe. Everything is heat like they've never felt. It's too much. It's too much. It's too—

"Your magia is a gift, tesoro."

Mar is nine years old. They've just accidentally burned Papá's arm after trying to hold their magia in for too long. It's the first and only time Mar has ever seen Papá injured. He should be angry, he should tell Mar their magia is dangerous, he should wish his child was never cursed with such a terrible burden.

He should wish for a child who isn't a monster.

Instead, Mar is crying on their knees and repeating, "Lo siento," over and over and over as Leo fills a tub with water for Papá's arm. Instead, Papá is smiling softly at them and caressing their cheek with his free hand.

Instead, he says, "Your magia is a gift, tesoro. Don't be afraid of who you are—you're beautiful."

"But I hurt you!" Mar cries.

"We all hurt each other, hije. We don't mean to, but we're human." The corners of his eyes crinkle. "This isn't the last time you'll hurt someone you love. And when that happens, you do what you can to make it better." Then he grins and gestures to the tub. "Now, come here and cool this water for me, hm?"

Mar steps toward the tub, shaking at the thought of calling on their magia again. "I can't," they say. "I can't use my magia. I can't control it. I can't—"

"You can," Papá and Leo say together.

Leo rubs Mar's back in comforting circles. "You can do anything."

Papá reaches for their chin and looks them dead in the eye. "Mije, you're a miracle."

Mar stops fighting.

Something clicks into place—the release of a deep sigh, an unraveling of tightly knotted rope. A rush of cold meets the heat at a breaking point inside them; like smoke, it dissipates. The pounding of their panicked pulse in their ears quiets and slows. All at once they can breathe again.

When they open their eyes, the markings on their arms and chest are glowing both orange and blue, weaving around each other like ribbons. It's never been like this before. It was always one or the other; balancing the two was too much, but they're here. Their skin buzzes pleasantly with magia, and it's . . . calm. Not demanding attention. Not threatening to spill over at a moment's notice. They can't remember the last time they've been this relaxed.

Until they look up at the crowd of gaping, wide-eyed people and remember where they are. Their heart drums faster again, louder in their ears, and they take half a step back, but all that's behind them is the burned husk of a building. There's no getting out of here unless they get through this crowd of people who could easily overpower them if they don't use their magia.

Mar really doesn't want to hurt anyone.

"I—I'm sorry," they stammer. "I'm just going to leave." *Please, let me leave.*

The child's mother steps forward. Tears have cleared trails on her soot-dusted face, and her voice is hoarse when she speaks, but it rings out clear. "¡Ángel! Thank you. You saved my baby. Thank you."

She thanks them over and over again, and Mar can't move. ¿Ángel?

The crowd murmurs, and Mar hears it again. *Ángel.*

Dios oyó nuestros rezos.

Milagro.

It feels like an impossible dream. The people aren't afraid of them; they're *thanking* them. Now with a street full of people who have come out of their homes, there must be close to three dozen people here. And all of them are watching Mar with a sort of wondering awe.

It's never been like this before.

Mar steps forward and no one stops them. The people all move out of the way, clearing a path for them. Walking by the people as they thank Mar, and nod respectfully, and send them blessings with tear-filled eyes. It all feels like an out-of-body experience. Mar can barely feel their feet, and soon they're running.

Their markings are extinguished like a snuffed candle flame. Mar blends into the night, and runs, and breathes, their very bones vibrating with power. They don't stop until they reach the shore, where they rip off their boots and walk ankle-deep into the ocean.

Papá was right. And Leo. And Bas, and yes, even Dami.

With the sun peeking over the horizon, painting the endless waves with the first dusting of light, Mar breathes in the salt-tinted air and laughs. Tears spill down their face as they tilt their head back and let the cool ocean breeze caress their face.

Mar's magia isn't a curse. It doesn't *just* bring death and pain and destruction.

They can do good with it, too. Bring hope to dark places. Save the unsavable.

For the first time that they can remember, Mar isn't afraid of what their magia can do.

"*Now* you get it," someone says beside them, and Mar doesn't have to open their eyes to recognize Dami's voice.

A smile curls Mar's lips as they look up at the burgeoning dawn. Finally, finally, they understand.

Now Mar knows exactly what they have to do.

CHAPTER 35

The door to Mar and Bas's room is locked, which of course makes sense, but Mar was certainly not thinking about that when they stormed out earlier. They stand just outside the door, debating whether to sit against the wall and try to get some rest that way, or to knock so Bas will let them in. But it's absurdly early—the sun has just started to rise—and they don't really want to wake him.

At least one of them should get some rest.

Mar sighs and moves toward the wall; the floor creaks so loudly they jump. "Shh!" they hiss at the floor, as if it has the faculties to listen.

The door whips open and Bas stands there, puffy eyes wide. His face is splotchy like . . .

Oh no. Has he been crying?

Dread curls in their gut like a viper about to strike. "What's wrong? Did they—? They didn't move the execution forward, did they? Dami said they could handle delaying it and—"

Bas throws his arms around them, pulling them into a

tight hug. He presses his face against their shoulder and takes a long, deep breath, holding them like they might slip away at a moment's notice. Mar gently returns the embrace, confused. He doesn't seem to be crying anymore. . . .

"Bas," Mar says quietly, "is the crew still alive?"

Bas doesn't move, but he croaks out, "Yes. It's not about the crew." He takes a deep, shuddering breath, then straightens, looking them in the face. He's so close, their noses are almost touching; his breath is warm on Mar's lips. "I went out looking for you," he says. "I couldn't find you, and I thought— You didn't have a shirt, and with your tattoos, I just kept thinking if the Spaniards spotted you, it would've been my fault for upsetting you and not going after you sooner and—"

"Bas, that . . . No." Mar shakes their head. "I'm fine, but if I hadn't been, that would've been my fault for my own carelessness, not yours."

"I shouldn't have pushed you earlier. I crossed a line, and I'm—I'm sorry."

Mar hugs him tight, settling in the warmth of his arms, in the incredible feeling of their flat chest against his. Just the reminder of the rightness of their new chest puts a giddy smile on their lips, but they quickly force it down. Now isn't the time. Even if Mar isn't done showing their chest off to the world.

"You did nothing wrong," they say into his ear. "I just needed some time to think. I'm sorry I worried you, but I promise I'm all right."

When they pull back, Bas's eyes are glistening with tears.

"I was so scared," he whispers. "I thought I'd never see you again."

"I'm not going to abandon you. I'm here." They offer a weak smile. "Something happened while I was out. And I think you'll want to hear about it."

Bas wipes his face, nods, and steps aside so Mar can enter.

Mar isn't surprised to find Dami lounging on the only bed, arms crossed behind their head, legs so long their boots hang off the end of the bed. They've changed since Mar last saw them; gone are the dress and heels and softer facial features. Dami's jaw has sharpened and squared, their shoulders broadened and arms and neck thickened.

Of course they're still dressed in their customary all-black, down to their dangling black crucifix earrings, black nails, and thickly kohl-lined eyes.

Bas stares at Dami. "What . . . When did you . . . ?"

"Oh good, you're finally done." They sit up and swing their legs around the side of the bed. "Now. Who's ready to talk about killing el Diablo?"

As it turns out, only Dami is ready to talk about killing el Diablo, since Mar first wants to recount to Bas what had happened. Dami makes sure to look utterly bored out of their mind the entire time, tapping their black-lacquered nails on their knee and even at one point hanging their head up-side down off the edge of the bed with their legs up against the wall.

But to their credit, Dami doesn't interrupt. And when Mar finishes, Bas is beaming, and Mar can't help but smile a little themself.

"You're amazing," Bas says.

Mar's face warms. They clear their throat and look at Dami, still watching them, dead-eyed, from the bed. "So, I think I'm ready to—"

"Finally," Dami says. They disappear in a plume of black smoke and reappear next to Mar, so close that the smoke makes Mar cough as they sidestep away and stand near Bas at the foot of the bed. "You'll be glad to know the execution's been pushed to tonight. It's the best I could do, but it buys us an extra twelve hours."

So it all falls to today, then. Either Mar kills el Diablo and frees Papá before the harvest moon along with *La Ana*'s crew, or all of them die. Mar turns the bullet in their pocket, breathing deeply through the panicked heat wrapping like a fist around their heart.

Less than eighteen hours until they save everyone or lose everything. For good, this time.

Bas nods, evidently oblivious to Mar's distress. "We can work with that. How did you do it?"

Dami waves him off. "More importantly, this evening el Diablo will be going to his favorite taberna right here in

San Juan just after sunset. It'll be the perfect place for Mar to confront him."

Mar's fingers stumble with the bullet in their pocket. They arch an eyebrow. "You want me to kill el Diablo in a bar fight?"

Dami wrinkles their nose. "That wouldn't be my first choice. Honestly, I don't particularly care *how* you kill him as long as you do."

"What *would* be your first choice?" Bas presses.

"Excuse me." Dami's eyes narrow at them both. "I'm not here to drop a fully formed, flawless plan in your lap. My job was to do what you *couldn't* do, which was make him accessible and buy your friends more time. I've done my end here. The rest is on you."

"Helpful," Bas says flatly.

"I'm sorry—would you like me to reschedule the execution back to eight a.m.? Because if I'm not being *helpful* enough for you, maybe you'd like to try it all on your own."

Bas's eyes widen, but it's Mar who speaks. "You've been plenty helpful, Dami, thank you."

"Sorry? What was that? I must not have heard right, because for a second there I thought you were actually being reasonable."

Mar rolls their eyes and looks at Bas. "So el Diablo will be at a bar. I can't just go in there blazing with magia. He'll see me coming a mile away, and innocent people will get hurt."

"To be clear," Dami says, "innocent people are probably going to get hurt either way, but you're right—that would be a terrible plan."

"Isn't he going to notice you the moment you walk in?" Bas asks. "He's met you before, right?"

"Twice." Mar reaches into their pocket and rolls the crushed bullet in their fingers. "But what if . . . he's paying attention to something else?"

Dami taps their chin and nods slowly. "A distraction could be effective, but it'd have to be something good. Something that'd get his full focus."

"How about a deal?" Bas asks.

"No," Mar says at the same time as Dami says, "That could work."

Mar turns on Bas. "You are *not* making a deal with el Diablo. It's not worth it. Bas, you *know* what happened to my familia."

"I know. I'm not talking about actually going *through* with the deal, but it's not like it's instant, right?" Bas looks at Dami. "There's a conversation first. Negotiation?"

Dami nods. "There's a negotiation, and the whole time, he's going to be focused on your emotions. Digging into your past, pulling on the things you want most. It takes concentration to do that while also working out the best terms for yourself."

Mar stares at Dami. "You use magia to manipulate people into making deals?"

"I wouldn't call it *manipulation*. More like . . . reconnaissance. In the moment. While being charming and persuasive. Anyway, you didn't really think we went into these things empty-handed, did you?"

Mar scowls, but when Dami puts it that way . . . it's not remotely surprising, no. Of course they'd use magia to get the upper hand. Why wouldn't they?

"All right," Mar says. "Fine. So would that be distracting enough?"

"As long as you don't enter until after the deal has started, it should be," Dami says. "But it'd have to be a deal worth his time. And he's only ever interested in souls these days."

Bas grimaces and glances nervously at Mar. "I won't go through with the deal. I promise."

Dami lifts a finger. "Just one problem with that. While I don't recommend making a deal with him, you can't go in planning not to agree to a deal. He'll know, and, quite frankly, Bas, your soul isn't going to be worth fighting over to him."

"Gee," he says. "Thanks."

Dami shrugs. "Just being honest. If there are holes in this plan, el Diablo will find them."

"This isn't going to work, then. Bas can't *actually* agree to give el Diablo his soul."

"Does it really matter if I do, though?"

Mar's mouth drops open, and Bas lifts his hands defensively. "Just listen for a minute. I obviously don't want him to have my soul, but if you kill him, our deal will be broken, right? So as long as you don't lose, it won't matter."

Mar's eyes narrow. "Because what I really need is yet *another* life hanging in the balance."

"Don't be so dramatic. I know you're going to win."

Mar shakes their head and looks away. "Well, I don't."

"Then you'll just have to interrupt them before they can complete the deal." Dami shrugs. "As long as Bas *intends* to make a deal, it doesn't really matter whether or not they make it to the end."

"Great," Bas says. "So how do I do this? I can't just walk up to him and ask to make a deal. I'm not supposed to know who he is, right?"

"Absolutely not—that would be very suspicious. But actually, this part should be pretty easy." Dami stretches their long arms over their head. "Diablos and demonios are drawn to the desperate and downtrodden. They're the easiest marks because they want something they no longer believe they can get on their own, and we can leverage their desperation against them to get the most favorable terms."

Mar glowers at them as Bas grimaces.

Dami rolls their eyes. "Don't look at me like that—you do the same kind of mental calculation every time you decide whether to attack a ship."

"Except our marks aren't the *desperate and downtrodden*," Mar says flatly.

Dami shrugs. "There isn't room for morality if you want to survive as a demonio. Now, if you're done being judgmental, I can tell you why this is going to work in your favor."

"Because I'm desperate to save my familia," Bas says. "So el Diablo will pick up on that."

Dami grins. "*Exactly.* As long as you're in that taberna thinking about the crew's upcoming execution and how badly you want to save them, you'll be irresistible."

Bas stares at them. "You do realize how wrong that is, right?"

"Oh, sorry, are we *not* done moralizing? Because I'm literally giving you all the information you need to trick one of the most powerful supernatural entities in existence, and all I seem to be getting from you two is how disgusting you think I am."

Mar sighs. "You're not . . . disgusting."

"Thrilling endorsement. I'm touched, really."

"I just can't help but think it's exactly this kind of predatory behavior that got my papá killed."

"And now it's my magnanimous behavior that's going to help you save him. Can we move on?"

Mar frowns but nods.

Dami looks at Bas. "So you'll go in first, before el Diablo is there. All you need to do is sit at the bar, order a drink, and think about how miserable you are."

"Great job," Bas says. "Can't wait."

"Perfect. Then el Diablo will enter; he'll see you brooding, sit next to you, and strike up a conversation. While you two are talking"—they turn to Mar—"*you* will enter and keep somewhere behind them, out of el Diablo's line of sight. You attack, Bas gets out of the way, you two have your little skirmish, and we all live happily ever after."

Mar's frown deepens. "What about the people?"

Dami blinks. "What people?"

"In the bar? It's not going to be empty. I don't want to hurt anyone."

"Of course you don't," Dami says flatly.

"I can get them out," Bas says. "Once you attack, I'll help get people out. I'm sure most of them will bolt for the door anyway."

Mar nods. "Good. How about the Spanish soldiers who are inevitably going to show up when the fighting begins?"

Dami laughs. When no one laughs with them, they clear their throat. "Oh, you were serious. You're not— You can't possibly be worried about hurting a Spaniard. Chances are they'll have been one of the ones who held your crew at gunpoint last night."

"I'm thinking about the opposite problem. I can't fight the Spaniards and el Diablo at the same time."

"I'm not convinced you can't, but even so, it won't be the whole army there."

"And I can help," Bas says. "You can focus on el Diablo. I'll keep them distracted."

"Bas—"

"I'm not asking for permission."

Mar wants to argue with him, but the truth is they can use all the help they can get. And it's not like they could really expect Bas to sit on the sidelines anyway.

He's a pirate. He can take care of himself.

"Fine," Mar says, as if they have a say in the matter at all. They turn to Dami. "And what will you be doing?"

"Staying out of the way." Dami shrugs. "I physically can't fight him—it's literally impossible for me to hurt the entity that holds my soul."

Mar shakes their head. "Better idea: You find my papá. If I do manage to kill el Diablo, I want to know he'll be safe. And if I don't . . ." They frown. "Well. I'll want him to know I tried."

"Melodramatic, but I can manage that."

"I believe in you." Bas throws their arm over Mar's shoulders. "If anyone can kill el Diablo, it's you."

"That's what I've been saying all along," Dami chimes in. "You're the only one I've ever met who's survived an encounter with el Diablo meant to kill them, Mar. That has to mean something."

Mar tries to smile. They can't help but think that the other side of that *if* may be true too: that it doesn't mean anything—they just got lucky; that they can't kill el Diablo, and neither can anyone else. Still, if this is Papá's only chance, then they have to try.

They glance at Dami. "Do you at least know how I can kill him? Or hurt him even? You know him better than anyone here—does he even have a weakness?"

Dami bites their lip. "I mean, he can only be killed with magia, but I'm sure you figured that out the night he took your papá."

Mar hadn't, admittedly, directly put that together, but they suppose in hindsight that what happened after Papá shot el Diablo made it pretty obvious he couldn't be killed by any worldly means.

"He forgets none of us are completely indestructible. He's

full of himself and underestimates everyone around him," Dami continues. "And he also has a *terrible* temper—he doesn't think clearly or act rationally when he's angry. You could use that to your advantage."

Mar frowns. That wasn't exactly the secret to killing el Diablo that they were hoping for, but they suppose if Dami knew exactly how to kill el Diablo, they probably would've told Mar already.

Mar looks at Bas, trying to ignore the warmth of his body pressed so close against theirs. "After it's over, we'll free the crew. I haven't forgotten about them, I promise."

"I know," Bas says, and somehow, impossibly, he's smiling. "I trust you."

Mar can't meet his smile. They wish it was as simple as trust.

Since neither Mar nor Bas has slept much and Mar is supposed to have the most difficult and dangerous fight of their life this evening, Mar suggests they try to get some rest. Dami promises to wake them up—not that Mar expects either of them to sleep the ten or so hours before sunset.

So Bas clambers onto the bed, turns on his side, then pats the empty space next to him. "I don't mind if you don't mind."

Mar has never minded anything less.

With their eyes closed, the comfort of Bas at their back,

his arm wrapped around their chest is hypnotic. They feel safe and calm in his arms, which is a miracle of its own given what awaits them just a handful of hours away.

But for the moment, they can push that aside. They can drift away in his embrace, pillow and surprisingly soft mattress below them, and the comforting heat of the boy who's starting to feel like home at their back. Mar has never had more pleasant sleeping quarters.

It feels as though they've just closed their eyes when Dami is at their ear, telling them to wake up, with the gentleness of a bullhorn.

"Up, up, up!" they're saying. "I may not be able to touch you during the day, but you better bet I can annoy you out of the most peaceful of dreams."

Bas groans, but at Dami's voice, Mar is awake. Their stomach gives a lurch as they remember what they're about to do.

"What time is it?"

"Noon." Dami may not be able to touch them, but their face is awfully close to Mar's in a way that, yes, could certainly be described as annoying. "There's about six and a half hours before he typically shows, so we should make sure you've both eaten before we get Bas in place early."

"All right. We'll be right down."

Dami arches a skeptical eyebrow.

"I promise. You can come back to annoy us if we aren't ready in ten minutes."

"Fine."

Smoke explodes where Dami was standing, and Mar coughs, their eyes watering at the smell. They sigh and nudge Bas at their back. "We should go."

Bas presses his face against Mar's back. "Ten more minutes," he mumbles.

Mar smiles softly. "No, we have to be downstairs in ten minutes. Time to get up."

Bas makes a pained noise, but to his credit he releases Mar so they can sit up. They reluctantly roll out of bed and grab their shirt, which they've hung on the door to dry. It's still slightly damp, so they hold it out, gripping the edges. A wave of heat races through them and into the fabric; steam puffs out of the shirt. Mar smiles and shakes out their now-dry top.

Bas hoists himself out of bed, rubs his eyes, and stretches his arms above his head. His shirt pulls up, and the sliver of his stomach just above his waistline peeks through.

Mar forces themself to look away and clears their throat. "So, Bas. If I don't win this fight—"

"You will."

"I just want to say—"

Bas gently presses his finger against Mar's lips. "I want you to tell me after you win. Please."

Mar frowns, their heart thrumming in their throat. But

there's something pained and desperate in Bas's eyes, and they can't bear to push it any further.

"All right," they whisper.

Bas nods, but his touch lingers on their mouth. His gaze searches theirs, and all at once their pulse is racing for a completely different reason. "I meant what I said, you know," he says softly.

Mar gulps. "About what?"

"You really are the most beautiful boy I've ever met." And with those words and a flash of a grin, Bas lowers his hand and waltzes out of the room, leaving Mar with a warm feeling in the center of their chest and a ghost of a smile.

CHAPTER 36

Waiting is the worst part.

Mar hates that they can't be in the taberna with Bas, hates that they have to just trust that he'll be fine on his own with el Diablo for some time. So they distract themself with the only thing that seems even remotely productive: their magia.

Calling on their magia after years of burying it is . . . freeing. And a little terrifying; the part of their brain used to fighting it sends little jolts to their chest as they breathe deep and let go. First the heat, roaring alive and overeager as it always is, racing across their markings and setting them ablaze. Then the breath of winter, settling over them like an incoming chill, weaving blue alongside the orange.

It's easier to hold both streams of magia now that they've figured out how. With their usual viselike grip released and energy humming in their bones, it all feels so familiar. Now that they aren't fighting it, it's so obvious that this power has been a part of them all along. They know how to use it like they know how to breathe. It's innate. Instinctual.

Sparks of magia dance on their fingertips and race over their arms. The light beneath their shirt looks like colored stars shoved into their chest. For the first time, they see it: Magia, in its own way, is beautiful.

With their magia they can save lives. Or destroy diablos. They're ready.

So when Dami's voice breaks the quiet out of nowhere to tell them it's time, they're out the door, markings extinguished, before the demonio can finish their sentence.

They don't slow until they're feet away from the steps of the beachside taberna, just outside the splash of lantern light. There, they finally pause to take a slow, steadying breath. They have to be discreet. And that isn't going to happen if they burst in there panting for air.

Mar looks at the coral building again and blinks. They've been here before; la Taberna Reyes, where the generous bartender gave them food for free. They hope that bartender isn't here tonight. The man was kind, and they really don't want him to get hurt. Just the thought of it sends a full-body shiver through them as their stomach twists nauseatingly. What if they hurt innocent people with their magia again?

They turn to the ocean for a minute, and their breath catches in their chest. The full moon is visible just above the horizon. It is huge and so bright; the night is washed in a silvery glow.

The time has come. And like it or not, they know what they have to do.

They just wish they knew how to do it.

Mar's heart doesn't quite slow, and their palms are clammy as they roll the bullet between their fingers in their pocket. When they can breathe quietly again, they steel their nerves and push open the door.

Though the moon is abnormally bright and there are several open windows to let in the silvery glow, la Taberna Reyes is still relatively dim. Mar pauses for a moment as their eyes adjust, slowly making out the layout of the room.

It's a relatively small room, though the counter extends across its width. Bas is seated on the far right, and a broad-shouldered man in a wine-red shirt beneath a black waistcoat trimmed in gold, black trousers, and a black top hat embroidered in gold sits beside him. Bas is hunched over his drink, but his face is tilted to the man, and he seems to be listening to him.

So, this is el Diablo.

The warning prickle of Mar's magia nips lightly at the base of their skull. A sign of potential danger, which makes sense given their proximity to who they're relatively sure is el Diablo. But the threat could just as easily be a Spanish soldier passing by outside.

Mar forces their gaze away before they draw his attention. The taberna, unfortunately, is full of people; Mar counts fewer than eight open seats scattered around the room, none of which are especially near the bar. At least there's a decent amount of space around Bas and el Diablo. Mar should be able to attack without hitting anyone directly behind el Diablo.

Mar can't very well sit down without a drink, so they walk to the far left side of the bar, put down the coin Dami nabbed for them, and order a cerveza. The bartender is a different man, to Mar's relief. Once he hands them a pint, they sit at an empty seat two tables back from Bas and el Diablo, keeping out of the latter's line of sight.

The chatter of conversation and clink of glasses fill the air. Bas and el Diablo are speaking too softly for Mar to pick anything out of their conversation. Which is a problem. They have to move closer for any chance to listen in on their discussion.

Unless, of course, they skip the whole "wait for the opportune moment" thing and just attack. They're not even entirely sure what the opportune moment would look like.

Mar presses their palms against the glass, willing their hands to stop sweating as they force themself to breathe steadily. They should get closer and hear what's going on. After all, are they absolutely *sure* that's el Diablo? It seems like the kind of clothes Mar would expect him to wear based on their two short interactions with him, but they can't see his face, and they've never seen him from behind before. He doesn't have his smoking coat like the last two times Mar saw him. What if some random man sat next to Bas and began talking to him? It's not exactly out of the realm of possibility, given how packed the taberna is.

Dami isn't here to confirm who it is—they said el Diablo would be able to sense them there, since he holds their soul.

Dami *did* tell them it was time, but it also took a solid fifteen minutes to get from the inn to the bar, and who knows what happened in that time?

But then again, wouldn't Bas be trying to signal them if el Diablo had left?

Mar takes a big gulp of the bitter, dry beer, wipes their mouth with the back of their hand, and dares a glance at the two of them again. They need to get closer, just to be sure. Mar doesn't even have to get close enough to hear *what* they're saying as long as they can hear his voice.

Mar will never forget el Diablo's voice.

The table Mar is sitting at is circular, and the empty stool directly across from them is closer to the bar; it might just be close enough to get within earshot. Mar stands, careful not to jostle the stool beneath them as they slide around the table and sit on the desired new seat, their back now to Bas and el Diablo. Their magia hums more loudly on their skin, setting their teeth on edge. They can't see Bas and the man anymore, but their voices carry just enough through the steady song of conversation.

"How do I know you can actually do what you've promised?" Bas is saying. "You don't look like a diablo to me."

The man laughs, and the sound is like nails running down Mar's spine. "And what, pray tell, should a diablo look like?"

It's him. Mar's breath shivers in their lungs. All they have to do is turn around and attack. It won't be an easy fight—of course it won't—and Mar can't even begin to imagine what el Diablo will have up his sleeve. He sank *La Catalina* and swept Papá away. According to Dami, el Diablo has the power of thousands of souls. Mar's never fought anyone with magia, let alone someone who likely has more magia than Mar does.

"Hola, mijo, ¿cómo estás?"

The loud greeting is so close, Mar jumps. They dare a quick glance over their shoulder and swear under their breath. An older man—probably in his fifties—has walked up to the bar, directly behind el Diablo, and is now having a lively conversation with the bartender. Which means if Mar attacks el Diablo now, they'll almost certainly also hit the newcomer and the barkeep.

"Move," they hiss under their breath. "Go talk at the other end of the bar."

But of course neither man does. Worse, the older gentleman pulls over a stool from a nearby table and takes a seat.

Mar could pound their head on the table in frustration. If they'd just moved a little faster—if they hadn't hesitated, Bas could have had the taberna cleared out by now. Instead, if they don't want to kill two innocent people, they'll have to wait until the men move.

But what if that doesn't happen before Bas and el Diablo are done?

Sweat drips down the back of their neck. The older man and the bartender lower their voices to a normal talking level, so at least Mar can hear Bas and el Diablo again, though the other audible conversation is certainly distracting.

"It all sounds too good to be real," Bas says.

"Just because something is good doesn't mean it can't be real," el Diablo answers.

"I just don't see why you'd want to help me. You don't even know me!"

"Well, that's true, but I see it less as helping and more as . . . a business transaction."

Mar barely suppresses the urge to roll their eyes.

The older man and the bartender are now talking about the bartender's wife, who apparently is the man's daughter and has had stomach problems lately. Which is already far more information than Mar wanted to have about any of them.

Wait—what did Bas just say? Focus!

". . . can make this mutually equitable with an agreement," el Diablo is saying.

"An agreement."

"Yes. I agree to set your crew free from prison, and you give me something equally valuable in return."

Bas swears. "So it's true, then. Diablo deals are real."

"As real as that drink in your hand."

Mar grinds their teeth, glowering at the scratched tabletop as the bartender and the man continue their inane conversation far too close to Mar's target. They can barely believe their rotten luck. Sure, Dami did say it was inevitable that innocent people would get hurt, but Mar really didn't want to start the body count with their first move.

They're running out of time. Bas and el Diablo's conversation is driving ever closer to the agreement Bas absolutely cannot make.

"So what is it you want, then?" Bas says. "My soul? Because I'm going to have to ask for a better guarantee of their safety than 'get out of prison' if that's what you're looking for."

"That's reasonable. We can continue ironing out the details to your liking. But it's not actually your soul that I want."

Mar blinks. It's not? But Dami said . . . and what on earth would be equivalent to saving the lives of an entire crew if not a soul? They look over their shoulder, frowning. Even Bas looks perplexed.

"It . . . isn't?" he says carefully.

El Diablo leans back and drums his fingers on the bar top. "No. As valuable as your soul is, I'm afraid it isn't worth the lives of sixty men. No, for an agreement of such magnitude, I need a soul with unique power and rarity. They're difficult to come by, I'm afraid, but you're very fortunate, Sebastián Miguel Vega."

The light prickling on the back of Mar's neck washes over them in a frozen flood, like someone dumped icy water down their back. Mar's eyes widen. Does he—

"I am?" Bas frowns. "I don't understand what you mean."

El Diablo laughs again. "Oh, I think you know exactly what I mean. After all, what are the odds that you would have befriended one of the very souls with enough rare potential to power such a deal? No, it's not your soul that I want, Se-bastián."

Bas pales. Mar should stand, they should attack, they should move *now,* while they can—but instead they sit para-lyzed, watching as el Diablo turns in his seat and looks di-rectly at Mar with those unfathomable black eyes.

"It's yours."

CHAPTER 37

The times when Mar woke up in a cold sweat, fresh from a nightmare replaying the horrors of the night they lost everything, they wondered if the intensity of the dream had distorted their memory of el Diablo. He always seemed so terrifying in their dreams, so insurmountably powerful, exuding the confidence of a man who knew he could take anything he wanted. Everything from his pitch-black eyes with a glow like embers to his intimidating stature and cold, haunting laugh—it all seemed too terrible to possibly reflect reality.

But now, sitting in a taberna with el Diablo standing to his full height, towering over them with a grin that could kill, Mar can no longer deny that sometimes reality is every bit as terrifying as fiction.

"Hola, Mar," el Diablo says. "How wonderful to see you again."

Mar can't breathe. *He knew.* Of course he knew, of course Mar never had a chance of taking el Diablo by surprise. Mar should attack, should do *something,* but if el Diablo has been expecting them, then won't he expect this, too? Is he prepared to fight Mar?

Does it matter if he is?

El Diablo crosses his arms, still with that sickly smile. The door opens somewhere behind Mar, but they can't tear their gaze away from el Diablo's terrible stare. He looks exactly as Mar remembers him, except he left his elaborate frock coat behind in exchange for a golden-threaded black waistcoat over his deep red shirt.

"Well?" he says. "Nothing to say? I'm sure you must have prepared something clever to say after you took me by surprise." He laughs gratingly.

"I don't need to take you by surprise to end this," Mar says, relatively certain that they're lying.

El Diablo smirks. "Even if you believe that, I imagine it would have helped."

"Mar?" Bas says nervously. He's looking at something over their shoulder, and his eyes are wide.

Mar almost doesn't want to look, but they do anyway. And their stomach all but plummets to their toes.

Facing down el Diablo evidently wasn't enough, because Spanish soldiers have lined the back wall, guns pointed at Mar and Bas. But how did they know Mar and Bas would be here?

The rest of the patrons have gone eerily quiet and still, save for one man at the taberna who has just continued drinking like none of this is worth his time. It's so quiet you could hear a pin drop, but then someone clears his throat. The bartender.

"Would it be possible to take this outside, Capitán García López?"

Mar gasps. García López? *El Diablo* is García López?

But if el Diablo is a captain of the Spanish army, then . . . they are all well and truly in serious trouble.

El Diablo grins at Mar. "Surprise."

Both doors slam open. A tall, immaculately dressed figure strolls through, coattails fluttering behind them, all legs and black makeup and black hair tied back in a bun. Mar blinks at Dami. They're not sure how they expected Dami to behave around el Diablo, but this beacon of utter confidence isn't what they pictured.

Dami glances at Mar and winks.

"Dami!" el Diablo says with a smile, like a father welcoming his child home. "So glad you could make it. Come, sit." He pulls out a barstool next to him and gestures to it.

Dami does as instructed, legs outstretched, crossing them at the ankles. Their polished boots gleam in the lantern light.

El Diablo turns to the patrons and extends his arms. "Now, because I am a gracious man, if my business does not concern you, you may leave."

They all file out the door, bartender included, except the soldiers. Which of course is exactly what Mar wanted—ten minutes ago. Bas stares at Mar wide-eyed, his gaze sliding from Mar to Dami and back again. They can practically see the questions in his eyes: Why is Dami here? And why does el Diablo look so happy to see them?

El Diablo claps Dami on the back. "You know, when you said you'd bring me Mar, I wasn't sure if you'd be able to pull it off, but I never should have doubted you. Well done, mije."

Bas's mouth drops open, and Mar glowers at them. But Dami doesn't so much as look at either of them; instead, their face twitches, and they cast el Diablo a sideways glance. "I'm not your hije."

El Diablo shrugs. "You might as well be. I raised you, didn't I?" Dami opens their mouth as if to argue, but el Diablo waves them off. "Of course, none of that matters, because we had an agreement, yes? I'm a man of my word. Your freedom is yours, if you still want it."

They don't move from their stool, but Mar recognizes the spark of hope in the demonio's eyes. Of course—it all makes perfect sense. Why *wouldn't* a demonio betray Mar for their own gain? Why risk the not-insignificant chance that Mar can't kill el Diablo when they could get a guarantee of their freedom without it?

"Traitor!" Bas yells. "We never should have trusted you!"

Dami snorts. "Well, I could have told you that much." They turn to el Diablo. "Of course I still want it. It's the only thing I want."

El Diablo shrugs. "I'll never understand your fascination with mortality, but it's yours. I free you from all that binds you to me, your soul is yours, et cetera. You're a free, utterly predictable human. You're welcome."

For a moment nothing happens. Dami looks at their

hands, then back at el Diablo with a deepening frown. Then they gasp and their head snaps back, mouth and eyes wide open, exploding with blinding white light.

Mar cringes and shields their face with their arms, but even with their eyes shut and their arms thrown forward, the light is so bright that it pulls tears down their face. They stumble back, nearly toppling over a chair and then into a body holding a bar that slams across their back.

No, not a bar. A rifle. The soldiers. Some of them yelling, all of them as blinded as Mar. Before Mar can think better of it, they spin around and rip the rifle out of the soldier's hands. He yells, and Mar jabs the butt end of the rifle in the general direction of his voice—it crunches wetly on something they don't want to think about.

Tears are endlessly streaming down Mar's face now, and the light is just beginning to dim. Mar can just make out the blurry wall of soldiers that seems significantly less wall-like now that some of them are on their knees, covering their faces. Mar kicks a dropped rifle out of reach and swings the one in their hands into someone else's face; then all at once the light disappears, and Mar can't see a damn thing.

Something hard slams against the backs of their knees, and Mar stumbles to the ground, dropping the rifle, which quickly is whisked out of their reach. They blink hard, swearing softly as they wait for their eyes to adjust.

When they do, el Diablo is holding Bas in a headlock with one arm and pointing a revolver at Mar with the other.

"That," he says, all too calmly, "was foolish."

Bas spits on el Diablo's boots. The man scowls and shoves Bas at Dami, who catches him before he falls over.

"You don't technically work for me anymore," el Diablo says to Dami, "but it'd be best for both of you if you kept him out of my way."

Bas lunges toward el Diablo, but Dami catches him and yanks him back. The boy yells and struggles in Dami's grip. The former demonio looks exactly as they did before they finished their deal with el Diablo; if it weren't for the light show, Mar might wonder if it worked at all. Dami says something in Bas's ear, and he suddenly goes still. And looks directly at Mar with something like terror.

Dami wraps their arms around Bas's middle and yanks him past Mar. Bas yells, fighting them at every step, but with Dami pulling him backward, he's off-balance, and Dami must be stronger than they look. Then Dami and Bas are out the door. Bas's screams begins to fade, and Mar does everything they can to hold it together.

The silence that follows is almost painful. The soldiers seem to have mostly recovered by now, save for the two who Mar attacked and who are now passed out on the floor. The rest have rifles trained on Mar. In case el Diablo and his revolver aren't enough.

El Diablo levels his gaze at Mar. "Perhaps it was rude of me to direct some of my attention to my former employee, but don't worry—I won't make that mistake again." He pulls the hammer back with a click. "Fortunately, I don't need to make a deal with you to get what I want."

It's not the first time they've stared down the firing end of a gun. But as they have every time, they can't help but wonder if this will be the last.

He doesn't think clearly or act rationally when he's angry, Dami said. While angering a devil pointing a gun at them doesn't feel like the most desirable of plans, the alternative is to stand there quietly and wait for him to shoot them. So even as everything inside them screams for them to run, Mar juts their chin up and says, "What, you can't take me on your own?"

El Diablo arches an eyebrow and laughs incredulously. "Excuse me?"

"It's not enough to point a gun at an unarmed young person, but you need an entire army to do the same?" Mar forces a smirk. "You must be terrified of me if you think you need a whole army to face me."

El Diablo's face reddens. "That's preposterous. Of course I don't need them."

Mar snorts. "Of course not. They're just here for decoration."

"They're here," el Diablos sneers, "because you're never unarmed."

"And neither are you. But you don't see me bringing a whole army to fight you." They shrug. "Suppose I'm just more confident in my abilities than you are. Somewhat embarrassing, seeing how you're supposed to be a supremely powerful supernatural being and I'm just a sixteen-year-old pirate who doesn't even fully understand their magia. But what do I know? I'm sure your men here will all remember you as the powerful capitán who needed half an army to take down a child."

If diablos could spontaneously combust, Mar suspects that García López would in this moment. Red face contorted with rage, he looks at his men and gestures to the door with his free hand.

"Go, wait outside. All of you."

For a second no one moves. Somewhere behind Mar, a voice says, "¿Capitán?"

"NOW!"

The thunk of boots on hardwood and the creak of the swinging door make it impossible for Mar to hold back their smirk.

"Enough," el Diablo says, wild dark eyes settled on Mar once again. "Enough games. This ends now." He steps closer, heavy boots on old wood, revolver aimed directly at them.

If they can just stall him long enough to focus. Mar takes a breath, calling on the heat in their chest—

Air catches in their throat like a fist clamped on their neck. Mar tries to gasp—their mouth opens wide, but no air comes. They can't breathe. They can't breathe. They can't—

El Diablo's free hand is balled into a fist, and he wears the smile of a wolf about to eat his prey. "I already gave you the chance to earn something from sharing your soul." He twists his fist, and the invisible clamp on their throat tightens. Mar claws at the skin on their neck, but there's nothing there, and tears are flooding their eyes, and their chest is burning but not with flame and

they

can't

breathe.

El Diablo's eyes flash bright with the orange spark of burning coals. "Now I'll take it for myself."

The blast of gunfire is a kick to the chest. For a brief moment their skull lights up with pain like fireworks. A rush of rust fills their mouth. Then they fall back into darkness, wishing the ocean were here to swallow them once more.

CHAPTER 38

"It's not going to work."

Dami leans against the wall, arms folded over their chest, watching Mar as they settle back on the bed. They've just finished talking about the plan, and Bas has gone out to find them both some dinner.

He hadn't been out the door thirty seconds before Dami spoke up.

"I think Bas is perfectly capable of finding us food," Mar says, even though they know that's not what Dami's talking about at all.

"Cute," Dami says flatly. "I'm talking about the plan."

Mar crosses their arms behind their head. "And you're mentioning this now, after we've agreed to the plan with Bas, because . . ."

"Because he doesn't need to know."

Mar barks out a laugh and looks at the demonio. "Bas doesn't need to know that the plan he's risking his life for isn't going to work?"

"No. He doesn't."

Mar shakes their head and closes their eyes, too exhausted with everything to argue. "All right."

Dami's clothes rustle as they near Mar, and when the demonio sighs, it sounds like they're sitting, weightless, at the end of the bed. The bed shifts as Dami's weight settles. Mar has half a mind to kick them, but that would also require more effort than they feel like exerting right now—and it'd be a futile effort, anyway.

"Don't you want to know why it won't work?"

"Not especially," Mar says, "but it sure sounds like I'm going to find out anyway."

"Mar, this is serious."

Mar groans and sits up. Dami is frowning at them in a way that makes it look like they actually care. Then again, they probably do care; if Mar fails, they don't get their soul back.

"Fine, Dami. Tell me why the plan that we just agreed was a good plan won't work."

"You're too powerful," Dami says. Mar arches an eyebrow at them, but before they can get a word in, Dami continues. "You're pumped so full of magia, you're practically a beacon to any sensitive entity paying attention. And he's always paying attention."

"But the distraction—"

"It won't be enough. Believe me, Mar, if you could see you the way anyone even remotely sensitive to magia does . . . There is literally no distraction big enough to drown out the caliber of magia you have."

Mar throws their arms up, exasperated. "So—what, it's all hopeless? Why did you even pretend you were helping us come up with a plan if you didn't think it could work?"

"Because I don't think it's hopeless," Dami says. "It won't work as is, but I think I know how we can fix it."

Mar looks at Dami expectantly. The demonio runs their hand through their hair. "This is going to be another case where you have to let me finish before you react."

"Great," Mar deadpans. "I already love where this is going."

Dami sighs. "Just—listen. The moment you walk into that room, el Diablo is going to know you're there. There's no way around it. You can't attack him by surprise if he senses you a mile away. So we circumvent that by making him expect you, make him think that he's the one ambushing you."

Mar stares at them. "And that's supposed to help me ... how?"

"I'm getting to that part—hold on." Dami rubs their hands together. "So instead of you trying to sneak up on him, which is impossible, I go to him beforehand and tell him I can get you to him in exchange for freeing me. When he asks how, I'll say I've tricked you into trusting me, so I've learned you're plotting to kill him to get your papá back. I'll tell him I've been pretending to be on your side and I'm helping you with this plot in order to deliver you to him instead."

"I'm failing to see the part where this benefits me."

"Wait. Remember what I told you about how he gets his power?"

"Through the souls he collects."

"And the souls that his demonios collect and the people they kill and he's killed," Dami adds. "So if he frees me, he'll lose the power he pulls from my soul and all the souls I've collected."

Mar frowns. "And how many is that?"

Dami grimaces. "I ... You need a lot to get to demonio status, okay? That's not the important part. The important part is that when he frees me, he'll be weakening himself significantly."

"But why would he agree to that?"

"Because he'll think he's getting you in exchange."

"He has to know that if I haven't yet, I'll never agree to give him my soul."

Dami nods. "But he doesn't have to make a deal if—"

"He kills me." Mar's frown deepens, remembering Papá's warning so many moons ago. "This still all sounds terrible for me."

"Right, well, I didn't say you should let him kill you."

Mar bites their lip. "Okay. Well, if he gets the souls of all he's killed, does that mean killing him will bring back my old crew too?"

Dami's face softens. "Not even el Diablo can bring back the dead."

"But Papá—"

"Isn't dead. El Diablo took him directly, like he does to all he's made a deal with. It's different."

Mar looks away, swallowing their disappointment. It's not

that they had really expected to ever see Leo or the rest of the crew again, but for a minute . . .

They take a deep breath and look at the demonio again. "Bas isn't going to like this."

"Under no circumstances can Bas find out about this."

"Are you serious?" Mar says incredulously. "I can't just not tell him a huge part of this plan."

Dami sighs heavily and looks at Mar as though they're about to explain something to a confused child. "Remember what I said about what happens during a deal? El Diablo will be poking around in Bas's head. If Bas knows I'm double-crossing el Diablo, then he's going to find out the moment he peers into Bas's skull. He can't know, or the whole plan falls apart."

Mar groans and covers their face. "That also means even if we don't do this, he's going to know we're there to kill him the moment he looks into Bas's mind."

"Yes."

"And you couldn't have mentioned that earlier?"

Dami shrugs. "There wasn't much point when I knew it'd all be solved with my version of the plan. And I couldn't very well say that in front of Bas—"

"Or el Diablo would find out."

Dami smiles. "Now you're getting it."

They were, but that didn't mean they liked any part of it. Mar rolls the bullet between their fingers absently. "If he can read minds, then isn't he going to know the moment he looks at me?"

Dami blinks, the smile dropping off their face. "He won't be making a deal with you, so he won't have reason to . . . but I guess . . . he could . . ." They frown. "I didn't think of that."

"So I can't know about this either."

"Right." Dami drums their fingers on their chin. "I'll have to make you temporarily forget about my involvement, then. Which means we'll have to make another deal."

"Lucky me." Mar sighs. "So you tell him about the plan, he pretends not to know to lure me in, he reveals he knew all along, and . . . what? You come in and finish your deal?"

"Pretty much," Dami says. "I'm fairly certain he won't drag things out with you after that. He's not going to want to be in a weakened state for long."

"And how weak are we talking, exactly?"

The demonio grimaces. "I mean, he's still going to have magia. But probably not the storm-brewing, ship-sinking kind. The deal isn't going to make him easy to beat, but it will make him beatable." They pause. "But only if you use all your magia. If you hold back, it's over."

Mar turns the bullet over in their fingers, smoothing their thumb over the crinkled, folded edges.

"Mar."

"I'm listening."

"This is really important. If you're too afraid to use the full power of your magia, you're going to die. You can't pull your punches."

Mar closes their fingers over the bullet and pulls their shoulders back. "I know what I have to do."

They tuck the bullet into their shirt pocket, relishing its comforting weight against their chest.

Hold on, Papá, *they think*. We'll see each other soon. One way or the other.

A pointed rock in the sand is sticking into the middle of Mar's back, and it is supremely uncomfortable. Mar blinks into too-bright moonlight as the muffled sounds of screams come into sharper focus through the ringing of their ears.

"You killed him!" Bas is screaming. "I'll destroy you! Let *go* of me, Dami. Mar is *dead*!"

Mar is certain they're not dead, but they're also fairly certain they should be. Also, weren't they in a bar? The gunshot. El Diablo shot them, and they died. Or at least they thought they'd died, but maybe they just passed out? And el Diablo must have dragged them out here, onto the beach. Onto a pointy rock.

Mar takes a deep breath, and it's then—far too late—that they realize something is lodged in the back of their throat. They bolt up, doubling over as they cough—hard.

Chest heaving, they stare, dumbfounded, at the crumpled bullet shining with spit in their palm.

"Mar?" Bas says, breaking a sudden quiet they hadn't noticed.

They look up, then slowly clamber to their feet, holding the bullet in their fist. Their heart gallops in their chest, alive.

Bas is staring at them, red-eyed; Dami is smirking; and el Diablo is gawking at them, openmouthed.

Mar walks right up to him, relishing the solid weight of their boots against sand, committing el Diablo's stunned stare to memory. They slip the bullet into el Diablo's shirt pocket with a smile. Then they pat it twice for good measure.

"Impossible," el Diablo says. "You should be dead."

"And yet," Mar responds, "I'm perfectly alive."

El Diablo's ordinarily pale face reddens with the kind of rage that would make a tomato proud. He takes two steps back, screams a terrible, echoing shout like thousands crying in agony, then throws his arms out.

Lightning jolts out of his hands, slamming into Mar's chest, but though they stagger back, the pain is distant. They stare down at the jagged light rippling over them; the pain quickly fades, replaced by a faint, buzzy warmth dancing over their chest. If they were to close their eyes, they're not sure they would feel even that much.

El Diablo's magia, it turns out, is less effective on Mar than a bullet.

This only seems to anger el Diablo more. He drops his arms and opens his mouth so wide, Mar is positive that he's unhinged his jaw. Black smoke pours out, shooting forward and surrounding Mar in a thick, choking cloud. They cough, wrinkling their nose at the sulfurous stench. They aren't sure what this is supposed to do, exactly, but they have a notion it's *not* supposed to just disappear when they wave their hand in front of their face, which is exactly what happens.

A realization settles over them as the smoke clears: The warning prickle of magia is gone. Which seems absurd, because if they aren't in danger from el Diablo, then they have nothing to fear.

At this, Dami snickers—then bursts into outright laughter. El Diablo's furious glare turns on the former demonio, and he opens his mouth, but Mar speaks first.

"You can't kill me." Mar looks at el Diablo as a memory clicks into place. El Diablo's glare settles back on them, but something like doubt flickers in his eyes. "You told me that night that deals can't be broken."

El Diablo pales just a shade.

Mar laughs. "It seems you forgot to be *very* careful with your choice of words. 'Sixteen years of prosperity and continuation of your legacy—your child's life.' That was the deal you made with Papá." They grin. "What was it you told me? 'Deals can't be broken, but we pay close attention to *exactly* what was said.'"

"The deal is *finished!*" el Diablo screams, spittle flying from his lips. "I ended your padre and the rest of your pathetic little crew!"

Flames burst to life in Mar's hands, an old friend waking deep in their blood. They release their hold on the magia they've kept locked away, breathing steadily as the rush of power makes their bones sing. Orange and blue lights race over their markings, weaving around each other; the world grows a little sharper, a little brighter. The potential energy in the air is so concentrated, so strong, that Mar can taste it: tart and sweet. Like lime.

When Mar meets el Diablo's gaze, they're not afraid of him anymore.

"I'm his legacy," they say with a smile. "And you can't kill me."

CHAPTER 39

The fire that explodes out of them emerges like a wave. El Diablo tumbles back onto wet sand, sputtering as the tide washes over him. Dami releases Bas and hands him a revolver; Bas looks perplexed for only a second before he grabs it and turns on the soldiers.

There are far too many of them on the beach for Bas and Dami to take on alone. There must be three dozen already, and their numbers are growing every minute as more rush over to help. Mar raises a low, three-foot-thick ice wall with one hand for them to duck behind while sending a fiery wave at the soldiers with the other.

Something hard slams into Mar's back, and they pitch forward into shallow, sandy water. The weight on their back is unmistakable—el Diablo's hand presses their face into the wet sand and doesn't let up as the cool ocean rushes over it. They can't breathe, and for a second pure animal instinct takes over and they flail, trying to buck him off. Then something baser takes over, something once locked deep inside them, and Mar relaxes.

Water rushes into their ears, submerging them with a roar and pulling back with a sigh, and Mar listens. It wraps around them like a blanket, welcoming them home as the ocean swirls around them faster, faster.

Mar wasn't named after the sea for nothing. Papá always said water speaks to those willing to listen, and now as the ocean lifts away from their face, they draw in a breath and laugh into the sand.

Bas was right.

They've always thought they understood the ocean's call before, but they've never heard her, not like this. Mar is the water lapping the shore, kissing Bas's ankles, depositing shells onto the sand, washing away footprints on the beach. They're the ocean crashing into herself, lifting lazy Spanish ships in the bay and swallowing the rocks at El Morro's feet. They're teeming with life, threading through seaweed, dancing with jellyfish, cycling through gills, sculpting the ocean floor again and again and again. Mar is stretching over miles, caressing the most buried edges of the island and filling even the deepest crevices of the ocean floor.

It was never like this before, but now Mar never wants it to end.

Levántame.

A roar rips through the underwater quiet. Water rushes beneath them, and Mar rockets into the air, throwing el Diablo off them. The ocean rises with them in a wave; below, the number of soldiers has ballooned four times larger, but it's not just Dami and Bas fighting them anymore. Inexplicably, Mar spots Eralia and five dozen others, and they're still outnumbered, but not nearly as hopelessly.

Mar can't begin to fathom how Eralia knew to bring fighters here, but it'll help to have the ocean on their side.

Mar doesn't even have to think a command; their magia knows exactly what they want. Directing it has never felt so natural, so seamless. With a turn of their head, the sea rises beneath the Spanish ships, lifting the fleet onto a wave higher and higher until the water no longer reaches the dock. With a released breath, the ships crash back down with obliterating force, smashing against rock and sand.

Mar glances at the beach below, and the ocean gently deposits them onto the wet sand before rushing around their ankles again. El Diablo is screaming at some soldiers and pointing at Mar; el Diablo may not be able to kill them, but that doesn't mean the soldiers can't. The men raise their rifles and take aim. At a movement from Mar's lifted arm, the ocean leaps in front of them, solidifies into ice as gunshots pepper the air, then liquefies and whisks the bullets away.

Mar presses their heels deep into the sand, grounding themself, then fills their lungs with air and awakens the heat in the center of their chest. Flames pour out of their mouth, racing at the soldiers who shot at them. They scream and dive out of the way as el Diablo throws his arms over his face, disappearing in a cloud of black smoke—

They spin back to Bas and Dami, still huddled behind the ice wall, firing off shots above and around it when they can. There aren't nearly enough barriers for all of Eralia's crew, though, as Mar raised only one. Cold races up their throat and bursts out of their mouth in a frigid white cloud. Mar flicks their wrist forward; the far edge of the ice wall races out, expanding across the beach to cut Eralia's fighters off from the Spaniards.

"Bas!"

Dami's shout stops Mar's heart. A soldier steps alongside the edge of the barrier where Bas and Dami are crouched. The soldier raises his rifle—

A scream explodes out of Mar as heat burns through them. The rifle glows red-hot, then melts over the soldier's hands. He shrieks and falls to his knees. Dami shoots him.

A black cloud explodes inches from Mar's face. They cough, and a hand bursts out of the smoke and clamps hard around their neck. El Diablo yanks them forward, and sharp, hot pain bites deep in Mar's gut. The man grins at them, his sweaty dark hair as wild as his red-veined, glassy eyes. Mar looks down, startled, at the small knife buried next to their navel.

"I don't have to kill you to make you suffer," el Diablo spits, tightening his grip around their neck. His breath is hot on their face, and his fingers are a vise. The crushing pain around their throat, combined with the searing pain in their stomach, is enough to blur their vision with tears, but even though they can't breathe, their body doesn't ask for air, and even though the knife is buried in their stomach to the hilt, they don't bleed.

Mar yanks the knife out, sighing as their skin closes over the wound—and slams the blade into the space where el Diablo's neck meets his shoulder. The scream that rips out of him rakes like nails over their back, and he releases Mar to pull the blade from his neck. Blood spurts out of the wound, but if he notices, he doesn't show it.

"You irritating child," el Diablo growls. "I never should have saved you. I will *destroy* you."

"No." Mar smiles. "You won't."

Feet pressed firmly into the ground, Mar reaches deep within the earth for the heat calling to them. Farther than they've ever pushed, far beyond any reach they ever thought possible, the fire inside them bristling with anticipation as they find that source to connect.

They press the heels of their hands together at their chest—and pull.

The ocean pulls back like an unnaturally low tide, sucking even the moisture out of the sand.

A large circle around el Diablo's shining boots sinks an inch, then two, into the earth. The heat is so close, they can almost taste it; they just need to call it a little closer. *Más.* El Diablo looks down, a question in his glowing coal eyes as bright red lava bubbles out of the sand and rises over his boots, cooling instantly as it meets the air and forming a thick crust around his feet.

El Diablo gasps and tries to yank his boots out but falls forward onto his knees instead, boots still glued into place. The call of liquid flame is intoxicating; the power in Mar's bones is wild and *alive*. There's so much more just beneath the crust of the earth; all Mar has to do is call it forward.

They shiver at their own power as a whisper of panic crawls up the back of their throat. It's familiar, this connection to the boiling blood of the earth. The last time they were here, so many people died.

If you're too afraid to use the full power of your magia, you're going to die. You can't pull your punches.

Mar takes a slow, controlled breath, even while their heart trembles with power.

Más.

The sand beneath el Diablo's legs sinks, and more lava rushes to meet him. He screams as it encases his legs in a molten hot prison. The lava works quickly, pouring out of the earth now, washing over itself and cooling layer over layer over layer, climbing up his thighs, then to his waist, as he thrashes. All the while Mar watches. And breathes.

Más.

Wisps of black smoke burst around el Diablo, but he can't escape. The black rock races up his stomach and back, over his chest, swallowing his arms and shoulders before slowing, at last, just beneath his chin.

If el Diablo were a mortal man, he would be dead. Instead, he stares at Mar with wide, bloodshot eyes, face red and sweating, teeth chattering.

With the full power of their magia's song unleashed within them, Mar has never felt so calm.

El Diablo looks Mar in the eye and releases a cold, pained laugh. "You've been running all this time from who you are. You may have won this battle, but now you have to accept what your magia made you: a monster." His grin stretches grotesquely wide. "Just like me."

They're words that even a day ago would've cut Mar to the quick. But now, with el Diablo himself kneeling before them and an army watching at their back, with Mar's friends fighting alongside them, prisoners waiting for release, and their magia's song free at long last, Mar knows that what they do with their magia can be its own kind of miracle.

And right now they're going to use it to pluck a monster from this world.

Mar crouches down to meet his face. "I'm not an angel or a monster," they say with a smile. "I'm just the pirate who beat you at your own game."

They rise with the lava spilling over el Diablo's jaw and into his mouth. It coats his cheeks, paints over his eyes, and slides over the top of his skull, enclosing him completely. The volcanic rock prison radiates heat as it glows through the cracks.

Then Mar releases a long, slow breath, and all at once the earthen shroud crumbles away in large black flakes of rock and ash, leaving nothing but a pile of charred bones.

Mar nods to the tide, and the water rushes forward once again, swirling around their ankles before sweeping the bones away to bury them deep where no one will find them. When Mar turns back to the battle on the beach and the soldiers drop their guns, they smile.

CHAPTER 40

Mar never imagined just a brush of their fingertips on iron would be enough to heat it to a melting point, but running their hand over the bars of every occupied cell is all it takes. Hallway after hallway of prison cells occupied by crew members and revolutionaries; Mar doesn't stop until the bars of the last cell are a hissing puddle of metal on concrete and Eralia confirms she isn't missing anyone.

"Thank you," she says after they free the last person and she reunites with her sister. "This never would have been possible without you."

Mar smiles. "You made it a lot easier by keeping the soldiers occupied so I could focus on el Di—García López."

"Well, we couldn't let you have *all* the fun." She winks.

Mar laughs a little. "How did you even know?"

Eralia arches an eyebrow. "Your amigue told us this afternoon what you were planning. I assumed you'd sent them."

They blink. "Bas? But he was—"

"Not Bas. The tall one. Dami."

Mar's mouth falls open—they snap it shut and smile.

When Mar emerges from the final group of cells, they stop dead in their tracks. The crew is waiting for them, watching, with Tito and el Capitán front and center. Mar swallows hard. They aren't sure how much the crew has heard about what happened, but at the very least they've seen Mar melt iron with a touch of their fingers. There's no sense in hiding, not anymore; the crew isn't any danger to them, even if only because they can protect themself.

But that reassurance does little to blunt the reality that a rejection from the crew would hurt just as much as el Diablo's bullet did. More, even.

"So," el Capitán says, "what are you?"

Mar blinks at the question. There are so many answers, each of them as true as the last. They're a person—mostly a boy, but not entirely. They're a crew member, a sailor, an explorer. They're an only child. A friend.

But with the crew watching them with unreadable expressions—except for Tito, watching them with a smile in his eyes—the words come to Mar, exactly right.

"I'm a pirate," they say, meeting el Capitán's eyes. "What are you?"

The grin that breaks across Vega's face is infectious. He laughs and pulls Mar into a tight embrace. The crew cheers, and Mar finds themself grinning too. Tito pats Mar's back with a proud smile. Then el Capitán leans close to Mar's ear.

"You took care of my boy, just like I asked. Thank you. I won't forget it."

He pulls back, and Mar barely has time to process before hands grab their waist and lift them into the air. Mar shouts with laughter while *La Ana*'s familia carries them on a wave of whooping pirates as they waltz out of the fortress.

Not a single soldier tries to stop them. They've all seen what Mar can do.

Later, with the plate-sized moon high overhead, Mar sits with their toes buried in the sand as Bas lies sprawled out beside them. They haven't seen Dami since the battle on the beach, and with the fight hours behind them, their hope that the ex-demonio will come through on the last part of their agreement begins to diminish.

They suppose now that Dami isn't a demonio anymore, they aren't tied to deals. Still, they can't help but think it's unfair that everyone got everything they wanted except for them.

Of course, it was probably foolish to believe Papá might be someone they could save.

"So, are you immortal now?"

Mar startles at Bas's voice—it was quiet for so long, they almost forgot he was there. "What?"

"El Diablo couldn't kill you because part of his deal was a continuation of your papá's legacy, and you're his legacy. So does that mean you can't die? Ever?"

Mar frowns. "I . . . I don't know." Their frown deepens. "I hadn't thought of that."

"Hmm." Bas shrugs. "Second question: What were you going to say?"

"What? When?"

"Before I left earlier today. You said you wanted to tell me something, and I told you to tell me after we win." He cracks a smug smile at them. "Well, we've won."

"Oh." Mar's cheeks warm. This morning feels like an eternity away, like a completely different version of reality. This morning Mar didn't truly believe they'd live to the end of the night. And they didn't dare to hope that if they did live, they'd have a victory to celebrate.

And yet here they are. They fought el Diablo and lived to tell about it. They used their magia in ways they'd never dreamed of. They called upon the deepest reservoirs of their power and never once struggled to maintain control.

Mar looks at the boy watching them from the sand. His quirked smile with the light scar on his lip. His mussed dark hair, sharp jaw, and that look in his eyes that says he knows exactly what Mar is doing.

They clear their throat. "Well. Don't get a big head—"

"Oh, I like where this is going already."

"But I suppose I've decided you're . . . not entirely terrible."

Bas stares at them. Then he sits up. "¿En serio? *That's* what you wanted to tell me? In those words exactly?"

"Hmm." Mar taps their chin. "Yes, I'm pretty sure that was it."

"You're sure it wasn't, I don't know, a little more flatter-ing, perhaps? Maybe with the word *alluring* or *handsome* or *wonderful*?"

"Definitely not alluring."

"You are shockingly difficult to impress, Mar León de la Rosa."

"Well, *someone* has to keep the two of us grounded."

"You're really, really sure 'not entirely terrible' is the last thing you wanted to tell me when you thought you were going to—"

Mar kisses him softly, quickly, a brush of lips lingering just long enough to render the boy mute. Bas's face is comically flushed when Mar pulls away, and he stares at them wide-eyed for a solid thirty seconds of silence. Finally, he wets his lips, clears his throat, and says, "Maybe I should have let you finish before."

Mar laughs and Bas grins, looking utterly pleased with himself.

Then Dami waltzes into view behind Bas's shoulder. And something else. *Someone* else. Mar gasps and Bas twists around, hand on his holster, but he relaxes when he sees who it is.

"Oh," Bas says. "Is that—?"

Mar nearly falls over themself bolting up to run. Their heart pounds harder with every step, tears springing to their eyes before they've even reached him. Mar doesn't slow, doesn't hesitate—they race right into his chest, throwing their arms around him and holding tight.

Papá chuckles softly and rubs their back. "¿Qué tal, mi tesoro?"

Mar can hardly believe it. They've hoped, but— "Is this real? Can you stay? Are you—are you actually here?"

Papá holds Mar's face so, so gently. "I'm not going anywhere, mije. I'm really here, thanks to you." He smiles and nods at Dami beside them. "Your amigue here told me what you did to save me and your new crew."

Mar looks at Dami, laughing through the tears that don't seem to want to stop. "You found him. Thank you. *Thank you.*"

Dami lifts a shoulder with a small smile. "I don't have to be bound to a deal to keep my word."

Bas steps up beside them, tilting his head. "So is this what you'll always look like now?"

"Hm? Oh. I thought it might be, but . . ." Dami releases their hair from the bun, then runs their hand through it. Mar's eyes widen as their shoulder-length hair grows down to their chest. "Looks like there are some perks to being an ex-demonio."

Mar grins and releases Papá at last, futilely trying to wipe the wetness off their cheeks. They look at Dami again. Dami has already said it's impossible but . . . "You didn't by chance . . . the rest of *La Catalina*'s crew?"

Dami grimaces and shakes their head. "I'm sorry. But at least with el Diablo gone, their souls are free."

Mar closes their eyes and presses their face into Papá's chest. Papá holds them tightly; Mar can almost imagine Leo coming up behind them to join in, like he always did.

The knowledge that they'll truly never feel that again aches deeply.

After some time Mar releases Papá, inhaling the salty air as they wipe their wet eyes with the back of their hand.

"Look at you." Papá beams at them with warmth in his teary eyes. "I'm so proud of you. I told you you're incredible."

Bas smiles. "He is."

"Mar's impressive, I suppose," Dami says.

Something hums inside them, the resounding thrum of happy, unobstructed magia. They can hardly believe how freeing it is to hear those words, to feel their magia and know they never have to fight it again. It may not be the first time Papá, or Bas, or even Dami has tried to tell them their worth. But with their magia free at last and surrounded by people they love, well . . .

This time they believe it.

AUTHOR'S NOTE

It seemed impossible to me that for all the famous stories we hear about pirates of the Caribbean, none of them were Latinx. I wasn't surprised to find that I was right—there *were* Latinx pirates (after all . . . it's the Caribbean). But I wanted to hear more about their adventures. So I made my own.

While none of the pirates in *The Wicked Bargain* were real, they were loosely inspired by real-life Latinx pirates like Roberto Cofresí of Puerto Rico and Diabolito of Cuba. There is, to be sure, a wealth of forgotten Caribbean pirate history beyond the European white men we all know from an abundance of popular media. Modern Western culture has also created a narrative that pirates freed enslaved people found on raided ships, but some historians have noted that often wasn't the case—and that many pirates used enslaved people on their own ships. That is why I decided not to include any real-life pirate crews in *The Wicked Bargain*, as I don't believe it's appropriate to rehabilitate the image of any slave owner, pirate or not.

Though the pirates of *The Wicked Bargain* aren't real, the locations of the story and revolutions of Latin America certainly are. The 1800s were a tumultuous time for Latin America as people all over Central and South America and the Caribbean broke free from hundreds of years of colonial oppression. While not every country in the region successfully claimed its independence then, many did, assuming the country names we know today. *The Wicked Bargain* takes place in the summer of 1820, on the cusp of Mexico's independence, which would be achieved the following year.

I did, however, do some minor tinkering with the timeline to better fit Mar's adventure—specifically, with Isla Mujeres. While *The Wicked Bargain* depicts a community on Isla Mujeres, in reality the first major community on the island wasn't founded until about thirty years later, in the 1850s.

Finally, I'd be remiss if I didn't discuss the queerness of the book. Queer and trans people have existed since the beginning of time. Popular Western media about pirates has largely straightwashed their stories, but historians have noted more than a couple of idiosyncrasies with cisgender heterosexual expectations. There are relatively famous accounts of people assigned female at birth living as men among pirate crews (see: Anne Bonny and Mary Read). There are also accounts of male pirates forming civil unions with one another in which they would agree to share their income and inherit their partner's belongings upon his death—a practice known as matelotage, which was relatively common on pirate ships. Queerness abounds in history, and I hope to shine a light on stories that, while fictional, spotlight queer and trans people who have always been here.

ACKNOWLEDGMENTS

Some stories evolve from idea to completed novel fairly quickly; others begin as a seed and require years of careful nurturing before blossoming into a book ready to be plucked from a shelf. The book you hold in your hands is the latter, and I'm so grateful for the host of people who encouraged it to grow.

I'll always be thankful for my rock star agent, Louise, and the Bent Agency team. Louise, you saw the potential in my words long before that first book deal and guided me through many uncertain years before helping me realize my dreams. Thank you.

I'm so grateful to my editor, Jenna—from that first phone call I knew you were just as excited about Mar's story as I was. That passion is so invaluable, and I'll always appreciate the way you helped me untangle the threads of this story and advocated for this book. To Mia and Angela for a truly stunning cover, to Michelle for an incredible interior design, and to the entire Random House Children's team, including Rebecca, Shameiza, Barbara, Caroline, Nichole, Tricia, and Jasmine, who all helped make this book a reality: from the bottom of my heart, thank you.

To Teo and Chayenne, thank you for your invaluable insight essential to my aim of writing a story safe for all readers. Y muchísimas gracias Polo y Denise, for helping me not embarrass myself in Spanish.

To my Simmons University Writing I class, and especially Elaine—thank you for seeing the magic in those early pages. To Emily, my MFA writing mentor, thank you for encouraging me along the terrifying journey of turning an idea and one chapter into the start of a book.

To my CPs Laura and Alice, thank you again and again for diving into every manuscript I send you and helping me pull out the story I'm trying to tell. And to my crew of awesome writer friends, especially Kit and Genie, thank you for cheering me on every step of the way.

To you, the reader holding this book right now: your support is what makes all of this possible. Thank you.

And last, but certainly not least, Jay. My love, I don't know how I would have gotten through this pandemic without you. For every hug, for every laugh, for every encouraging word and mug of steaming tea, and for always listening while I talk your ear off about publishing, thank you, thank you, thank you. I love you so much.

A teen demon who wants to be human.

A boy cursed to die young.

A friend looking to escape.

And a murderous island destined

to bury them all.

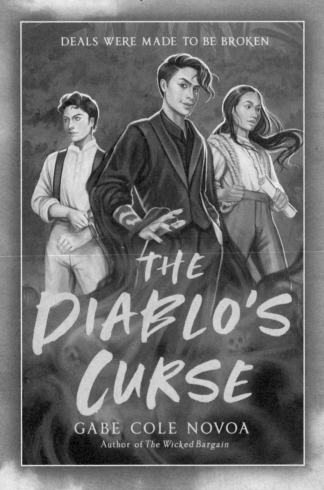

DEALS WERE MADE TO BE BROKEN

THE DIABLO'S CURSE

GABE COLE NOVOA

Author of *The Wicked Bargain*

Turn the page for
a sneak peek at Dami's story.

·····················

There are two sets of doors at the entrance to the Boston Athenaeum library: on the outside, intricately carved and wooden; on the inside, studded red leather. Dami supposes the former protect the latter from the elements, and they can't help but appreciate the ostentation.

Naturally, in the middle of the night, all the doors are very much closed. But this would only be a problem if Dami were there to see the books, or the statues, or even the impressive building itself. They have more pressing matters at hand.

Matters like their mouth still tasting of ash.

Dami waltzes up the two smooth steps, their boots crunching on fresh snow, and stops directly in front of the threshold. They clear their throat and say in an unwavering voice, "Juno."

For a moment nothing happens. The night is quiet and still. A cold breeze blows, carrying the faint scent of salt and winter. Dami shivers. But they stand firm, waiting until—

"*Enter.*" The voice is barely a whisper, easily mistaken for the wind. But this isn't Dami's first visit to the Diablo of Knowledge. They step forward, not even flinching as the wooden, then leather, doors ripple around them like the sea—and Dami walks *through.*

The Boston Athenaeum is intimidatingly beautiful during the day—an enormous building full of vaulted ceilings, statues, and multilevel bookshelves—so it's not really a surprise that at night it takes on the eeriness of a crypt. Each of Dami's footsteps echoes on the polished brown marble floors, breaking the hush of emptiness with an unsettling staccato.

Because, of course, no one is here. Except her.

Of course, she could be anywhere in the enormous building. It would take Dami hours to check every room and comb through the shelves, so they don't. Instead, they take a left into the reading room, their footsteps muting as they step onto the large plush rug and settle in a comfortable chair in the middle of the room, positioned across from a matching chaise. They lean back, sighing into the soft fabric, then cross their legs at the ankles and drum their fingers on the chair's arm.

They don't have to say anything. Juno knows they're here.

"Well, well. The prodigal child returns."

A tall woman with olive skin settles in the seat across from them, her silky black hair swaying down to her hips, matching the movement of her equally black dress. She peers at them with unfathomably dark eyes over spectacles she surely doesn't need, but they suit her. Silver moonlight spills in from a nearby window, washing over her and giving her the quality of a beautifully rendered statue.

"Miss me?" Dami asks.

"More like already missing the peace and quiet."

Dami tries to laugh, but it's . . . hollow. Juno's eyes narrow; they've known each other too long for her not to notice Dami's malaise. Juno was the one who explained to Dami what being a demonio meant. She taught them what they needed to survive.

What they needed to escape.

Of course, she didn't do so for free. Juno was a diablo, after all. She didn't do charity.

"I need information," Dami says. "And I have some to trade in return."

She looks at them over the frames of her glasses. "And is what you need equal in value to what you're willing to trade?"

"If it isn't, I'm sure you'll let me know."

She smirks. "Let's start with what you want."

Dami grimaces. If they start with their request, she'll get to name her price. And Dami has a sneaking suspicion her price is going to be far more expensive than, say, a juicy piece of gossip.

But what choice do they have? Bread and booze turned to ash in their mouth. It was far too reminiscent of—they can't even think it. Don't even want to entertain the idea. And yet, when it comes to unraveling magic, ignorance isn't bliss.

"Something's happening," they say at last. "With me."

"I hope I don't have to explain puberty."

"This is serious." Dami runs their hand through their hair—startling at the short curls. They'd forgotten they still looked like Charles. Dami closes their eyes, focusing on returning to themself. With a sigh, their shoulders relax, hair turning black and long, chest reshaping as their silk shirt and breeches become a black dress that flows like water studded with shimmering silver—like the night sky. The dress sleeves stop at their elbows, showing off the smokelike tattoos spanning from elbows to wrists. When they speak again, their voice is softer. "I need your help. He's dead, but el Diablo's been haunting me for months. Food turned to ash in my mouth. I don't know what's happening."

Juno regards them for a long, alarmingly silent moment. "I think you do."

Dami frowns. "What do you mean?"

"Let me ask you something, Dami. How many humans do you know who can change their appearance at will?"

Their blood goes cold. The answer to this is obvious: none, as far as they know, including people they've met whose sense of gender is as fluid as Dami's—but they've brushed off this reality as a stroke of luck. A token, for losing years of their life to being a demonio.

"I just thought . . ." Even trying to say it aloud now feels foolish. They thought what? That el Diablo would do something nice for them? That the universe would look upon them favorably? Were they really that naïve?

Not naïve, they think, *just in denial.*

Dami tries to speak again, their voice fading with every word. "Are you saying I'm not . . . actually . . . human?" They finish on a near whisper. Just saying it aloud restarts the panicked gallop of their heart, heat attacking their chest.

But if they aren't human, what are they? "I'm *not* still a demonio," Dami says, strength returning to their voice. "Everything is so different now. I can *taste* and *smell* and *feel*. I can be corporeal during the day. I would know if I were still a demonio, and I'm *not*."

Juno nods. "You're not a demonio, not entirely." She pauses. "Not yet."

They can barely breathe. "Not yet?" they croak. "You can't mean . . ."

"You can't taste anymore, can you?" she says softly.

The ash.

No. No, no, no. It can't be. It *can't* be. Anything else—they can't go back.

They won't survive it.

"That's not . . . possible," they croak out. "I had a deal. El Diablo . . ."

Juno arches an eyebrow, locking eyes with Dami. She doesn't have to say it, not really. Dami spent the entirety of their existence around el Diablo. They know all too well how he worked, how he was never—not once—up-front about what the full terms of his deals really meant.

Of course, most diablos and demonios aren't, and when Dami was a demonio, they were no exception. Otherwise humans would never promise away their souls.

"What did I miss?" Dami asks at last. "I can't go back to being a demonio. What do I need to know?"

Juno drums her perfectly manicured nails on the arm of the chair. They're painted deep red, shiny—like blood. "Your happiest memory," she says at last. "That's my price."

It doesn't surprise them. This is how Juno operates—where most diablos and demonios deal in souls, Juno derives her power from knowledge. Memories, primarily, but also skills, expertise, even rare artifacts. Dami has always been a little jealous of the demonios who work for her—amassing knowledge sure sounds less terrible than collecting souls.

Dami knows instantly which memory it'll be: their first night as a human. San Juan. They said goodbye to their friends, Mar and Bas, astonished by the notion that they could say for the first time in their life that they *had* friends. They ate their first meal at a nearby taberna and nearly died of happiness as they experienced flavor for the first time. Those maduros were *divine*—sweet and soft, freshly fried, crisp and chewy at the edges and still piping hot. A handsome boy started talking to them, and after laughing together for an hour they went to the beach together.

There, with the waves lapping at their ankles, bathed in moonlight, the boy held Dami's face in his hands and called them beautiful, so beautiful.

It felt so good to be seen. It was everything.

Dami's stomach squirms at the thought of losing that moment. That euphoria of first human contact. But if they refuse the deal, they risk losing everything. If Dami is really reverting to a demonio, back to that miserable unlife . . . the thought of it makes them cold.

"Okay," they whisper. "My happiest memory—but you'll tell me what I need to do to stay human. Everything, Juno. No details left out."

Juno nods. "Everything you need to know." She holds out her hand, black ring glistening in the moonlight. A single piece of obsidian carved into a rose, the band like woven thorny stems.

Dami stands and approaches her, holding the memory tight in their mind.

The boy's fingers are soft on their cheeks. Warm. His smile— magnetic. "I've never met a boy like you," he whispers. "You're so beautiful."

Dami's eyes sting. No one has ever called them beautiful before. Looked at them the way the boy is looking: with awe and wonder. Not a hint of hatred or anger, just pure admiration. The cool sand shifts under their toes as Dami moves closer to him—chest to chest. Hips to hips. Warmth and muscle and the softness of his gaze.

So beautiful.

Something hot splashes on Dami's hand, yanking them to the present. Their cheeks are wet. They're crying? It's just a memory—they'll make more. And it's not like he was the only one to call them beautiful over the past few months.

But he was the first. And in a mere moment Dami won't remember him.

Their throat aches. "I don't want to do this."

"I know," Juno says. "It's a treasured moment—that's what makes it a powerful deal. If it didn't mean anything to you, it wouldn't be worth it."

"You'll tell me everything." Dami meets her eyes. "If I do this—"

"You have my word." Juno pauses. "I don't do charity, Dami, but I'm not going to cheat you. You deserve better."

Dami isn't sure that they do, but they nod anyway. They don't trust many people—and even fewer diablos and demonios—but they trust Juno. She's always been honest with them, even when they didn't want honesty. She doesn't sugarcoat, but she doesn't deceive, either. She doesn't need to.

Biting their lip, Dami takes her hand. They close their eyes, savoring it one last time: *so beautiful.*

It's a mercy, in a way. They can't miss something they don't know they had.

D ami blinks, clearing away a fog in their mind. They're kneeling, holding Juno's hand, their lips on her ring. They pull away, blinking hard as a full-body shiver rolls through them.

What did they give her?

Juno sighs and slips her hand out of Dami's fingers. "Delicious." If she can see the question in their eyes, she ignores it. Instead, she nods to the seat behind them. "Why don't you sit while you get your bearings?"

Dami stands on shaky legs, relieved when the plush seat catches them. They won't ask what they gave away. It's better this way, not to know. Not to wonder.

"As you guessed, you're reverting to your former self. A being of the dead. A demonio." Juno leans back in her seat. "Your deal with el Diablo may have freed you, but he never told you how to tether your soul. Without that, you'll return to the plane of the dead—and this time you won't be able to leave. You'll be as you were before, forever."

Dami's stomach flips. "So I need to . . . tether my soul."

Juno nods. "You can't be fully human as long as you have active demonio deals with living humans. You need to end your deals with each of them. Once that's done, you'll be fully mortal. Fully human." She pauses. "Of course, if you make any new deals with a human using magic—even one—or if you die, you'll become a demonio again immediately."

Sure. Right. End every active deal they have left. That's . . . how many? Dami takes a minute to run through their mental list. As a demonio, Dami always knew how many deals they had running and with who; it was innate knowledge, impossible to forget. That they can recall it now so easily probably should have been a warning sign on its own.

One hundred twenty-seven. One hundred twenty-seven active deals they have to end. With people all over the world.

"And . . . how long do I have, exactly?"

"A year from your first day as a human. The closer you get

to your deadline, the faster the reversion will be. You'll lose everything that tethers you to the plane of the living—your senses, then your corporeality—until you become fully as you were. A demonio."

Dami grimaces, staring at their palms. They became a human on September 22. It's now January, which leaves them with a little less than eight months. That would mean ending a deal every two days, give or take. As a demonio it would have been easy—they could zip around the world in a blink. But as a human? It takes days to get to another city, let alone across the world.

It's impossible. Unless . . .

Dami looks up at Juno. "Yes," she says, "you'll need to make a deal with a diablo to give yourself a chance." She must see the concern on their face because she adds, "Humans make deals with diablos and demonios all the time, so you won't revert. Only making a demonio deal with a human will untether your soul for good."

They swallow; their throat is paper-dry. "Okay," Dami rasps. "Another deal, then."

She stands, towering over them as her heels clack on the tile before stepping onto the rug. Dami resists the instinct to shrink in their seat as she runs her nail over the arm of their chair with a grating sound like a hiss. "I must admit, I'm curious about how this will turn out. I'll transport you to each person—once. In return, I'll know everything you do about how your little adventure is going. I'll have access to your memories about your journey—but I won't take them from you."

"Deal. Absolutely. Yes."

Juno chuckles softly, offering her hand once more. Dami

reaches for it, but she pulls her hand away. "Remember, only *once* each. If you lose track of them after I bring you there, you're on your own to find them again."

"I understand."

She offers her hand again. Dami takes it and kisses her ring. A burst of magic rushes through them like hot sparks running through their veins. When the sensation fades, Juno takes her hand back and turns away.

"Well, what are you waiting for? Time's ticking."

Underlined

A Community of Book Nerds & Aspiring Writers!

READ

Get book recommendations, reading lists, YA news

DISCOVER

Take quizzes, watch videos, shop merch, win prizes

CREATE

Write your own stories, enter contests, get inspired

SHARE

Connect with fellow Book Nerds and authors!

GetUnderlined.com • @GetUnderlined

Want a chance to be featured? Use #GetUnderlined on social!